Wasted Away

Away Series, Book 1

M. Marie Evans

DEDICATION

To my Mom, Janet. You are my rock and my best friend. I
love you very much.

PART 1

1 ADAPTATION

Travis

I was at happy hour when I first saw the unknown number with the New Jersey area code light up my cell phone. I never answered numbers I didn't know so I hit the button sending it straight to voicemail. I was in a heated debate with Mike, my best friend and roommate, over whether the blonde next to me had fake boobs. We were in Boca Raton after all. Here everyone had a fake something or other.

After I dared Mike to ask her, and he chickened out, I saw the voice message light up the screen. Telemarketers never left messages, but I decided that maybe it was an automated message so I let it go.

The night went on and happy hour turned into happy evening, as it usually did with Mike and me. It was 10:00 p.m. before I realized that I had three missed calls all from the same unknown Jersey number, and three messages. A little buzzed, I decided to step outside for a smoke and listen to the messages.

The first message was from an Officer Thompson of the Jamesburg police force. He sounded hesitant to leave the message. I could hear him pause before he finally left his number and said he needed to talk to me. My heart started to race when I realized that the second message was again from Officer Thompson. This message was a little more rushed. The third and final message was left only moments before I stepped outside. This time he left me his cell phone number, since he was going off duty, and explained that my parents had been in an accident and I could call him back at any time.

The cigarette started to shake in my hand, and I could feel the shock take over as I dialed his cell number. As soon as I heard the tone of his voice I knew it was bad. He explained how the truck had run a red light and hit them. They most likely never saw it coming. The emergency team had tried everything, but the injuries to both were too severe. My mother, Anne, had died on impact since the truck had hit the passenger side. My father, Tom, had died on the way to the hospital from internal bleeding.

The officer expressed his condolences. Apparently, he had worked with my father years earlier when my dad was still on the force. I thanked him and was about to hang up when he cleared his throat and hesitantly asked, "What would you like to do about your sister?"

I was so stunned by the news of my parents' death that I hadn't even thought about Samantha. She must be fifteen or sixteen years old now; admittedly I wasn't sure. I asked if anyone had told her and Officer Thompson explained how he'd visited the house earlier and told her in person. I asked how she took the news, and he responded, "It's not news that anyone takes well. Mr. Harris, your sister is a minor and legally I can't leave her alone in the house. You need to either fly here tonight or have a relative go stay with her." I couldn't get on a flight right now. That was insane. I would have to call my Great Aunt Alice and break the news to her. I thanked him, explained how I would make sure she wasn't alone tonight and hung up. I knew the call to Alice, who I hadn't spoken to in years, wouldn't be an easy one. She was old and I was hoping that she could make it over to the house this late at night.

I made the call, but no one answered. She was most likely sleeping. I figured that Officer Thompson wouldn't know either way. I would call Alice again in the morning. I felt a twinge of guilt for leaving my sister home alone tonight, but I was hoping she would call a friend.

I stood outside the bar, I'm not sure for how long, lost in my own blank thoughts. I wasn't that close to my parents. I was a bad son and I knew it, but they weren't saints either. I never called except on holidays and rarely returned their phone calls. If I ever did, it was via text message so that I didn't actually have to talk to them. Now that they were gone, I felt the guilt sink in.

I decided the best way to deal with this was to do what I do best, drink. So, I went back into the bar deciding not to mention the news to Mike just yet.

When I say bar, I don't mean some rundown, shoes stick to the floor hole-in-the-wall. We went to happy hour at Morton's Steakhouse, an upscale steak joint that charged $15 for a martini, my typical drink of choice. It was close to the law firm where I worked, and a lot of guys from the office went there regularly. It had a decent drink menu, and they called their happy hour "power hour", which a lot of my fellow lawyers liked since it made them feel superior.

I went back to the same seat I had just left minutes before and ordered the same drink I had just finished: a Tanqueray martini on the rocks. I didn't realize it then, but my life had just changed forever.

* * *

In order to understand how my parents' death impacted my life, you first need to understand who I am.

3

My name is Travis Harris. I am a defense attorney living in Boca Raton, Florida. I live what I like to think of as a privileged life. I am single and what most would call a workaholic. I would sleep in the office if I could. In South Florida, no matter where you go, as long as you are a big tipper, everyone knows who you are. It's one of the only locations where money can buy your importance. Be sure not to confuse importance with respect because, as I have learned, money makes you important for that one night only.

I left home right after high school and headed to the University of Miami, also known as "The U," where I worked my way through the first four years of college. I did well in school and got into law school with a full academic scholarship. I never looked back to my life in New Jersey or the family I left behind. Some may think that I'm selfish, coldhearted and insensitive. I've been called all of those things before, mostly by ex-girlfriends. I'm not. I'm self-preserving. My father was a drunk, and my mother was a timid, quiet woman who made excuses for him. There's a difference between selfishness and self-preservation. Selfishness is when you only think and care about yourself, even though there are others that care about you. Self-preservation is when you only think and care about yourself because you have no other choice. It was survival of the fittest, and that was how I lived my life.

Now you can see why taking on the responsibility of my sixteen-year-old (I think) sister was not in the cards for me. Since I was a lawyer, I knew that I had no real choice, given that she wasn't eighteen yet and I was now her legal guardian. I could always leave her with friends or Aunt Alice. All I knew for sure was that I was not moving back to New Jersey to take care of her. I knew Samantha was probably heartbroken over my parents' death. They'd changed when they had her. My father had stopped drinking and my parents had actually been loving to her. Deep down I knew that was why I secretly resented her.

4

She'd gotten everything my parents had been too broken to give to me. Either way, she was probably lost, and I knew that feeling all too well.

I realized I had to go to New Jersey. It was in my best interest while I was there to figure out what to do with Sam. And I owed my parents at least that much. Of course, it would be best for her to be with anyone but me.

Samantha

Have you ever felt lost? So lost that you don't know what you are going to do in the next minute? Then that minute turns into an hour, and that hour turns into a day? You are stuck, unable to move forward, too busy living in the past. Well, that is where I am: stuck, lost, alone and scared.

I was home alone when I heard the news of my parents' death. It was Monday around 5:30 p.m. and it was raining outside. I was lying on my bed listening to the latest "hit" song, a song I now hate. The doorbell rang and I almost missed it…what if I had? What if I had never answered the door that night to hear the news? Once that doorbell rang, my life as Samantha Harris was over. Of course, my name would be the same, but the rest of my life would change forever.

At the door was Officer Thompson. I knew him because my dad used to be a cop in this town. After he said hello, everything became blurry, and I only remember pieces of information. I listened to him explain how the truck ran the red light and hit my parents' car. I was waiting for him to say that they were okay, just a little banged up, and then I realized if that were the case I would have received a phone call and not a personal visit. Or he would have rushed me away to take me to the hospital. When he said, they had not survived, I was confused. I didn't understand. You always see those cop shows where they tell the family that their loved one is dead, and the person breaks down right there on the spot. I didn't see how that was possible, since I didn't even understand what he was saying. It was like my body was protecting me because, instead of freaking out, I just froze. He offered his condolences. I thanked him and closed the door. I stood alone in the foyer unable to react.

I turned around and took in the quietness of the empty house. What do I do now? All of a sudden, the brightness of the lights in the house were too much for me to take. I needed darkness. I walked around and turned off all the lights and locked all the doors. I went upstairs to my bedroom and walked into the bathroom. I had my own bathroom that my father and I painted blue the year before. One thing every teenage girl needed was her own bathroom. Why was I thinking all of these random things? It was as if my mind couldn't grasp the news of what it just heard. I stood holding the towel rack to steady myself as I ran my fingers through my hair. I tried to react...cry, scream, shake, something, but nothing happened. I just stood there for what seemed like hours. Then my head started to pound uncontrollably. Like a wave, it washed over me. I grabbed the wall and stood there with my cheek pressed flat against it. It was cold and felt good against my hot, tear-drenched face. I sank to the floor, still pressed up against the wall, and stayed there all night, not moving. I had never known this feeling. I had never lost anything before in my life. Nothing that I loved so dearly and relied on so much.

That night and the next day were a haze of grief. All I did was sleep on the bathroom floor where I felt safe. I knew it didn't make much sense, but my mind and body had shut down, and I needed the seclusion and safety of my private little room. I didn't eat, I didn't shower, I didn't really move. My Aunt Alice stopped by at one point and cooked for me, but I wasn't hungry. My best friends, Jacob and Lisa, came over and banged on the door, but I needed to be alone. Their parents both invited me to move in with them for the time being, but I could not leave my house. Even though I realized I couldn't spend every waking moment in the bathroom, my house was still the place where I felt the most comfortable. Some people say, that after you lose someone you've loved, the house that you shared becomes a constant reminder of loss and sadness. I disagreed. I needed this house. It was the link to my life. It made me feel safe. It was the place where my bathroom was…just in case I needed it.

2 THE MEETING

Samantha

Today I met with my parents' lawyer about their will. His name was Milton Freeman and, given my current hermit-like behavior, he was nice enough to come over to the house. It seemed that they had left me all of their valuable possessions including the house and just about everything in it. I also got the old Buick that my father owned. The other car, my mother's station wagon, was totaled beyond repair in the accident. Not that I would have wanted it. Unfortunately, the house was not really worth much money. My parents had taken a line of equity out about five years ago, to pay for my school. They had decided to send me to a private Catholic school after there had been a string of bad events at our public high school. Two kids got beat up after a football game, a girl in my class got pregnant, and a teacher had admitted to an affair with a student. My parents had a life insurance policy, but it had to go into a trust for me until I was eighteen and could only be accessed by my guardian. I also learned that I wasn't the executor of the will. Apparently, you have to be eighteen to have that authority as well.

The final line of the will read "Travis Harris is to retain custody of and have full guardianship over Samantha Harris until she is eighteen years of age." I suddenly couldn't breathe. It was like the life was being sucked out of me. I wasn't sure why my body reacted like that to the news of my brother's guardianship, but I knew to always trust my gut. I was only sixteen (almost seventeen); I had another year and two months before I was eighteen. I wondered if I could file for emancipation from him. I remembered hearing that Macaulay Culkin did it when he was younger. Why would my parents send me to live with a brother I barely knew when my aunt lived close by? Yeah, she was my great aunt and pretty old, but at least I knew her. And most of all, she knew me.

After the reading of the will, I was told that I had a letter. It had Sam written on the outside of the envelope in my mother's handwriting. I was scared to open it. This was definitely not something that I wanted to share with anyone, let alone a strange lawyer. I thanked him, folded the letter, and slipped it into my back pocket. I was not ready to read it. Not yet, maybe not ever. For now, I wanted to pretend like it didn't exist. So, I did. I showed Mr. Freeman to the door and returned to the bathroom. I decided I could easily live there with a mini-fridge and pillow.

Travis

I received a call today from some lawyer named Milton Freeman. At first I thought it was some sleazy salesman lawyer who found out about my parents' death and was trying to exploit it somehow. That happens more than you would think here in Boca. All of those scummy lawyers advertising on TV, saying things like "Did you slip and fall? YOU could be entitled to a settlement." Those lawyers are always a scam, and they all have names like Milton Freeman.

"I am looking for Travis Harris."

"Why?" I snapped. Every time you say "why" or "who's asking" or any other smartass comment when someone asks for you by name it totally gives away that you are in fact that person. I completely lost my anonymity.

"I am calling about your parents, and first let me say that I am deeply sorry for your loss."

Yeah, right, I thought to myself. "Thank you".

"My name is Milton Freeman." This was when I figured he was some sleazy lawyer. "I am, or was, your parents' lawyer. I was hoping we could schedule some time tomorrow to meet in my office and review your parents' will."

I hadn't even thought about my parents having a will. They still seemed so young to me. "Unfortunately, I won't be able to make it to your office tomorrow. I don't arrive in New Jersey until after dinner." I had been planning on arriving earlier, but I had a big drug case fall into my lap, and I needed to do depositions, so I had to push my flight back to late afternoon. I knew it was going to make me look bad, but I figured my parents would have understood. They knew my job was important to me. Anyway, I figured I would only be in New Jersey for a couple of days for the funeral anyway.

I was not a coldhearted person; I was just realistic. I loved my parents, in my own way, but I had a life, a job, and responsibilities to get back to. I was an adult. I left my parents fourteen years ago. They had raised me and supported me financially, and I appreciated them for that. But let's face it, I was not going to win any awards for child of the year. Although I loved them I was far removed from my family.

"Well, you do have some responsibilities you will need to take care of regarding things that were left to you in the will," Milton explained.

I knew my parents didn't have much money, so he

must've been referring to my sister. I thought back and tried to remember as much about her as possible. I hadn't seen her much over the years. The last time I saw her was at her tenth birthday party, but that was not the Sam I chose to remember. The first image that came to mind was of a little two-year-old girl with wavy brown hair and crystal blue eyes, playing on the beach. After she was born, my parents started taking us to Myrtle Beach, South Carolina, for summer vacations. We went there twice before I moved away for college. I remember taking her to the beach and her running along the sand collecting sea glass. She was so happy then. A lot was different now for both of us.

"Yes, of course. Tomorrow is Thursday, and the funeral is probably going to be Saturday." My Aunt Alice had called me the previous night, crying and giving me the funeral details. It was the first time that I had spoken to her since I called to tell her the news and ask her to check on Sam. I was glad she had taken care of the arrangements, since I really hadn't wanted to deal with any of it. "Is there any way for me to meet you Friday? Maybe first thing that morning?"

"Of course, I will definitely make time for you. How is 8:00 a.m.?"

I agreed to the eight o'clock meeting and hung up the phone. I wondered what Milton thought of me. Probably muttering under his breath about how I was a stuck-up snob or horrible son. Not anything I hadn't heard before.

I arrived at Newark International Airport at 5:53 p.m., two days before my parents' funeral. I had finished the depositions on my drug case the night before but kept my later flight time. Honestly, I was procrastinating as much as possible. One, I did not want to go to the reading of the will. And two, I did not want to face my sister, Samantha.

I hadn't seen Sam face-to-face since her tenth birthday party. I had always resented Sam for getting the love and attention I'd never received. But now that feeling of resentment turned to feelings of sympathy. I had never gotten close to my parents, and throughout the years we just grew further and further apart. Sam was their pride and joy, their reason for living. She had to be taking this hard.

I am not a nurturer, if you haven't figured that out already. It's just not in my genetic makeup. I am a loner and a pessimist. So, the gooey feelings that most people have toward a younger sibling, I just don't possess.

I picked up my rental car from the Enterprise counter at the airport: a Ford Focus. I cringed at the thought of driving this car, but it was New Jersey, not South Florida, and I was sure that everyone owned a Ford Focus here. As I drove down the long, winding, tree-lined streets, I remembered what it was like to live in a small town...the quiet, the isolation—and I felt bad for them. All of them. They didn't know the excitement of South Beach on a Saturday night. Or waking up on a Sunday morning and going five minutes down the road to the beach.

I drove up to my parents' house at 6:45 p.m., just in time for dinner. Then I remembered that my mom wasn't there to cook for me like she used to. The lights were all out. There was no one home. I wondered where Sam was and then remembered that she was probably staying with my Aunt Alice, who lived just two towns over.

The house was a white two-story. In New Jersey, we called it a colonial. I strolled up the center walkway to the rickety old porch. My father had built this porch before I was born, and it definitely looked that old. I'd swear this was a hazard that should be removed before it collapsed and killed someone. I muttered this under my breath as I climbed up the porch stairs that creaked under my weight.

I stared at the exterior, thinking that if we were going to sell this place we really needed to fix it up a little.

I unlocked the door with the spare key that I found hidden in the back of the mailbox. Even with the crime in the area, and the State Home for Boys about ten miles away, my parents still left a spare key in the mailbox. Like the back of the mailbox was the best hiding spot ever and no one would ever think to check there. Just as ingenious as under the potted plant or the doormat, I supposed.

As I opened the door to step into the foyer, I heard a sniffle, and then all of the sudden something knocked the wind out of me. I keeled over in pain, and as I looked up to see what just hit me, I got hit in the side of the head with the same object that hit my stomach. As I fell to the floor, a few choice words came out of my mouth. When the darkness subsided, I looked up and realized that my baby sister was standing over me with the baseball bat my father had always kept hidden in the kitchen pantry. This was the first time I had seen my sister in six years, and I was now seeing three of her. I decided to roll over slowly and succumb to the pain and darkness.

Samantha

All I wanted was to be left alone to wallow in my own self-pity, but now I had to deal with my brother who was passed out on the floor in the foyer. Okay, so I guess it was more like he was knocked out on the floor in the foyer. But how was I supposed to know he was the one trying to break into my house? Okay, well, I guess it was not really breaking in if you had a key, but at the time I didn't think of that. I just figured someone found the key in the mailbox and was trying to rob my dead parents' house, although with Travis I was probably not that far off.

I wondered if I should help him. I did hit him pretty hard. I must admit, even though I felt bad that I'd basically beat the hell out of my brother, I felt good, too. Not as helpless. Maybe I could live on my own.

As he lay on the floor unconscious, he looked older than I remembered. I hadn't seen him since my tenth birthday, and even then, I only saw him for a few hours.

There weren't a lot of pictures of Travis around the house. There used to be more, but as the years went on and he showed up less and less, it was almost like he started disappearing from the walls. My favorite photo was one of the two of us on the beach in South Carolina when I was a toddler. I was told it was taken on one of the family vacations we used to go on when I was little, but I don't remember them. It amazed me how happy we both looked, me and this stranger.

He was not a bad looking guy, but he definitely looked tired. His dark brown hair was darker and straighter than mine but was still long enough to reveal that there was a wave to it. I could see the red welt the bat had left on the side of his head and worried I might have really hurt him. Then I heard him start to groan and figured he was fine. When he opened his eyes, I realized that was the one family trait we shared. We both had clear blue eyes, like my mother's, and his were staring at me with a look cold as ice. For some reason, I felt no love lost. No overwhelming urge to help him. I was almost content watching him lie on the floor in obvious pain. This was the first time I'd felt anything but emptiness all week. The first time I was having an emotion, and it surprisingly brought a smile to my face. Was it wrong that I was feeling this way? Then I thought back to all the times I saw my mother cry over Travis's clear lack of caring for her, and I realized no it wasn't. Maybe I just needed someone to blame, someone to take my aggression out on. Why shouldn't that person be Travis? I hadn't seen or spoken to him in years.

As Travis started to roll over and get up, I stood my ground, leaned up against the side of the wall, and spoke first.

"Are you okay?"

No response.

"Are you okay?" I asked again, this time a little louder with less sympathy in my voice and more annoyance. Maybe I damaged his hearing with the shot to the head.

"I am fine," Travis admitted, although I could see he was lying.

"Let me get some ice for your head," I said as I walked toward the kitchen, seeing that he was dazed. I wasn't sure if it was from the pain of just getting beat upside the head with a bat, or if he was just taking in his surroundings. He looked confused, almost as if he was a stranger in his own house. Then I realized, he was.

As I started to pack the ice in a Ziploc bag, Travis slowly hobbled into the kitchen, still looking overwhelmed and taking in his surroundings. Again, I wasn't sure if it was because he forgot what the house looked like or if he was still stunned from the hits he'd taken.

"Here." I held out the ice for him.

He grabbed the bag, held it to his head, and let out a little moan. "Geez, I had no idea you were so good with a bat. Maybe we should sign you up for softball." Little did he know I had been playing softball since I was ten. This made me start to steam again.

"I thought you were breaking in. What were you thinking just dropping in without telling anyone? Do you know how bad this neighborhood has gotten over the years? How was I supposed to know that you weren't a criminal here to kill me?" My rant sounded more like a planned speech than a genuine concern for my safety.

The truth was that I really didn't care who was at the door; I was ready to hurt whoever it was. I admit, after the first swing I knew it was Travis, but I took the second swing for good measure. I had so much anger and rage inside of me from what had happened to my parents that I was ready to unleash it on the first person who challenged me, and there he was.

"I am sorry if I hurt you, but next time ring the doorbell. Don't break in like a criminal."

"I had a key!"

Travis was clearly right on this point, but I wasn't one to back down. My dad always said, even if I was wrong, I would still battle to the death before admitting it. As I thought this to myself and remembered my father, I decided that it was not worth it this time. I wasn't going to argue a moot point with a man I barely knew.

I conceded with a slight motion of my shoulders.

Silence then filled the room like a rush of cold air. It made us both shiver. I suddenly felt uncomfortable, vulnerable. Not a mood I wanted to share with him. I decided that we'd had enough "bonding" for one night.

"Well, make yourself at home. I only ask that you sleep in the spare room and not in Mom and Dad's room." It was the first time I had said their names since the accident, and I choked on the words as they exited my mouth.

I turned and left the room. Not looking back at my brother, whom I barely knew, and not thinking about what would become of this house or our relationship.

Travis

As the throbbing in my head started to subside, the pain in my side got worse. Beat up by my little sister. I was such an idiot. Why hadn't I called first to find out where she was? Why didn't I suspect that maybe she wouldn't want to go stay with my aunt?

I slowly moved myself to the couch in the living room where I decided to sleep. It was close and required the least amount of movement for me to get there. Also, after the crack in my sister's voice with the mention of my parents, I realized she needed her space.

As I lay there, I replayed the events of the evening in my foggy mind. I never remembered my sister being as stubborn and mean as the person I just encountered. She was always such a happy child, but the truth was I didn't know her at all. Maybe she had turned out like me after all: a stubborn cynic. What a shame if that was true.

3 GETTING ALONG

Samantha

The sun shined in through my window and woke me a little before 7:00 a.m. the next day. I lay in bed recounting the events of last night. Around 2:00 a.m. I had decided to move out of the bathroom and back to my bed. After hitting Travis, I was feeling adventurous. I couldn't believe Travis would break into the house and ruin a perfectly good evening of self-wallowing. The nerve of him. This was my house; I owned it! He hadn't been here in over six years. He had no right to just invite himself in and pretend like everything was normal.

As I worked myself into a frenzy, which I was very good at doing, I decided his morning was going to suck as much as his night had.

As I brushed my hair, I reenacted last night's events in the mirror and came up with what I should have said. I was always better at telling people off after the fact. For some reason, I could never think of the perfect thing to say in the moment, so afterwards I would always act out in the mirror what I should have done or said. It made me feel better about myself, like I had the ability to be mean, even though I didn't have the guts in the heat of the moment.

To Travis's "I had no idea you were so good with a bat" I should have said, "Maybe I should show you my pitch, too." Then I would have grabbed a softball and thrown it at his balls. That image brought a smile to my face.

Instead of conceding last night after he'd said he had a key, I should have said…" A key that you stole from somewhere! Obviously, no one would ever give you a key to this house, since you aren't welcome. You are a lowly, rotten, terrible son and brother. Where have you been for the last six years?"

What would he have said to that? I wondered if he would even care enough to give a response if I confronted him like that.

I'd definitely conceded too early. I should have challenged him more than I did, but last night I was unprepared, not in the right mindset. Today, however, was a different story entirely. I figured he must be hurting pretty bad this morning. I did hit him really hard with that bat, after all. I was even a little sore in my shoulders from the hit I landed.

I decided to continue on with my attitude. I could be a bitch. I'm a sixteen-year-old girl; it's practically instinctual.

I realized that I had entered into a new stage of grieving, hatred, and it was invigorating. I looked at myself in the mirror and marveled at how great it felt to hate my brother. It was better than the emptiness I had been stuck in for the last several days.

When I didn't hear him come up the stairs last night, or his car drive away, I figured that he'd slept on the couch. Just in case, I made sure to check all of the rooms before heading downstairs. When I got to the bottom of the stairs I peeked into the living room. There he was, lying on the couch drooling all over our throw pillows. I could see a red mark on the side of his head from where the bat made contact. I tried to hold it in, but a small smile crept across my mouth. I then thought to myself: what would be the best way to wake him up? Of course, I could just walk over and shake him, or kick him in the side or hit him with a pillow. All too nice. That's when I formulated the noise plan.

I'd only been drunk twice in my life. The first time was last year when I had slept over at my friend Lisa's house. If we were going to try liquor it had to be at her house, since my parents didn't keep liquor in the house. We swiped some vodka from her mother's liquor cabinet and decided to drink straight from the bottle. Her parents were not big drinkers, so we figured they wouldn't notice, or we could just refill what we drank with water. We both ended up drinking until the room spun. Let's just say it was no fun at all. I was sick all night and could barely breathe the next morning without my head pounding. The second time was after our softball team lost in the second round of states this year, and I had made the final out. Needless to say, my teammates thought a few shots of tequila would make me feel better…it didn't.

Anyway, both times I'd been drunk I remembered my head pounding like someone had hit me with a baseball bat. Since that was exactly what I had done to Travis, I formulated the noise plan. The noise plan was simple, make as much noise as humanly possible. My best bet in executing the noise plan without screaming or breaking things would be the kitchen. Pots and pans made a lot of noise when banged together. I could also disguise the noise as cooking. Again, a little smile started to form as I realized my sheer brilliance.

I decided to go with the frying pans. They are large, loud, and in the very back of the cabinets. That meant I would have to move a lot of things around in order to get them. And when my brother finally came in I could ruefully offer him eggs.

The only flaw in my plan was that it was taking longer

to wake him than I'd initially thought. I mean, I could bang pots and pans "on accident" for only so long. Then I realized, what did I care if he knew I was doing it on purpose? I didn't.

The next thing I knew, Travis was standing in the kitchen doorway with both hands over his ears, looking truly miserable. Mission accomplished.

Travis

As I awoke the next morning, the pounding in my head was now accompanied by a loud clanking. It felt like I had finished off an entire bottle of Jack Daniels last night and then fallen down the stairs. As the banging got louder I realized that it wasn't my head, it was coming from the kitchen. I slowly threw my legs over the side of the couch and sat up. Suddenly the room was spinning, and I thought I might throw up. My palms got clammy, and I had beads of sweat forming on my upper lip. It was a cold sweat though, one you got when you were either hung over or deathly ill. Then I tried to remember what happened last night. Did I drink an entire bottle of Jack Daniels? It had happened before on numerous occasions. Then I remembered my sister and the baseball bat. Did having a concussion also cause this reaction? My head was throbbing and felt like it might fall off. I also realized that I must have a cracked rib because with each beat of my heart came a terrible pain in my side. I put my head in my hands to stop the room from spinning and dull the nausea I was feeling.

I sat there until I could focus on one object. I chose the TV. It was not on, but I imagined it was, and I started to feel a little better. I decided I should try to stand, and even though my legs were wobbly, I didn't fall over. Now I just needed to stop the tremendous noise coming from the kitchen. My confusion and nausea turned into anger and rage when I saw that the noise was coming from Sam, and she was obviously doing it on purpose.

"What the hell are you doing?" I yelled, standing in the doorway of the kitchen, hands clamped over my ears holding my head together.

Samantha

"I am making eggs. Did you want some?" My mouth was shaped into a wide, obviously fake, smile. I made one last reach and grabbed the big frying pan. I pulled it out of the cabinet with one final clank.

"Do you have to make so much noise while you're doing that?"

"Oh, I'm sorry. Does your head still hurt?" Of course, I knew the answer to that question, especially since he entered the room holding his head, and there was a giant welt on the side of his face.

Now he was the one wearing the wry smile. "Are you enjoying yourself?"

"I have no idea what you mean."

"Sure, you don't." He paused. "My head's fine. Thanks for asking. It must be from the warm welcome I received."

"I apologized to you last night for that," I said innocently. "Besides it was an easy mistake. You do look like a criminal dressed like that." I pointed at his black collared shirt and black slacks. They looked expensive. I knew he would get insulted if I went straight for his looks, and by the expression on his face, I was right. One point for me.

"This is Armani and costs more than that couch in the living room," he snapped back. "By the way, I will take some eggs."

Crap, I didn't actually want to make eggs. One point for him, I guess.

"We are out of eggs. Maybe you should go sell that outfit so we can afford some." Two for me.

"Okay, I'm not doing this with you this morning," he

said as he started to leave the room.

"Where are you going?"

"Out to the car. My luggage is still in the trunk. I need a hot shower and change of clothes, obviously, something less suspicious looking." He turned back with raised eyebrows, clearly upset by my clothes comment.

I heard the door slam behind him. Mission accomplished, I thought to myself. Then my stomach growled. All that talk about eggs, and I was actually hungry. I got the frying pan and decided to make myself breakfast. Just enough for one.

Travis

My head was still pounding as I headed to the car to get my bags. I couldn't believe that snot-nosed little brat. I guessed I deserved it to a point. The bad attitude, I mean, not the beating I got last night. I just needed a hot shower, and then I could get what I needed done today, meet with the lawyer about the will. The funeral was tomorrow. If I could get through that, I could be back home in Florida on Sunday and back to work by Monday.

As I reentered the house I smelled the bacon cooking. My stomach growled, but I refused to go back into the kitchen to get food. I wouldn't give her the satisfaction.

As I walked up the steps to the guest bedroom, the old wood creaked under my feet. Much like the front porch. How did I not hear her come down this morning? Oh yeah, my concussion.

As I walked up the stairs, the memories of my childhood came flooding back. The upstairs wasn't quite as I remembered, since my old bedroom, the first door on the left, now had a sign that read "Samantha's Room." The second door was the bathroom and the third was the guest room, now my room. There was one double door on the right side of the hallway, which I knew was my parents' room. The bed in the guest room was made up with clean sheets and had one empty dresser in the far corner of the room.

As I walked in, I realized that the old bed and dresser were mine from when I was a kid. It was the smallest room in the house. It was not my room growing up; it was Sam's nursery and then her little kid room. As I looked around and took in my surroundings, I realized that there was a picture of me in this room. Just one picture. It was of me and a two-year-old Sam taken at Myrtle Beach. It was the image of the little girl I remembered when talking to the lawyer back in Florida. I guess this was my room now.

When you grew up and left your parents' house you had to wonder how long they'd keep your old room "yours." Like the longer they kept a shrine to you the more they loved you or something. I'd always figured my room had been changed into a game room the second I left.

I couldn't believe they still had a room for me. Granted, it was not a shrine. None of my old posters hung on the walls, and none of my old clothes were in the closet. But with my bed and my dresser there, it still sort of felt like me.

I realized that I needed to snap out of it. My parents were gone, this was not my house and not my life anymore. I was here for only two reasons, to bury my parents and figure out where Sam would live. Then, I could get back to reality and the life that I loved.

Samantha

I was now making a full on breakfast with eggs, bacon and toast. I went with bacon because I knew that the smell would permeate throughout the entire house. Travis had to be starving by now. I just heard him get out of the shower, and I figured he'd come down and beg for some food at any moment.

I started thinking of what I'd say when he came

downstairs and begged me for breakfast, when I heard the front door open and close, and the car start up. "What the…?"

I ran to the living room window just in time to see Travis in his Ford Focus heading down the street, away from the house.

Damn. I guess I wouldn't be torturing him anymore this morning.

With my plan foiled, I moped back to the kitchen, depressed again. I hadn't realized how much joy it had brought me to torture my brother. Then I realized it took my mind off of things. For the first time all week I hadn't thought about my parents' death. For once I had a feeling other than loss. I hadn't realized how much it had consumed me.

"He'll be back," I said out loud to no one. Then I started to think of what I could do next to piss him off. I wondered when he'd be back. He left his stuff, so I assumed he would be back sometime today. I would just have to wait until then. In the meantime, I finished cooking breakfast. I ate alone at the kitchen table, realizing it was the first time I had cooked for myself or eaten at the kitchen table all week.

I took in the moment. It was sunny outside, another first all week. Maybe it was getting better, I thought to myself. Maybe this was what it was like to pull yourself out of the pits of hell.

I decided to call Jacob and Lisa today. Maybe they'd help me with my new mission and give me ideas on how to best piss off Travis. But before that, I decided I should also take a shower and put on some makeup. I couldn't torture him when I looked like a boxer who'd just gone through twelve rounds and lost by split decision.

4 REALIZATION

Travis

While I was in the shower I thought about the meeting I had scheduled with Milton Freeman this morning at eight to review my parents' will. Milton had left me a message last night to confirm the appointment and to let me know that Sam had already met with him about the will.

When I got out of the shower, the clock read 7:24 a.m. I had a little more than thirty minutes to get from Jamesburg to Milltown. I would be cutting it close.

Worst of all, the smell of bacon was permeating through the house. I couldn't decide if it was making me hungry or more nauseous. I needed coffee. I decided to hurry up and maybe I could stop at Dunkin Donuts on the way.

I gave myself a quick once over in the mirror before throwing on my clothes. My side was red and blotchy, definitely a cracked rib. My face was not too bad, just a little red, but it would definitely be a bruise by tomorrow. If anyone asked, I decided to tell them that I had fallen through the old rickety porch steps. That was believable.

When I left, I walked straight out the front door. I'd

already had too much Samantha for one morning. Anyway, she had already met with Milton, so I figured she wouldn't miss me much.

Luckily, I had just enough time to stop and get a coffee. I pulled into the parking lot of Milton Freeman's offices right at 7:56 with four minutes to spare. There was only one other car in the lot, an old white Cadillac with a navy blue ragtop. I figured that belonged to Milton.

Milton Freeman's office smelled like stale coffee and rubber bands. There was a dusty fake palm tree in the corner of the waiting room, and the chairs were metal with faded pink fabric. There was no receptionist, so I just strolled through the office until I found the door that read "Milton Freeman Esq."

I knocked on the faded wooden door. "Come in," I heard from inside.

When I entered the room, I was surprised by his appearance. I had expected a short portly man with no hair. Instead, Milton was a tall, thin gentleman with a full head of silver shiny hair.

Milton rose slowly from behind his oak desk and extended his hand. "You must be Travis Harris," he said with a smile. "You have your mother's eyes."

I shook his hand and nodded. He motioned for me to sit in one of his blue leather sling back chairs, so I did.

I was suddenly nervous and uncomfortable. I felt like a kid who was sent to the principal's office, about to get lectured on something I'd done wrong. I wasn't sure why I felt this way, since I was a lawyer myself, but I started to sweat nonetheless.

"Thank you for being on time." Milton smiled again.

"Of course," I replied nonchalantly. I was trying not to seem nervous, but I wasn't doing a good job. I shifted uncomfortably in the chair, which made me even less confident. This was not like me. "Um…I'm here to review my parents' will. You mentioned over the phone that there were some responsibilities that I needed to take care of." A bead of sweat started forming on my upper lip for the second time today.

"Yes. Were you in contact with your parents much in the last few years?"

Like I didn't feel bad enough about it already. "No, unfortunately, I was not. I am…um…a very busy man." It wasn't exactly a lie. I was very busy, but that didn't mean I couldn't call my mother on the weekend to say hello. It meant that I chose to go to work instead.

"Your mother mentioned to me that you were a very important person. A lawyer, right?"

"Yes, like you, I guess," I said, joking.

"Oh. Are you a personal liability lawyer?" He didn't get my sarcasm.

"No, actually, I am a criminal defense attorney. I just meant that we are both lawyers."

There was now an awkward silence in the room.

"Well, let's get to it, then. In your parents' will, they leave the house and all of their important named possessions to your sister, Samantha."

"What? She gets everything?" I was truly shocked. This was not what I expected. I grabbed the will out of his hands and started to scan it. It was true. Sam got the house, the car, some collectibles and the insurance policy. "What do I get?" I asked out loud, even though this question was to myself.

Milton cleared his throat. "Well, Travis…you get Samantha."

I looked up in disbelief, not comprehending what the stranger sitting across from me was implying. "What do you mean I get Samantha?"

"I'm sort of astounded that you're so surprised by this news. I mean, you are a smart man. Where else would she go?"

He was right. I knew even before coming to New Jersey that I would probably be the legal guardian to Sam, but hearing the words made it real, and knowing it was real made it that much scarier. Honestly, I'd always had a glimmer of hope that my parents would entrust Aunt Alice with the custody of Sam. I knew Aunt Alice was pushing eighty, but Sam was sixteen years old. I could totally take care of myself at that age. And did.

"I guess I just never thought that my parents would want me to take care of her." As I flipped through the paperwork in my hands, desperately looking for something else, I said, "Is there nothing in here stating that I have the option to appoint Aunt Alice as guardian?"

Milton looked ashamed. "No Travis," he stated. "I guess you need to step up and take responsibility."

I attempted to stand up and leave the room to digest this information, when Milton quickly held out a sealed envelope with my name on it. The writing was my mother's. As I took the letter, Milton said that it was a letter she had written to me "just in case." Did people really write letters to their loved ones when preparing a will? Could she have known this would happen? I decided not to read it in the office. I was on the verge of passing out as it was.

As I left Milton's office my head was throbbing again. Somehow, I had been hit in the stomach twice in less than twenty-four hours, once physically and now metaphorically, but the reason for both was the same: Samantha.

I now had my mother's letter folded in my back pocket. I never thought my right back pocket could feel so heavy.

My Ford Focus drove me to the local park instead of home. I needed to think and find a quiet place to read this letter.

I removed the letter from my pocket and sat on a swing. I stared at my name written on the envelope. When you're a kid growing up, you see your mother's handwriting on notes in your lunch box or notes on the fridge, but you never think you'll see it on the outside of an envelope containing a letter saying all the things she could never say to your face. I sat for a moment imagining what was written inside. Maybe it was just a quick "I love you" note like she used to leave in my lunch box. But I knew that was not what this letter contained.

As I opened the envelope, I realized that the letter was only one single page. I was a little disappointed. Although I knew how my mother felt about me, since she used to tell me all the time, I thought it would be longer. We hadn't really spoken in years and I thought she might have more to say.

My Dearest Travis

I know it is a cliché to say I have written this letter a thousand times, but that is the truth. If you are reading this, then I have met an unfortunate end too early in life. I want to start by saying I'm sorry. I am truly sorry for all of the things that pushed you away from us, for all of the fights that we had, and all the hurtful things I have ever said. You are my son, and I love you more than you will ever know.

People say it all the time, but I learned the hard way that it's true. You were my first, and unfortunately, I made all of my mistakes with you. I allowed us to grow apart, and for that I will never forgive myself.

I know that through the years you felt like I have asked a lot of you. I have asked for your forgiveness and your sympathy. Two things you could never give. Now, after everything that has gone on, I ask you to take care of your sister. I know that you have always felt like she was our favorite, but we loved you both equally. The difference is that she got the best of us. She is a wonderful young woman. Smart, confident, funny. She reminds me a lot of you.

No matter how you feel about your father and me, the truth is you need family. Everyone does at some point. Please give things with Sam a chance. You will be good for each other.

Remember what we used to say when you were a little boy. I love you up to heaven.

Mom

I had a lump in my throat as I read her last words. As a couple strolled by me with a baby in a carriage, I rethought the public park idea. I hadn't thought the letter would have this much of an emotional effect on me.

I folded up the letter and placed it back in the envelope. I wondered when she wrote it. It couldn't have been that long ago because she referenced Sam as "a wonderful young woman." I was guessing about five years, but then why didn't she say any of these things in all that time? Probably because I never let her.

I had really cut ties with my family over the years. I called at Christmas but made sure to do it when I knew they would be at mass so I could leave a message on the answering machine. I was not a good son and, thinking over the feelings my mother shared in the letter, I was sure she agreed. But she still loved me surprisingly enough.

I collected myself and got up off the swing, still uncertain of what to do about Sam. Could I really take care of another person? Maybe my mother was right. Maybe Sam would be good for me; maybe she would make me grow up. We would have to see how the rest of the weekend went. As for now, I needed a drink. It was just about lunchtime, which was late enough for a drink, in my opinion.

I decided to head to one of my old favorite places, Sayreville Bar. They used to have the best chicken fingers with barbeque sauce, and I needed some grease and a beer.

Samantha

It was 1:00 p.m., and Travis still wasn't back. I found out from Aunt Alice that Travis had an appointment with Mr. Freeman this morning to go over the will. Mr.

Freeman had called Aunt Alice to tell her. I was guessing that he'd found out he was my guardian and, on top of that, he basically got no money. He couldn't be too thrilled. I wondered if he would ever come back.

I couldn't bother myself with worrying about Travis today. Tomorrow was the funeral, and I needed to pull myself together. Good thing Aunt Alice had done all of the planning, knowing that I was too fragile, and Travis was useless.

I had been holed up in this house for close to a week now, and I needed to get out. I decided to call Lisa and see if she wanted to go shopping with me. I had very few items in my wardrobe that were black and nothing that was fitting for a funeral.

After shopping, I ate dinner at Lisa's house, and her mom dropped me off at my house around 8:00 p.m. I knew that her family was trying to be supportive, but the sympathy at dinner tonight was a little much. Lisa wanted me to stay, but I couldn't take it anymore.

When I got home, my house was empty and quiet, no Travis. I guessed he wasn't taking the news of being a "new father" all that well. I headed to my room, not looking forward to the weekend like I used to. I didn't know what was going to happen to me.

Travis

After lunch I just couldn't bring myself to go home. I still needed to think. How was this going to work? I was not moving back to New Jersey, that was for sure, which only left two options. One, I let Sam live with Aunt Alice, who was old and frail and had trouble taking care of herself. This would be ideal for Aunt Alice, since Sam could help her around the house, but it would probably be torture for Sam. I knew my aunt would take her, and it was only for two years until Sam graduated high school and went to college. Two, Sam could move to South Florida and live with me. Option two was more difficult for me to comprehend. It meant that my whole life would change, and I liked my life as it was. I didn't deal well with change.

I needed to go someplace where I could think. The park idea did not work out so well for me earlier. And the waitress at the bar was far too distracting. I'd forgotten how desperate Jersey woman were. She must have hit on me six times in the hour and a half I was there.

I decided to just drive around. I was in a rental, what did I care. There were a lot of suburban roads in Jersey that were surrounded by woods, so I figured I could clear my mind if I just drove. I drove all the way to Trenton, taking back roads and listening to the classic Jersey shore station 94.3. They played all the best oldies like Billy Joel, Elton John, and of course The Boss, Bruce Springsteen. You couldn't be from New Jersey and not love The Boss.

By the time I got back to Jamesburg it was after 9:00 p.m. I was hungry so I stopped by the White Castle drive thru. I took my bag o' burgers and went back to the house. I could see that the light in Sam's room was on.

The drive had done me good. It gave me time to clear my head and collect my thoughts. I knew what I had to do. It was for her own good…and mine.

5 THE FUNERAL

Samantha

I had finally fallen asleep last night at around midnight. I heard Travis get home around nine thirty and could smell the White Castle from my room. If you have never had the privilege of smelling White Castle, it was a very distinctive smell. Like greasy dog poop. Only someone who was either really drunk or really hungry could eat it. Travis was probably both.

Last night I was stressed about the funeral and couldn't sleep, so I decided to watch an old Clint Eastwood movie on AMC. When I woke up the TV was still on, but instead of Clint Eastwood I woke to Judy Garland singing and dancing in some super frilly outfit with a parasol. Just what I needed, to be creeped out first thing in the morning.

Why does every funeral parlor look like the haunted mansion at Disney? An old Victorian house, creaky wooden floors, dark flowered wall paper, weird paintings on the walls and you never know if there is a dead person behind each door. It makes the whole experience that much more torturous.

My parents' funeral was held at Feldman's Funeral

Parlor in Morristown, New Jersey. It's a small town with old buildings and quaint-looking houses. The last time I was on this side of town was for a 4th of July barbeque at my parents' friends' house. I couldn't remember their names. It was painful to think about that night because it was a happy memory for me. We had such a great time barbequing and playing with the glow stick necklaces my father bought us. I remember the fireworks, bright and loud, and how they made us all smile. I was not smiling today, back here in Morristown. I wasn't sure when I would smile again. Probably not for a long time.

Why did people act like you had some deadly disease when you lost someone who was really close to you? Everyone looked at you differently and smiled all of the time. They weren't genuinely concerned for your loss, but secretly evaluating their own lives and thanking their lucky stars that they still had what they did.

I had decided to go to the funeral with Jacob and his family. I felt more comfortable with him than I did with my Great Aunt Alice, who was the one who'd put the funeral together. I also didn't want to go with Lisa and her family. Although they were wonderful, her mom was a little too emotional for me and I just couldn't deal with that right now.

I looked at myself in the mirror one last time before heading downstairs to meet Jacob, who had been patiently waiting for at least ten minutes. I didn't have any makeup on. I couldn't cover up my sadness with eyeliner and mascara. I stared at the long black skirt and charcoal gray top with little black flowers that I'd bought while shopping with Lisa, knowing that I would never wear this again. I wouldn't throw it away, but I would keep it in my closet as a reminder of this horrible day. I knew that wasn't healthy, but I knew it was what I'd do.

We arrived at the funeral a little late. I had trouble pulling myself away from the mirror at home, because I did not want to be here. As I walked through the parking lot into the funeral parlor, I noticed my brother's rental car parked close to the front of the lot. I wondered if he went in early to view my parents' bodies. It was going to be a closed casket funeral, per my request, but they did give me the option to view them if I wanted. I refused, but I wondered if Travis said yes. As I walked in the front door I saw my brother in the distance. By the look on his face I could tell that he had seen them. His eyes were a little swollen and bloodshot. I hadn't noticed the wrinkles on his face until that moment. He looked much different than when I last saw him just yesterday morning. Did I feel sorry for him? I guess I did. Not as sorry as I felt for myself, but he had missed the last fourteen years, and he couldn't get them back. What a shame, I thought to myself.

Travis

When I arrived at the funeral parlor I was nervous and a little scared. I thought that seeing my parents before the funeral would give me some closure. I was wrong. Instead, I found myself staring at my parents in matching dark wood caskets with silver trim, reflecting on my own life. In thirty-two years of living, this was my first time seeing a dead body. I knew that seemed unbelievable, but I hadn't been to many funerals, and all the ones I had gone to had been closed casket. I was not surprised to hear that Sam had chosen a closed casket for my parents and refused to see them before the services. I could only imagine how hard this would have been for her. It was hard for me, and I hadn't seen them in years.

The individuals lying before me looked like wax museum versions of my parents. I immediately regretted seeing them this way. Now this would be how I remembered them instead of rosy-cheeked and smiling like the previous image I'd had before entering this room. I wondered if I could or should touch them. I decided not to. What if they were cold? I didn't think I could handle that.

I found myself focusing mostly on my mother, as I'd done in life. Her hair looked different, and I thought to myself that the mortician was probably working off of a picture from the '80s. Her curly hair looked frizzier than normal. You could tell that they put makeup on her to make her look less pale, but up against the lavender satin casket lining it wasn't working.

I thought back on our relationship over the years. What had gone wrong? I knew what had gone wrong, and so did she, but we never truly confronted it. We ignored the problems, figuring that they would go away, and eventually they did...with me when I moved to Florida.

When I moved, I let go of everything that was holding me back at home. I thought that a fresh start was just what I needed to be happy. I figured that eventually I would be able to come home, and my mother and I would be able to have a "normal" mother and son relationship. I was wrong. I held onto grudges when she pleaded for me to return home for holidays and family events. She'd forgiven me, but I hadn't been able to forgive her.

There was nothing I could do about it now. I lowered my head and wondered how I'd gotten to this moment. Where had the hours, days, weeks, months, and years gone? I leaned forward over my mother's head and whispered, "I love you." I felt my throat start to close and the tears well up in my eyes. My stomach started to churn from the grief and sorrow that was overwhelming me. I tried to remember the last time I told her that. I realized I couldn't.

As I walked out of the room that held my parents' lifeless bodies, I glanced at my father. I had so many mixed feelings about him. I'd always wanted his support and his pride, but I'd never received it. He was always so distant and obtuse. In death I treated him the same way he had treated me in life...I walked past him without a second glance. I knew I would regret that later, but right now I was filled with so many emotions, and one of them was anger.

People were starting to arrive for the funeral, so I closed the doors behind me and informed David Feldman, the owner's son, that I was done. I asked if he could close the caskets for me and ready the room for mourners. He was a nice kid, probably eighteen. I could tell his father had instilled professionalism in him because he wore a suit and his hair was neatly sculpted. He nodded and hurried into the room that I had just left.

I really needed some air. As I turned to walk outside, I noticed my sister walking in with a boy about her age and a group that must have been his family. She was staring at me.

"Have you been crying?" she asked.

I brought my hand to my face and realized that my cheeks were wet. I guess I had been crying. How could I have not realized it?

"I'm okay," I replied.

"Did you see Mom and Dad?" What a weird question. She said Mom and Dad so nonchalantly, unlike the other morning when she'd barely choked out the words.

"Yes, I saw them."

"Oh," she said and walked past me without a second look.

When I got outside, the crisp, misty air hit my face, and I felt a little better already. It was April and still cold. As I was gathering myself, I realized that the parking lot was filling up with cars. Were all of these people here to pay their respects to my parents?

As they walked closer, I realized they were. People I had not seen in years were arriving, and since I was at the entrance to the parlor, I guessed they thought I was here to greet them. I saw my old kindergarten teacher, Ms. Showers, although I didn't really remember her much. I even saw some of my old high school friends that I had not kept in touch with other than that they were "friends" on my Facebook. Not that I had time to use Facebook, but I had created an account a few years ago. I couldn't believe some of the people that were showing up. My old baseball coach, the police chief, the principal of my old high school. That's what a small town was all about.

After the initial rush of people entered the funeral parlor, I saw a break and took it. I decided it was the perfect time to sneak out back and have a smoke. I didn't smoke often, just when socially drinking with friends or when I was really stressed out. I figured that my parents' funeral counted as a stressful event, and lord knew I could use a cigarette.

As I made my way through the crowd to the back door, I noticed a woman out of the corner of my eye. I stopped to look. Tall, thin, and wearing a long black skirt and dark green top, she was consoling my sister. I couldn't tell who it was at first because I only saw the back of her, but as she turned I realized who it was and knew I really did need that smoke.

It was Madeline Walsh, my high school girlfriend. She looked just as I remembered with her long dark hair and piercing green eyes that could see right through me.

A rush of nerves ran through my body and panic started to take over. I fumbled for the door handle to try and sneak out, but as I tried to push I realized it was a pull. I pulled as hard as I could just to get out of there, and the door swung open so much I knocked over the lamp on the console table. Everyone turned and looked, but it was too late for them to see who caused the ruckus. I was already out the door and panting on the other side.

Samantha

What was wrong with Travis? I couldn't tell if he was freaking out from seeing my parents or if it was because there were so many people from his past here, especially

Maddy. I had known that Maddy was always a hot button topic for Travis. They'd been high school sweethearts, or so I was told. I was too young to really remember my brother in high school or any of his girlfriends. From what my mother told me, they were pretty serious. My mother was afraid that they were going to run off and get married before either one of them got a chance to "experience life," as she put it. Was he that freaked out by seeing her that he just knocked over what I was sure was a very expensive lamp, while trying to escape through the back door? It was quite the scene and internally made me giggle. I'd had a bit of a reality check when I saw the tears in my brother's eyes earlier, but it quickly turned into resentment and bitterness when I saw him happily greeting my parents' friends. He was such a fake.

I was surprised to see so many people show up for the funeral. I hadn't realized how my parents' death affected so many people. They were all being nice and sincere, telling old stories about my parents. Lisa and her family had shown up about ten minutes ago, and I had already thanked them for coming and hugged them all. I was still standing with Lisa making fun of the scene my brother just caused when I felt Jacob's eyes on me from across the room. When our eyes met he smiled. I had arrived with Jacob and his family. They were not a very affectionate family, and that worked for what I needed today: my space. But Jacob was looking at me now in a different way than I was used to and it was making me a little nervous. Maybe he felt sorry for me. After he realized he was staring, he got up to go talk to my aunt. I was so tired of people feeling sorry for me, and I made a mental note to tell him that later.

I knew that the funeral would be starting in a few minutes, so I figured I'd go get Travis from out back. When I turned to walk to the door, I realized that I was too late. Maddy was already on her way out there. Even though I couldn't stand my brother, right now I decided to give them a few minutes before I interrupted. Maybe she was going to tell him how much she hated him, or that he broke her heart all those years ago. After everything he had put our family through, he deserved a little extra pain today. So I waited.

Travis

I couldn't seem to catch my breath. Was I having a panic attack? I was definitely on a roller coaster of emotions today and, given that I had not felt this much emotion about anything in about ten years, I didn't know how to cope with it. I fumbled in my pocket to try and find the pack of cigarettes I'd bought after my experience in the park yesterday with my mother's letter. I lit a match and inhaled. That was better. I could feel the nicotine doing its job.

Maddy Walsh. What was she doing here? I hadn't seen her since the night before I left for Florida. She was truly the only woman I had ever loved. Even though we were technically kids, it was real. She always knew how to make me feel special, unique, loved. Back then it was all I wanted. But my parents thought that we were too young, and so did hers. She chose to go to Rhode Island University and I went to Florida (for so many reasons). I begged her to go with me. It was quite pathetic now that I think back on it. But she was different that night. I remember trying to kiss her, and she just wasn't there mentally. You can always tell when a person doesn't want to kiss you but they do anyway. You can almost feel them daydreaming.

We were supposed to have a week left together before going our separate ways to "experience" life. We went out to dinner at the local pizza shop, and then we went to the little airport near our high school. It wasn't a commercial airport; it was for small Cessna planes, the ones that you always see on the news because rich people crashed them.

There was a spot right at the end of the runway where you could park your car and watch the planes take off and land. It was very cool and it was our place. We would usually go there to make out or make love, but that night she was not in the mood for either. I figured that she was just anxious about leaving me, but then she dropped the bomb on me. Very casually, she told me that she didn't love me anymore and needed a fresh start. I remembered feeling like someone was playing a joke on me. Like it was a bad dream, and I would wake up at any moment. But I didn't.

She got in the car and asked me to take her back to her car. I did. She gave me a reaching hug when she got out, like you do with someone you barely know. She drove away that night in her red Volkswagen Jetta, and I never saw or heard from her again. It was too much for me to handle. I left the next day for Florida, a week early. I didn't care that my dorm wasn't ready or that I had no money for a hotel. I just had to get out of there. I ended up sleeping in my car my first week in Florida. Great way to start fresh. I was a mess for a good six months after that. Since then I'd never been in a real relationship with a woman. Sure, I had dated girls and had my share of one-night stands, but I was never going to let anyone get that close again. My shields went up and had never come down since. Well, not until about three minutes ago.

I was almost done with my cigarette when the back door opened. I figured it was someone coming to tell me that the funeral services were about to begin. I didn't figure it was going to be Maddy. Oh boy, I was going to need another smoke. She looked great, even better than I remembered. She had grown up and was now a sophisticated woman rather than the young, bright eyed, bubbly girl I knew all those years ago. She looked at me with a judgmental glare. I knew she wasn't a fan of smoking.

"You smoke now," she said flatly. No hello, how are you, sorry to hear about your parents. Sam gets a hug and I get that?

"When the occasion calls for it. I would think my parents' funeral would be just that occasion." I tried to sound as firm and steady as possible, trying to forget the scene I had just relived in my mind. Clearly, she knew I had seen her inside and was the reason why I made such a fool of myself. I needed to pull it together now.

I could tell that my statement hit home with her. And she quickly looked to the ground.

"I apologize. Where are my manners? You're right. This is certainly a sad occasion. I wanted to come and pay my respects. I didn't know if you would be here," Maddy said, still looking at the ground.

"Of course, I'm here. They were my parents, and Sam is my sister." I repeated myself for effect. "Of course, I am here."

"Of course," she said, and she looked awkwardly up at me. "It's just that I, no one, has seen you in years."

"Well, I live in Florida, and I get busy." Now I looked at the ground. I wasn't sure why. Up until now I had been so strong and confident. I never backed down from a confrontation, and I never gave in to anyone. That was why I made such a good lawyer.

"Well, you look good. I mean, it's good to see you." She smiled. "How did you get that bruise on your face?" She reached out and almost touched my cheek. She hadn't even touched me and I felt heat course through my body. Was she flirting with me? At my parents' funeral?

"Let's just say I didn't have the warmest family reunion." I felt the bruise, but it barely hurt anymore. "You look good too," I said, sounding like a school boy. Was I flirting back? What was wrong with me?

Suddenly, I found myself asking the one thing I did not want to happen, but I couldn't seem to stop the words. "Did you want to maybe grab a drink later? After everything today, I know I'll need one," I said, hopeful that she didn't think I was asking her out, secretly knowing that was exactly what I just did.

She hesitated. Never good. Did I read the signals wrong? Was she just being courteous and not flirting with me?

"Sure," she finally said with a smile. "It would be nice to catch up." She turned to look at the door. "We should get back inside. I think they're about to get started."

Even fourteen years later, her smile still gave me chills and butterflies in my stomach. I smiled back.

Just as Maddy had said we should go inside, the door opened and Sam was standing there.

"Time to get started." She looked back and forth between the two of us, wondering what was going on out here. I knew she was not ready for this funeral, so I walked past Maddy to my sister. I grabbed the door from her with one hand and put the other on her shoulder.

"Let's get this over with," I said. She nodded in agreement.

Samantha

Travis, Maddy, and I walked into the funeral room while everyone was getting seated. When I'd opened the outside door, I had expected to see her yelling at him or Travis defending himself against Maddy beating him with her purse. But I was totally wrong. It almost looked like they were smiling at each other. I guess I always figured that he broke her heart and left without telling her, but maybe I was wrong about that, too. Maybe they ended as friends.

I never really asked Maddy when she moved back to Jamesburg a few years ago. She had run into my mom at the grocery store, and Mom had invited her over for dinner. She explained that she used to date Travis in high school, and then they went their separate ways for college and left it at that. I never asked more questions because I really didn't care. I liked Maddy. She was nice to my family and came over for dinner every month or so. I hadn't seen Travis in years and, before these last couple days, probably wouldn't have been able to pick him out of a lineup.

As people saw us enter the room, they all looked back at us. Almost like a wedding where the bride walked down the aisle but morbidly different. No one was smiling. Everyone had tears in their eyes, even the men. That was the worst part for me, seeing men cry. It always made me cry no matter what. I just thought men were always so strong and rarely cried, so when they did, it had to mean it was a really bad situation. And this was a really bad situation.

I kept my composure as I took a seat in the front row. Travis sat next to me on my right. Maddy had broken off from us and taken a seat in the back somewhere. I saw someone coming up on my left and turned to see that it was Jacob. He took my hand in both of his and held it on his lap. I looked at him while he did this, and we smiled at each other. His hands were hot but not quite sweating. It was comforting and sweet. Something I thought a boyfriend might do, but it was exactly what I needed. I did notice that Travis looked over and saw what Jacob had done. He squinted his eyes, critiquing our body language. At that moment, I didn't care much about what anyone thought.

We both looked up front to the pastor. I didn't know his name, but he was kind enough to preside over the funeral. I was lucky that my Aunt Alice took care of this; I would never have been able to handle it. He stood on a podium next to the set of coffins that held my late parents. In front of each casket were stands with their pictures on them. Looking at the caskets was surreal. My whole body went numb. It was almost like Jacob knew this so he squeezed my hand as if to make me realize I still had feeling in my limbs. But he couldn't help me suppress the heaviness that sat on my chest. It was a familiar, overwhelming despair, the same that I had been feeling for the last week or so. I was getting used to that feeling, which I figured was a good thing since I would probably carry it with me for the rest of my life.

The pastor started by thanking everyone for coming and reading some of my mother's favorite bible passages. My Aunt Alice then said some kind words and told a nice story of how my mother used to dream about being an angel when she was a child. Aunt Alice said to everyone that my mother was always an angel on earth and now she was where she belonged with the other angels in heaven. It was a touching sentiment and made tears well up in my eyes.

As Aunt Alice left the podium, she gave my brother and me a hug. The pastor asked if anyone else would like to say a few words. I was surprised by the amount of people who wanted to share stories and condolences. It was a testament to how many friends my parents really had, how many lives they had touched. But with each new person I was getting more and more annoyed. I just wanted it to be over with already and these people were just stretching it out. I had never intended to say anything myself, and apparently, neither had Travis. I just wasn't ready; I wasn't strong enough. I figured anything I wanted to say I would say to them alone after they were buried. Everyone here knew how much I loved my parents, and I didn't feel the need to share with people who were practically strangers to my everyday life.

After a grueling hour of tears, stories, and hugs, the funeral finally ended. I turned to Jacob and asked him to get me out of there. I couldn't stay any longer and figured everyone would understand. I would see them all in an hour at my Aunt Alice's house for lunch.

Jacob and I stood, still holding hands, as he led me down the row. We walked out together, and I noticed out of the corner of my eye, Lisa watching us the entire time. I guess everyone was watching us because we were practically running out, but Lisa was staring daggers at me.

I brushed it off and kept walking.

6 FEELINGS

Samantha

I was finally out of that place and riding down Route 9 at sixty-five miles per hour. Jacob was about six months older than I, he had just gotten his license and his parents had bought him a car to use with their permission only. Lucky for me, they had suggested that he and I ride separately from them to the funeral, just in case I needed to leave. Clearly, they were right. When I was sitting in the funeral listening to all of the nice things people had to say about my parents and the stories they were telling about our family, I realized that part of my life was over. We were no longer a family. My entire life was about to change. Most likely I wasn't going to be able to stay in my house, our house. I was either going to have to live with my Aunt Alice or move to Florida with Travis. Neither scenario was appealing, but leaving the state, my school, and my friends was definitely the worst.

We had been riding in silence for about ten minutes before Jacob asked me if I was all right.

"I'm fine now, thanks to you." I smiled and grabbed his hand. The same hand that had comforted me during the funeral.

He smiled back and squeezed my hand as he had done earlier. A slight chill ran through my body, even though his hands were so warm.

"What am I going to do now?" I asked him, more in a rhetorical sense.

"Not sure. What are your options?"

I realized I hadn't really been talking much to my friends about my situation, and they were nice enough not to pry. They had been giving me my space, and I had been grateful to them for that.

I decided to give it to him straight. "Well, the way that I understand it, I can either live with my Aunt Alice or I can move to Florida with Travis."

"Move to Florida?" he sounded shocked. I guess he never thought of that option. "But will your brother even allow that? I mean, no offense, but he hasn't cared at all about you for as long as I can remember. And you have always bitched about what a horrible brother he is."

I was a taken aback by his abruptness and I pulled away a little, which he acknowledged.

"I mean, am I wrong?" he asked.

I hesitated. "Well, no, I guess not. But you just asked me my options, and as I see it those are the only two I have."

He shook his head like he was disappointed with me.

"What?" I asked rather bitterly. "Am I missing something?"

Maybe I had taken his reaction the wrong way because he tried to pull my hand closer.

"I guess not. I just never realized it would be something you would consider." He sounded like he was being honest. "And you don't think they will let you stay in your current house? I mean, what if your brother signs off on that? You could use the insurance money to pay off the mortgage." He sounded like he really believed this to be an option.

"I'm not sure. I don't know if I can touch anything since it's all in a trust until I turn eighteen. Technically, I am still a minor for two more years." I looked at Jacob, and he looked back at me with his big brown eyes.

"One year and two months." He sounded defeated. "I just don't think I can lose you." We were stopped at a red light, and he ran his free hand through his thick brown wavy hair.

I was starting to feel like the conversation was taking a turn in a different direction, one that made me uncomfortable. Jacob was acting very weird; a weird I had never seen from him before. He was usually so cool and collected, the voice of reason to my normal neuroses.

He also looked like he was starting to feel uncomfortable, so I tried to save the conversation. "I know. I feel the same way about you." Uh oh, that didn't come out right. I saw him sit up a little straighter in response to my comment, so I quickly added, "And Lisa of course," to make him realize I meant it in a friend way. Yeah, I did have the jitters before when Jacob took my hand, but I didn't want him to know that.

"I mean, what would I do without you guys? You're my best friends," I added. Even though I knew I probably should have stopped there, I continued on. "I love you guys." Yikes! Why did I add in the "L" word? Maybe I was just overreacting to the situation and reading it all wrong like I normally did. Maybe there was no real tension in the car, and I was just imagining it all. Maybe it was just a combination of all of my emotions coming to the surface.

At that moment, Jacob pulled off the exit and into the parking lot of a Fudruckers. I guessed I wasn't reading the tension in the car wrong, after all. I had a bad feeling where this was going, and I started to get that panicky feeling in my stomach. My heart started to pound really hard, and my cheeks and ears started turning red. Damn Irish blood. It was so obvious when I was angry or nervous. I blamed my Irish ancestors.

Jacob turned into a far parking spot and shut off the car. He had taken his hand back so that both could hold the steering wheel when he abruptly turned off the highway. They were still resting on the wheel at ten and two as he stared at the center of the steering wheel like he was building up the courage to say what was clearly in the air.

I decided to take control of the situation. "Don't," I pleaded.

He turned his head to me wearily, hands still on the wheel. He looked like he was either hurt or relieved, or maybe both.

I had to finish my thought. "I have been through so much this last week. I have a lot ahead of me in the next few days. I need you as a friend right now." I was being as honest as possible, hoping it would get me out of this situation.

"But I have to tell you." He hesitated and then and added, "In case it makes you stay."

I looked down and shut my eyes. Why now? I sort of always knew there was an attraction between Jacob and me. We always held each other's gaze longer than friends normally should. He always teased me a little more than normal. We always touched each other whenever we had the excuse to, whether it was an arm over the shoulder or a hand on the knee when the other told a good joke. I knew it was there, but always figured it wouldn't go any further than friendship, because there would always be Lisa.

You see, Lisa liked Jacob. I'd known for some time now. She had never come out and told me, but girls could tell when their friends liked a guy. She always talked about Jacob when he wasn't around, and when he was around she was always trying to put the attention on herself. I never minded much. She was the beautiful one, so I naturally assumed that Jacob would one day decide to be with Lisa anyway. I thought about all of this during the long pause that now filled the air.

Jacob didn't speak again until I looked up at him. He had to know I knew what he was going to say, and I guess he was giving me time to formulate a response.

Jacob finally took his hands off the steering wheel and faced me. "You see, I have feelings for you."

There it was, he said it, and now he could never take it back. Now I needed to decide if I wanted to be with him and potentially ruin my friendship with Lisa, or try to figure out a way to forget he ever said this and be friends with both of them.

I let him continue. "I always thought we had something," he paused, "something more than just friends." He was right. We did and we both knew it.

"I see the way you look at me, and I know what it means because I look at you the same way," he said plainly. "I know you better than anyone. You're panicked right now, thinking that I'm ruining our friendship because I just said what neither of us wanted to say."

"I am not panicked," I stated defensively.

Jacob smiled and looked down for a moment before responding. "Your cheeks and ears are bright red."

Damn. It was a clear giveaway every time.

I wasn't sure how to respond. "I'm not sure what you are looking for from me. I wasn't expecting this. It's just too much for me to handle right now." I was on the verge of tears. I had thought I was all cried out, but it seemed I was wrong.

I went to put my head in my hands, but Jacob grabbed my hands so that I couldn't hide. I just wanted him to stop talking, to let it go for now. Why did he have such bad timing?

"I'm not trying to force you to say it back, but I have feelings for you, Sam. I like you. I thought you should know before deciding what to do." I had never seen this side of Jacob before. His six-foot tall baseball player body did not look so strong sitting in this car. Right now he looked scared and vulnerable. He looked really afraid that I didn't feel the same way he did, even though he had seemed so confident a few moments ago.

I had trouble doing it, but I forced myself to look at him. His eyes were truly beautiful, and I really wanted to tell him the truth about how I felt. But there were other things I needed to consider and think about. I couldn't give him the answer that he wanted right now.

I said the only thing I could think of saying, "Thank you." It sounded so lame and I knew it the moment I said it. I couldn't end it this way; I needed to be more honest with him. "Honestly, Jake, I don't know how I feel right now about anyone or anything." He nodded at me, so I continued on. "I just can't think about it today. There are a lot of things going on, and I need a friend right now. Maybe we can talk about it more later. I just can't right now," I repeated. Tears started to well up in my eyes. I didn't want to suffer the loss of my parents and my best friend in the same day.

Jacob nodded again and seemed to understand.

"Can you take me to my aunt's house?" I asked, trying desperately to get out of the current situation.

He put the car in reverse and backed out of the spot. Once we were on Route 9 again heading to my aunt's house, I realized that neither of us was talking, so I flipped on the radio to fill the awkward silence. It took me five stations until I could find one that wasn't playing a love song. Suddenly I couldn't wait to get to my aunt's house when only two hours ago, that was the last place I wanted to be.

Travis

My Aunt Alice's house was full of people and the last place I wanted to be. I hadn't seen Sam in over an hour, after she walked out at the end of the funeral with a boy I was guessing was her boyfriend. The funeral had been harder for me to take than I'd thought it was going to be. I was relieved when I realized that Sam wasn't going up to the podium to say anything. I was anxious about how I would deal with her words. Everything that had happened over the last few days had really thrown my world for a loop. I hadn't expected for this to be so difficult. I just assumed it would be more of a bother. I assumed that I would just have to deal with the will and put the house up for sale. I would be back in Florida by Sunday and back to work Monday. But tomorrow was Sunday, and at this point I couldn't see how everything would be dealt with by tomorrow. And what was I going to do about Sam? Bring her back to Florida with me?

I was standing by the makeshift bar, pouring myself a gin and tonic, mulling over the weight of this responsibility, when a side thought entered my brain. I couldn't help but think about Maddy Walsh. I knew that I had more important things to consider right now, but I couldn't stop thinking about how smooth her skin looked and how tight her skirt was. A smile came across my lips as I had these thoughts. Of course, it was the worst possible time, but I was a man and I had a hard time controlling myself. Just as I tried to refocus my mind, I realized Maddy was standing beside me.

"What are you smiling about? Don't you know this is a funeral?" she whispered in my ear. The gesture and tone were so intimate that my skin got goose bumps as I felt her hot breath so close to my neck. If she had only known the thoughts swimming around in my mind were of her.

I turned to face the room of people, but instead saw only Maddy. I had to remember that she'd left me all those years ago, and I was still resentful of her for it. Well, maybe not, but I should've been. Over the years, I had definitely grown up. I was no longer the boy she once knew. I was a man and was very good with women. I had a charm about me that women were attracted to, and I'd used it to my advantage on several occasions. You see, I loved women. Not emotional love, but physical love. And

I was good at it. Let's just say I was not the type of person that would fall so easily under the influence of Maddy Walsh, as I once had. I wanted her, yes, but I also wanted to let her know that I was not a pushover. Was I going to fall in love with Maddy again? No, but I could still sleep with her, right? That was the beauty of my experiences over the years. I learned how to detach myself. If I was going to get her, I needed to act like I didn't want her at all. That was what you needed to do with women like Maddy, who were confident, beautiful, knowing they could get any man they wanted.

"I was just thinking of the past and the good times I had in this house," I lied. Women didn't want the truth from men. They liked the lie better.

She smiled and let out a quiet laugh at my response. I couldn't tell if she thought I was being sweet or if she knew I was lying.

"So how are you handling everything? It must be hard on you even though you've been out of the picture for so long," she flatly stated.

This comment infuriated me. Who was she to cast judgment? Had she been a saint these last ten years? I was sure the answer was no.

"Excuse me." This was a statement, not a question, and I walked away. Even though I had lusted for her seconds earlier, she didn't have the right to imply that I was a bad son or brother. Clearly, I was overreacting to this comment, but I didn't care. We were at my parents' funeral. I figured I had the right to overreact if I wanted to.

I headed toward the front door, stone-faced, and Maddy hurried to follow. When I arrived outside and started to head down the stairs she grabbed my arm to stop me.

"I didn't mean to insult you."

"Too late." I turned to continue down the stairs.

She followed me again, like I knew she would, but this

time she jogged to get right beside me. "Listen to me. I really didn't mean it that way. I was trying to be sympathetic!" Now she sounded angry at me. Like I was insulting her.

Surprisingly, this aroused me. We were halfway down the long driveway of trees. I stopped abruptly and grabbed her hand to swing her so that we were facing each other. With my other hand, I grabbed her neck and pulled her to me and kissed her. The kiss was hard and wet. She resisted at first out of shock and then grabbed my lower back to press me closer against her. Her warm tongue felt good, and we moved in perfect motion. I had forgotten how good of a kisser she was and thought that she had even improved over the years.

The kiss was long and full of aggression and passion. My hands were entangled in her hair, and her hands were on my lower back pressing my body into hers. This felt good, and I started to feel warm and hard in all the right places. Then, she suddenly pulled away. She must have felt me, realizing where this was headed.

Even though she had broken our kiss, her face was only inches from mine, and we were both breathing hard like we had just run wind sprints.

She stared into my eyes. "We can't."

Why do women always do that? She clearly wanted to sleep with me, and I wanted to sleep with her. But it was like she was struggling with her inner morality, deciding whether or not sleeping with me right now would make her a slut. Men never thought that way. If the situation arose for me to have sex, I did it. I never worried about what she would think of me or what happened next. I guess that was a luxury that men had over women. Well, that luxury was screwing me right now, no pun intended.

"We are at your parents' funeral." Okay well, she had me there. It was a reality check, and I realized this was not the right time or place.

I still tried to lighten the situation. "Well, technically we are at the after party," I said with a smile.

I was still holding her face in my hands. Her skin was smooth, and she smelled like vanilla. I decided to kiss her cheek and let go. "We still on for drinks tonight?"

"Tonight?" I could see a sense of panic cross her face. "Haven't you been through too much today already?"

I suddenly realized I didn't know anything about her. Maybe she had a boyfriend that I didn't know about. Maybe he was bigger than me and could kick my ass. "Do you have a boyfriend?" I needed to know.

She laughed at my suggestion. "No. It's just that you seem, um, vulnerable. It's been a long day for you. Maybe we should wait a few days."

"Well, I leave tomorrow so I only have tonight," I said. "We should head back to the house now."

I thought about taking her hand, but that seemed too intimate. Holding hands would send the wrong message. So we just walked back to the house side by side, my hands in my pockets and hers swinging casually by her side.

As we walked back up to the house, I turned to ask Maddy what time I should pick her up, when I saw Sam walking into the backyard. She looked weary and confused. Different than I had seen her earlier. I decided to go talk to her. I wasn't sure what I was going to say, but it felt like the right thing to do.

I told Maddy that I needed to get something from the back patio. We agreed to meet at the local bar at 7:00 p.m. I wasn't sure where she lived, and I didn't have time to ask or get directions. Meeting there was just more logical and made it feel less like a date.

As I headed to the back I saw Sam sitting on the brick retaining wall at the far end of the yard. Something was wrong, and I had a feeling I was the last person she wanted to talk to.

Samantha

I was late to my aunt's house. My head was still reeling from the car ride with Jacob. Why was all of this happening to me now? I knew why. Jacob thought he was going to lose me. I hadn't even thought of it much because all week I'd been stuck in my own personal hell. I realized now that I was going to have to make a decision, and soon. The stress of everything and massive grief that I was still feeling over the loss of my parents was too overwhelming. Just minutes ago, I couldn't wait to get to my aunt's house to escape the uncomfortable tension with Jacob. Now that I was here I didn't feel like going inside and facing everyone.

I stared at the house thinking of where I could go hide for just a little while longer, and then I decided to sneak to my aunt's backyard. She lived on a huge piece of land, probably over five acres. Most of it was woods, front and back. The driveway was long and winding and lined with trees on either side. As Jacob and I pulled up we saw Travis and Maddy walking to the house. I didn't think much of it, since I was so focused on getting out of the car. When we finally parked behind an older Volvo, Jacob went in the house after I told him I needed some time to myself.

The backyard, much like the front yard, was filled with trees and woods. I was sure there were lots of tics in those woods, but as kids we never thought of that stuff and would build forts and go on expeditions looking for Indian arrowheads, which we would sometimes find. In the center of the yard there was a circular eating area surrounded by a brick retaining wall. There was a built-in brick barbeque that was stained black from years of charcoal grilling and an old wooden picnic table with benches. I sank onto the bench at the picnic table and took in my surroundings.

We'd had so many family gatherings in this backyard over the years, it was filled with memories of my parents. My dad at the grill, my mom setting the picnic table, my aunts, uncles and cousins all being their crazy selves. I lost track of time in my daydream, when I felt the bench sink next to me. I hadn't even seen my brother walking out to join me. He was undoubtedly the last person I wanted to talk to right now, and I guessed he realized it when I rolled my eyes as I looked over at him. During all my family reminiscing I hadn't once pictured him.

"Hey, Sam, are you okay?" he said, sounding half concerned and half annoyed.

"I'm fine, thanks. I just need some time alone to think for a while." Hint, hint.

"Oh, okay. You just looked a little weird, so I thought I would see if you needed anything. A soda or some food maybe?" Travis seemed legitimately concerned. What was happening to everyone today? Was I in the Twilight Zone?

"Um, no, I'm fine. I'll be in to grab some food in a bit. I just need some time to think." I didn't really feel like sharing anything with my brother. He knew just as well as I did that we were going to need to make some decisions in the next few days, but now was not the time for that discussion. I'd already been through enough today. But Travis didn't seem to take the hint. He stayed sitting next to me.

"I remember coming here when you were little, and we would look for arrowheads in these woods. Do you remember that?" He pointed to the woods in the direction of a path that we had made through the trees and brush. I didn't answer, not wanting him to know that I did remember looking for arrowheads, but not with him. "Nah, probably not. You were just a baby, no older than two. You loved it, though." He paused as if reflecting. "I guess we are lucky we never got Lyme disease from tics in those woods, huh?"

I shrugged. I was trying to give him as many hints as possible that I just wanted to be alone. Finally, he got it.

"Well, I will let you be alone, then." Travis stood and was about to walk away when he turned back and ended with, "You know we're going to need to talk. I had planned on going back to Florida tomorrow, but I don't see that happening. I am going to cancel my flight until we can figure things out here." I nodded in recognition of his last comment, and he headed back up to the house.

I sat in silence for a good fifteen minutes thinking about my current situation. First, I needed to figure out the best way to cope with the loss of my parents. Sitting on my bathroom floor was clearly not a good long-term strategy. Second, I needed to decide if my feelings for Jacob were strong enough to potentially ruin my friendship with Lisa and keep me in New Jersey. And finally, I needed to decide where I wanted to live. A pretty big decision, if you asked me. The final dilemma hinged on the conversation with Travis tomorrow, which made me nervous. I had no idea how he felt about the situation or what he was going to want to do.

Sitting here stressing over these things was not helping as much as I thought it would. I decided to join the rest of the guests in my aunt's house. The sooner this day was over, the better off I would be.

Travis

I never thought that I would be the one to stick around and help my aunt clean up after everyone had left, since usually I was the first to leave any family function, but I did.

My conversation, or lack thereof, with my sister didn't go so well. I realized after the funeral that I would never be able to leave tomorrow like I had originally planned.

I made sure to keep an eye on Samantha throughout the day. I felt uneasy about her mood. I knew that she was grieving our parents more than I was, but it felt like more than that. She was probably stressing about what was going to happen to her, where she was going to live. I knew because it stressed me out more than I wanted to admit. I also noticed that her boyfriend—or at least who I thought was her boyfriend because I was never introduced to him—was visibly upset the entire afternoon, and they didn't really talk much. Did something happen after they left the funeral? I probably should've been more curious, but I honestly didn't care much, as long as we were both on the same page with her staying here while I headed back to my life as soon as possible.

I also spent the majority of my afternoon distracted by Maddy. I couldn't get that kiss out of my mind. It was different from when we were kids. We were both more experienced, and the kiss was more aggressive and heated than I remembered from our past. I found myself looking for her every time I walked into a different room. I tried not to be obvious and to be cooler about it, but clearly it wasn't working. Every time I seemed to look at her I found myself staring. She caught me doing this at least three times. Each time I knew I had been caught and just smiled and chuckled at her. I was actually looking forward to drinks with her. Partially because I was interested in knowing more about her current life, but mostly because I wanted to get a few drinks in her and rip off her black skirt. Before she left, we had decided on where to meet up and exchanged numbers. Actually, I asked for her number, and she seemed hesitant to give it to me but eventually caved in.

By the time the last person left, it was almost five thirty. Sam and I helped Aunt Alice finish straightening up and were finished around six. We got in the rented Focus and headed back home. It was a short drive, only about fifteen minutes, and the car was silent the entire time. I didn't want to push Sam to talk to me. Also, I didn't have much time to get ready if I was going to make it to my drinks with Maddy. I was afraid that if Sam did talk to me she would never stop. Not that I had firsthand experience with Sam, but it was a typical woman thing to do. Once you get them started, they'd go on and on about their feelings.

When we got back to my parents' house, Sam jumped out of the car like she was in a hurry to get somewhere.

"Hey!" I yelled, standing next to the car. "I'm going out tonight just in case you were wondering."

She turned around at the top of the porch. "Okay, I'll order Domino's and have them deliver." Then she was gone, into the house.

I was ready and out the door twenty minutes later. I had just enough time to shower and cancel my plane ticket for tomorrow. I was wearing my dark designer jeans that had embellishments on the back pockets and a black button down collared shirt. I was told once that dark clothes make my light blue eyes stand out with my dark brown hair. My hair was slicked back and it was still a little light out so I wore my Serengeti's. I looked good and knew it.

I arrived at the bar before Maddy, so I found a seat and ordered a beer. I had been drinking gin and tonics earlier in the day but figured beer would last me longer. I could handle beer better than gin, and I didn't know exactly what was going to happen tonight, so I needed to prepare myself just in case. I hadn't really eaten so I ordered some chicken strips, figuring it couldn't hurt to have some food in me.

After finishing my chicken strips and my second beer, I realized that Maddy wasn't going to show. She was already forty-five minutes late and Maddy was never late. I sat at the bar, and suddenly felt alone. It was nothing drastic. I mean, I had been through a lot this last week, and I was sure that the gin earlier and the beer now didn't help much, but I had never been stood up before. I had been dumped (by Maddy), I had been yelled at, and one time even slapped, but I had never been stood up. Not that I was completely stuck-up, but I was a good-looking guy and knew how to turn on the charm with a woman so that she at least gave me a chance in the beginning.

I guessed this was a little different. Maddy and I had a

lot of history. But after everything that had happened, the least she could do was call my cell and give me some explanation, no matter how pathetic it was. Then, as I thought more about being stood up, my loneliness started to turn into resentment. I couldn't believe that she had done it to me again. She built me up, gave me all this expectation, and then left, or never showed, whichever circumstance you wanted to relate this to. I was stirring in my barstool, getting increasingly mad with each passing minute, when I decided I was going to confront her about it. We weren't kids anymore, and she would have to answer to her decisions. I quickly realized I didn't know where she lived. I could go to her parents' old house, but I doubted that she still lived there. I wondered if she was listed. I took out my blackberry and looked her up.

There she was! Gotta love technology. From my phone I could see a street view of her house, and to my surprise, she did still live in her parents' old house. That made me wonder if she lived with them or if they had passed away and I didn't know. Either way, I paid my bill and was out the door.

As I drove up to the old blue house, I realized that the lights were on and only one car was in the driveway. Even if she didn't live here by herself, she looked to be alone right now. Her home was just as I remembered it. The house was a one-story ranch style located right off one of the heavier travelled roads in town. Her driveway was short and wide so about four cars could fit next to each other. It wasn't paved but had a decent amount of gravel so that it wasn't too bumpy. The front walk was made up of white stepping stones, and there was a wind chime that stayed silent on this calm April night.

As I walked up to the porch, my resentment and anger that had filled me at the bar were quickly turning into nervousness and doubt. Should I be here? What was I going to say to her? Had I had too much to drink? Would she think I still had feelings for her? Which clearly, I did, whether I wanted to admit it or not. I hesitated as I approached the first stepping stone on the path that lead to the front door. After all these years of not feeling much of anything for anyone I realized that maybe I miss it. Maybe the wall that I had put up all those years ago, was brick to everyone else, but water to Maddy where she could just walk right through. The realization that someone could affect me in this way made me have doubts as to whether I wanted to let that person into my life, to give up control. I thought for a moment and then realized that coming here tonight was a mistake. This wasn't the right time or place to deal with feelings that I didn't know what to do with.

I quickly turned around and headed back to my car. When I got halfway across the driveway, the outside porch light flickered on. Maddy must have seen me pull up and was probably watching me the entire time I was debating with myself. I realized it was too late to retreat. Even if I made a mad dash for the car, I would eventually have to face her, right? Could I get away with telling her that I just came to check on her since she didn't show for drinks? I could tell her that I was worried about her so I looked up her address and decided to come over. But why had I been standing in her driveway so long? I would've had no logical answer for that.

As I turned around I saw Maddy standing in the doorway, looking puzzled and annoyed at the same time. Her arms were crossed in a protective way over her chest. She had on faded blue jeans and a green T-shirt that said New York Jets in white print. She looked beautiful in the way that women do when they aren't trying. The green shirt brought out the green in her eyes, which I was always a sucker for as a kid. While I took her whole body in, I realized that she was waiting for me to say something. I quickly snapped back to reality.

"Hi." It was a weak start, and I knew it. She didn't respond. "I thought that you were gonna meet me for drinks tonight and when you didn't show I wanted to make sure you were okay." There. End of story, I thought to myself.

"Oh." She looked puzzled, clearly that was not the response she was expecting. See? I could still think on my feet even while looking into her piercing eyes, which were making my head fuzzier than the beers I drank earlier. I was a defense lawyer, after all, so I was good at coming up with alternative intentions.

"Sorry about that," Maddy said after a few seconds of awkward silence. "I just thought you'd had a long day and that it would be best for me not to complicate things for you too much."

Yeah, right, I thought to myself. She was not as good as I was at thinking on her feet. Well, I had a decision to make now. I could confront her as I had planned on doing at the bar or I could just leave, walk away, and not turn back. I'd never been the type of person to take the easy way out, and I thrived on confrontation. I loved a good fight. But I knew I might not win this one and that it could open up feelings that I had closed off years ago. I made my decision instantly.

I took a few steps up the stone walkway. It was too late to make a scene, and I felt like I had a better chance of taking her face on if I was closer.

"So you let me sit at a bar for almost two hours by myself, with no phone call, because you were looking out for my best interest?" I wasn't even close to raising my voice, but it did have a bit of an edge to it.

"Ok so maybe I thought it was best for the both of us. I mean, you are leaving tomorrow, you just lost your parents, and we haven't seen each other in a really long time." She didn't take one breath through that entire sentence. I could tell from the look in her eyes that she was remorseful. She was clearly regretting her decision to stand me up.

"I cancelled my flight tomorrow." As I said this, I

instinctually looked down at my feet. My own insecurities made me think I couldn't look her in the eyes. I didn't want her to get the wrong idea, like I had cancelled my trip home to stay here to be with her, but that was how it ended up sounding. I wasn't ready to go back to Florida yet. I still had to deal with my parents' estate and my sister.

"Why? I hope you're not staying for me," she said. That was a shot in the gut if I'd ever felt one. I would have preferred to get hit with a baseball bat again like I had the other day. I needed to clear this up fast.

"No," I said defensively. "I still have a lot to do with my parents' estate and I have some stuff to discuss with Sam." There. All cleared up.

Maddy fumbled a little at the door. I could see that she hadn't realized I would have other reasons to stay until I explained the most obvious. "Of course, you have a lot to do. It's just that after that kiss today I didn't want you to get the wrong idea."

Wrong idea? We practically jumped each other in the front yard of my aunt's house. She groped me like she was going to the electric chair and I was her last conjugal visit. Then she said she would meet me for drinks, knowing I was leaving tomorrow, which of course meant back to her place to have wild meaningless sex.

I played it off like I didn't have the "wrong idea" at all. "Of course not. I just thought it would be nice to catch up." I was definitely playing it cool. "It was a surprise for me to see you today at the funeral. I didn't even realize you still lived here in town. I figured you would be married with three kids by now." I didn't know that much about her anymore. She could be married with three kids and just lied about it earlier.

"Oh." She seemed taken aback. "Nope, not married and no kids." She looked a little uncomfortable as to what to do next. "Well, I would invite you in, but it's late, and I have to get up early tomorrow. You know how it is."

She was blowing me off. Clearly, she was

uncomfortable with the discussion of the kiss today and fearful of where the night might lead if I were to stay any longer. She looked vulnerable and scared. I decided it was best for me to leave. Maybe I could take some time tomorrow to think about where Maddy and I could go from here. As I turned to leave, Maddy looked relieved. She had never been much for confrontation and she was obviously confused about her feelings for me, much like I was with my feelings for her.

I drove home in silence. I needed to think, so I left the radio off. The streets of the suburbs were so dark and quiet compared to the city. There was no one on the roads even though it was only 10:00 p.m.

I spent the time thinking about what I was going to do tomorrow. I needed to try and figure out what should to be done with my parents' estate and who could handle it for us. I also needed to have a talk with Sam. I didn't want to, and I knew she didn't either, but we needed to get things out in the open. I liked my life, and Sam was just an added complication and responsibility. She had a life here, school and friends. The question we would have to face tomorrow was how could we both keep the lives we wanted?

7 DECISIONS

Samantha

Last night had been another late one for Travis. I wasn't sure exactly where he went, but he left the house looking pretty done up. He was different from what I remembered as a kid. He seemed more vain and self-absorbed, but Travis had never been one of those brothers who cared more about his family than he did his friends or himself. He was a solo teenager all the way. I remembered when my mother would try to make him take me to the park on the weekend or play with me in the pool he'd always put up a fight. He would eventually give in, and from what I remembered, we had so much fun, but he would put up a fight every time. I thought he secretly liked playing with me all those times. I always remembered him smiling and laughing when my mom wasn't around. It was almost like he wanted to hide from her the fact that he liked me, like he was ashamed to be having fun with his little sister. When he left, I was so little that I didn't remember much. I did remember the fighting my parents went through for what seemed like years. Looking back now, it was probably only a few months. My mother always blamed herself for Travis going so far away to college. I wasn't entirely sure what his reasons were and feared that I might never know.

My brother and I had never been close. Of course, I got courtesy cards on my birthday and presents at Christmas that I was sure my mother bought and just signed his name to. I'd never really thought too much about it. In my mind, I was an only child. I grew up that way and was so close to my parents. Every now and then my mother would bring up Travis, things that he had done in law school, cases that he had won. But we never went to his college graduation or law school graduation. We never saw him argue a case in court. Never received postcards when he was on vacation.

It was weird now having him here. It was like the entire mood of the house had changed. Initially, I was resentful and angry that he stayed here. I never saw this house as his, even though he had grown up here so many years before I had. I felt like he made enough money to stay in a hotel. Somewhere less personal and more detached, exactly like he had been all these years. But he had decided to stay here, maybe because he realized he would rarely actually be here. Yesterday was a very difficult day for me, and I couldn't believe that Travis tried. It was a pathetic attempt, and of course I didn't talk to him about what I was feeling, but he did try nonetheless.

Today was going to be a rough day for both of us. Sooner or later we were going to have to discuss the elephant in the room. Where was I going to live? I knew that Travis didn't want or need the responsibility of taking care of me. I used the phrase "taking care of" loosely because most likely I would be taking care of myself and of him. But I knew that he liked his life so far away from New Jersey, or else he would have come home to visit more.

I was sixteen, almost seventeen and practically an adult. I could definitely take care of myself, and I wanted to stay in New Jersey with my friends. But deep down I felt a little hurt. I felt like I was sixteen and all alone. I knew that Travis didn't want me, and I knew that I didn't want to live with him or have anything to do with him, but it would still be nice if he did want to take care of me. I sometimes thought of what it would be like to have a brother. Not just a biological brother, which was what I had, but also a real older brother who looked out for me and made sure that I was safe and happy. I wasn't sure if that was what I wanted from Travis, but sometimes I thought about what it would've been like to grow up with a brother like that. I wondered now if that was something we'd ever have. What if I were to move to Florida? Could I make us a family? I wondered all of this while I lay in bed staring at the ceiling. A few seconds later my alarm clock went off. It was eight on Sunday morning. I closed my eyes one last time and thought to myself yet again that I just needed to get through the day. By tomorrow I would know what the future held for me. With that final thought, I got out of bed and started the day determined to make some decisions.

Travis

I heard my sister get up around 8:00 a.m. and figured it was a good time to also get started on the day. I had a rough time getting to sleep last night after my encounter with Maddy. There was so much going on right now that it was hard to determine if I actually had feelings for Maddy or if I was just reminiscent about the past and the once romance we'd had. I decided that I needed to focus on finishing up my parents' estate business today and dealing with Sam and her future living arrangements. I knew it would be a hard conversation to have with her but one that needed to be had. I thought it was best to start with the estate stuff.

I got down to the kitchen before Sam, probably

because she took much longer than I did getting ready. I made a pot of coffee and called Mr. Freeman at his home. He told me yesterday that it was okay to call him on a Sunday, given that he knew I needed to tie up loose ends rather quickly. We spoke for about twenty minutes about the timeline of settling the estate and the normal procedures that went into it. Luckily, there was not much that I had to do except sign some papers when the time arose. He asked me what we were doing with the house. We could sell it, pay off the mortgage with the insurance money, or keep the mortgage and move the payments into my name for now so that I could keep them up. I decided the house would have to be part of my discussion with Sam today, so I made a note to add it to the list and told Mr. Freeman that I would get back to him later on today with our decision.

I decided the best thing to do was make a list of topics to discuss with Sam today. I feared that things might get a little emotional for her, and I needed to make sure I covered everything and that nothing was forgotten in the heat of the moment.

The first item was the house. I had just gotten off the phone with Mr. Freeman, and it was the first thing on my mind. The options were: buy with insurance money, sell, or Travis to make payments (I starred sell since that was my first preference).

Second, the distribution of allowance from the estate to Sam. My parents had left all of their money and possessions to Samantha, but they had left Samantha to me. Given that she was still a minor, she couldn't collect any of the money because it would go into a trust until she is old enough to access it. I decided to set some aside for her college and other future purchases. The rest I would get in monthly allowances for her care. I would either keep it for myself, if she came to live with me (not what I wanted, but a legitimate consideration to note), or I would deposit it into a joint account that she would have access to. If we opened up a joint account, then I would need to trust that she could handle the money herself and not spend it all. That would have to be a job for whoever was taking care of her in this scenario.

Third, was going through the house. If we sold the house, someone would need to go through all of my parents' things and figure out what we should keep and what we should give away or sell. I knew that would be a huge job and hoped that Sam and my aunt were up for the task, given that I wasn't planning on staying that long.

Fourth, and most importantly, was where Sam was going to live. That was the big one and the one that I deliberately wrote down last. Technically it should have been the first item on the list, given that the answer to this question would be the basis for the answers to the other three questions, but I knew it was also the touchiest. Neither one of us wanted to broach this subject, so I left it for last.

If Sam moved to Florida with me, then we would get a joint bank account that I would be in charge of, and we would spend an extra couple of days going through the house to clear it out for sale. If Sam stayed in New Jersey, then she would most likely have to move in with my aunt. However, she might want to keep the house to move into when she turned eighteen or keep it until after college. These were all things I was leaving up to her to decide.

Analytically speaking, I had all the points that I wanted to discuss, but what was I going to say if Sam wanted to live in Florida with me? The odds of that happening I knew were slim to none, but there was that chance. If that happened, then what would I do? I would be responsible for a sixteen-year-old girl. I couldn't even imagine how much that would change my life. No more working until nine at night and then going out with my friends to a club until 3:00 a.m. No more sleeping in on weekends until two in the afternoon and waking up to start off my day with a beer, hair of the dog and all.

But I might've been going about this all wrong. Sam was sixteen, which was practically an adult. She seemed pretty tame. Maybe she would do my laundry and cook me dinner? Maybe she would clean my house, and I wouldn't have to pay for the maid service anymore? I knew this was a pretty selfish thought pattern, but it could have its advantages.

And at the end of the day, I liked my life how it was. I didn't want a sixteen-year-old girl coming in and messing with it. I didn't like the fact that I was here at all, dealing with these decisions or dealing with my feelings for Maddy. I wanted to just get this over with and head back to my normal life in Florida.

It was time for a second cup of coffee as I waited for Sam. I was as prepared as I would ever be, or so I thought.

Samantha

I walked into the kitchen and realized that my brother was already sitting quietly at the kitchen table reviewing his notepad. He looked very much like a lawyer as he sat there reading.

"Good morning," I said to get his attention.

He looked up. "Oh, hi. Sleep well?"

"Better than the night before, I guess."

Clearly, we both were a little nervous about the discussion we knew was coming and the chitchat was just getting us by.

"So how was the pizza last night?" he asked.

"Okay, I guess. It was no DeSalvo's, but it was good." I went to the coffee pot glad that he had already brewed some and left enough for me. As I poured in the creamer I realized he was staring at me. "What's up?" I asked, even though I already knew the answer.

"I spoke to Mr. Freeman today about the estate and getting some things completed before I head back to Florida."

"When do you leave?" I honestly wasn't sure how long my brother planned on staying, and I hadn't even cared enough to ask before now.

"I'm not sure. I was supposed to leave today, but I cancelled my flight yesterday. I wasn't sure how long it would take to settle things here, and I don't really need to be back so soon. I have a lot of vacation time coming to me. I spoke to my boss, and he understands." He explained, "I don't plan on staying much longer, but to go back today is just too soon."

I considered the manner in which he was explaining his reason for staying. It made sense. I mean, three days was not nearly long enough to settle a life that two people had spent thirty-five years building. It made me wonder how he thought he could do it in the first place. Then I realized he probably didn't care enough to think about it.

I grabbed my coffee mug off the counter and sat down next to him at the kitchen table. We had a beautiful bay window in the kitchen and the table fit in it perfectly. The sun was strong today and I realized that at least outside it was going to be a nice day, not so much in here.

"So what's the notebook for?" I asked, making a gesture towards the notepad that had consumed his thoughts before I entered the kitchen.

"Just some notes on things we need to settle today for Mr. Freeman." He looked a little uneasy as he tapped the pen on the notepad.

I braced myself for the conversation we were about to have. "Okay, hit me with them."

Travis read through each one of his points without stopping, so that I couldn't give my thoughts or opinions on each too soon. I could see he was determined to go through them all before we made any decisions. I realized why when he got to his last point. Where was Sam going to live? He read it just like he had written it, like I was another object on his list and not a person with a real life. After he was done reading, the room went silent. He looked up at me like he expected me to say something. I was still trying to digest all of it. The fact that he just summed up my life in bullet points took me a few seconds to comprehend.

There was no time to be petty I needed to act mature and show Travis how much of an adult I really was. I knew what I wanted, and now I just needed to convince him it was the right solution.

I wanted to stay here of course. I didn't want to move to Florida. I didn't know anyone in Florida, not even my own brother. I was a junior in high school. Do you know how difficult it will be to start new in high school at sixteen? Plus, I had Lisa and Jacob here. I wasn't sure what my feelings were for Jacob right now, but I knew I wanted to stay and figure them out. There was something there between us more than just being best friends. I owed it to myself to figure it out. Maybe I could convince Travis to let me live in this house by myself. I was only two years away from that happening anyway. He was so self-absorbed that this idea might work. It was a perfect solution all the way around.

I started off negotiations. "So, I've been thinking about this a lot since I found out that Mom and Dad made you my guardian." I decided to keep it as formal as possible. My plan was to not get emotional. "I would like to use some of the insurance money to buy the house and then live here on my own until I decide what to do about college." I got right to the point. This was my life and there was no need for me to beat around the bush.

Travis stared at me with a perplexed look on his face. Clearly this was not what he had planned or thought I would say. I figured that we would both have different ideas on what should be done, so I sat patiently and waited for his response, trying to brace myself for anything.

He shifted in his chair before he started, almost like he was on a plane about to crash land. "That is definitely a different way to look at it." He was being very diplomatic.

Handling me with kid gloves. "I never thought about a scenario where you would be living here alone. I mean you're only sixteen."

I didn't think he was trying to insult me, but that is exactly what he had just done. "So, are you going to make me change my entire life because of a year and two months? You think I'm not adult enough to live on my own in this house? You don't know anything about me." I was desperately trying to calm my emotions and sound adult, but I didn't think it was working. My "stay calm" plan lasted about a minute.

"I just don't think that it would be responsible of me to leave a sixteen-year-old girl alone in a house with no protection. What would people think? I don't even think that legally it's an option. I would get arrested. It's called endangering the life of a minor." He was so selfish and this proved it.

"So, you only care about what happens to you and what people think of you? What about me? You are asking me to turn my life upside down, move out of my home and leave my friends?" I knew I wasn't going to be able to hold it together for long. But he totally dismissed my idea. No matter how impractical, it was still good enough for consideration.

"So, what do you think we should do?" I asked, even though I was afraid to hear the answer.

Travis folded his hands together over his notepad. I knew he was trying to be calm, but he was getting ready to lay it all out on the table whether I liked it or not. I realized at that moment he must be a very good lawyer. I felt more like his client than I did his sister.

"I think we should sell the house, and you should go live with Aunt Alice." He said it very matter of fact and did not falter. When I didn't yell or scream or have a hissy fit, he continued. "It's the most logical solution. You still get to stay in your same school with your friends. Aunt Alice loves you and could use the help around the house. You would get all of the profit from the sale of the house, and it would go into your future, college, home, whatever."

I knew that my brother was making perfect sense, and I had figured this was the solution he would push on me. It was the easiest for him. He would get off scot-free. It was also the easiest for me. Everything he said was right, but tears started welling up in my eyes, and I couldn't stop them. I thought about my future, taking care of my aunt, and it looked grim. Don't get me wrong, I loved my aunt, and she had always been good to me, but it wasn't a burden I wanted to carry at sixteen. It felt like Travis was pushing off his own responsibility of taking care of me onto me taking care of Aunt Alice.

Travis saw my tears coming and his hands started to shake in a "no" motion. He clearly didn't want me to cry, but I couldn't help it, the tears started streaming down my face. He leaned back on his chair and combed his hands through his hair, leaving them there as if he was going to rip his hair out.

"Come on, Sam, don't cry." He sounded a little desperate. Good. It was a desperate situation for me.

"I don't want to move out of this house." I said just what I felt. If Travis was going to take me seriously, he had to know the real feelings behind the tears. "I don't want to be burdened with taking care of Aunt Alice. I don't want to get stuck in that life. I know that you don't want to take responsibility for me…I get that, but I don't like this solution. It's the best road for you, not for me." It was hard to get it all out through choking back tears, but Travis got the point.

He nodded and looked up at the ceiling with a big sigh. "Well, I can't let you live here by yourself. I just can't." That was the end of that pipe dream for me. "We can buy the house with the insurance money if that's what you want, but you can't live here alone until you're eighteen." He sat silent for a few moments deep in thought.

I figured I might as well throw out a crazy notion. He

just might go for it given that I was crying. "What if you were to move back here?" He was not expecting that, and he quickly looked right at me. I knew that was a mistake the second I said it, but I was getting desperate.

"Hell, no." He looked almost insulted.

I continued on, even though I knew I should've dropped it. "Well, you're asking me to change my life to suit you. Don't you think it's fair for me to ask you to do the same? You are my brother and supposed to look out for me, which you have never done. Here's your chance."

I had gone straight for the jugular. I knew that Travis had probably thought exactly that at some point throughout these last few days. I had to go for broke if I was going to get anything I wanted. If he had any regrets at all, I needed to take advantage of them.

He was still staring at me in amazement. Maybe he didn't think I could be as mean as him, or that I had it in me to insult someone so personally. He let out a little laugh and went back to staring at the ceiling, his hands still on his head.

After a few very long minutes he spoke.

"You know, you're right. I haven't been a very good brother. I never wanted a sister, and I was always resentful that Mom and Dad loved you more."

I was not expecting to hear this, but I had gone for his heart and this was what I got in return.

He continued on. "Here is what we are going to do. We are going to compromise. We are going to buy this house with the insurance money. It's your money, and if buying this old broken down house is what you want then who am I to stop you." He was very firm and a little scary.

I couldn't seem to respond except to sit there and stare at him with unbelieving teary eyes.

"You don't want to live with Aunt Alice and you don't want Aunt Alice to live here, right?" I nodded slowly. "Then that leaves only one option. Given that I won't let you live alone and I'm not moving back here..." he paused as he considered what he was about to say, "we will stay here for another week. That should give you enough time to go through Mom and Dad's things and decide what you want to keep and what you want to sell or get rid of. After a week, you are coming back to Florida with me. It's almost summer so you won't have to be in school for very long down there. During your summer break, you can come back here and stay with Alice for a few weeks to visit with your friends and pack up the rest of your things. Then you will come back to Florida, and we will live there until you are eighteen. After that you can do whatever the hell you want." His speech was done, and his decision was final, so he got up to leave the kitchen.

I was still sitting there in shock, and as he passed me I grabbed his arm to stop him. He looked down at me. I whispered, "no." But he just walked off.

He looked determined, and I knew that there was nothing I could do or say at that moment to change his mind. This had ended so much differently than I expected. I sat in the kitchen for another hour just staring out the bay window into my backyard. I didn't cry and I didn't scream. I just sat there feeling even sorrier for myself than before. I had one week to change his mind.

8 DISCOVERY

Travis

As I walked out of the house, I grabbed my keys from the holder hanging on the wall next to the door in shock at what I had just done. My intentions had been to figure out a way to tell Sam that she was going to have to stay with Alice and that we would sell the house. But while I was sitting there thinking about what to do with Sam, I couldn't help but think about my mother's letter. I heard her voice in my head and did what I thought she would have wanted. For the first time in my life I listened to my mother. After all, Sam was only sixteen and not old enough to take care of herself or make decisions on her own, so said the law. She didn't even have her driver's license, for crying out loud.

I needed to think about what just happened so I decided to take a drive. I had been doing a lot of that lately.

I opened up the windows of my car and let the fresh crisp air in to help me come to my senses. The truth was I had made up my mind. Sam was right about the fact that I hadn't been a good brother. I had always skirted my responsibilities when it came to my family, and it was something that would stop today. I had no choice but to face this head on.

My mother specifically told me that Sam was my responsibility now, for better or worse. I needed to step up and do what was in her best interest whether I liked it or not. I knew this was very much out of character for me. The first person I always thought of was myself and this was not the solution that bode best for me. Maybe this could be my big gesture to make up for all of my past misgivings. Okay so maybe I was doing this a little bit for me and my own peace of mind.

As I drove through the winding roads, I worked out some things that needed to be done. Now that I had made this decision I had to get things in order. First, I needed to call my boss and tell him when I would be back. Then, I needed to extend the rental car reservation another week. I didn't want to be stuck here without a reliable car. I also needed to figure out what school district my neighborhood was in back home. I'd never had any reason to care. Then I needed to get Sam enrolled for the final few months before summer break.

Wow this was a lot and kept adding up as I went through it in my mind. I decided I needed a smoke and a place to rest and really think. I went back to the same park where I had read my mother's letter. How ironic. When I had originally read that letter I thought that there was no way in hell I would ever bring Sam back to Florida with me, and now that was exactly what I would be doing, because of that letter.

Samantha

After sitting in the kitchen for a while I started to have a mini freak out (and when I say mini, I mean major). I wanted to call Lisa and tell her about the jail sentence that my brother had just imposed on me for no good reason. I wanted to vent on the phone to her and have her tell me what a jerk Travis was and that we would figure out a way to work through this. But I couldn't call Lisa, not after the funeral yesterday. I knew she saw Jacob and me walking out of the funeral proceedings before they had concluded. I knew that she saw us holding hands and shot me a dirty look. Did she know something was going on with me and Jacob? Well, not that anything was going on, but that I maybe wanted something to be going on and Jacob clearly did. I knew that Lisa secretly has a thing for Jacob. She would be mad at me if I explored my feelings for him. Even though I had just lost my parents, there was no way she would be supportive. She would ask me what happened between Jacob and me yesterday, and I didn't know what I was going to tell her. Technically, nothing happened, if you consider Jacob spilling his guts about how much he cared about me as nothing. We didn't kiss, and I didn't give in to my temptation to tell him how I felt, because I wasn't entirely sure how I felt.

Bottom line was I didn't want to have to deal with Lisa's drama right now. I had enough drama of my own. The only other person I could call was Jacob. I sat and looked at the phone for a moment while I considered what would result from that call. I was sure Jacob would rush over to be with me and listen to all of my screaming and yelling and crying. I was sure he would agree with everything I said and give me ideas on how to convince Travis to change his mind. But then what? Would he continue down the path he paved yesterday? Would he push me to know how I felt? This all made me very nervous.

Did this mean I had no one to confide in and complain to? Maybe I was better off starting fresh in Florida. Okay, Sam, clear that thought from your brain right now, I told myself. I would not be better off in Florida, in a strange school with kids I didn't know. It would be too hard to start from scratch.

I had to call someone to help me formulate a plan, and when it came down to weighing my options I went with Jacob. After all, I did have feelings for him, and I was scared and lonely and could use some affection from someone who truly liked me. I realized this was selfish, but I didn't care much right now. I was too mad at Travis to think logically.

Just as I suspected, Jacob answered the phone and was more than happy to listen to my detailed telling of this morning's events in the kitchen. When I got to the news about leaving in a week, Jacob quickly said he would be right over. Uh oh. I thought that might happen. I wondered what would happen when he got here. I ran upstairs and fixed my makeup and changed my clothes just in case. I had still been in my sweatpants, and even though Jacob had seen me in them several times, it didn't feel like the kind of time for sweatpants. I wasn't sure what kind of time it felt like, but I wanted to look presentable.

Jacob was at the door ten minutes after we hung up the phone. He had just gotten his license, and I was assuming his parents let him take the car when he said he was coming over to see me. They were really nice people and sympathetic to my situation.

He was wearing a royal blue shirt and jeans. The blue really brought out his blue eyes against his dark hair and olive skin. I had been crying earlier, but I put on enough eye makeup to cover up the puffiness. When he saw me, his face lit up into a smile, and I couldn't stop from doing the same. He walked in slowly and gave me a hug. I started to tear up a little again. It was nice having someone here who cared about me. I'd missed that lately.

"Can you believe he is making me move in a week?" I sounded muffled because I was talking into Jacob's shoulder. He was still hugging me and I hadn't pulled away.

Finally, he let go and looked down into my eyes. He gently cupped my cheeks with his warm hands and pulled me into him. His lips were so soft, and his breath smelled like spearmint. He clearly had prepared for this moment. At first I was in shock, since I hadn't seen this coming. I imagined it might happen eventually, but I thought I would have ample warning to figure out what to do. I did the only thing I could think of: I kissed him back. This was a side of Jacob I had never seen or experienced before, and his kiss made all of my worries fade away, at least in that moment.

After several minutes, I realized that I needed to break away and bring us both back to reality. I was out of breath and starting to sweat a little, even though I had goose bumps all down my arms and legs.

"Jacob," I breathed, since I couldn't think of anything else to say. We just stood there with our foreheads touching, thinking about what had just happened. We had just crossed the friendship line. This was the number one reason boys and girls couldn't be best friends. The relationship always got complicated. In my case I had another friend that liked Jacob, which complicated matters even worse.

"I had to know," he said.

I wasn't exactly sure what he meant at first, but I quickly figured it out. Jacob wanted to put it all on the table once and for all before I left, to see if maybe I felt the same way he did. I guess he got his answer.

"So much is happening to me right now." I started to tear up again. I had thought only a few days earlier that I was all out of tears, but I was wrong. "I just don't know how I'm going to deal with this."

"I know." Jacob always said the right thing. "We have all week to figure it out." He sounded sad and heartbroken, which surprisingly made me feel good. He cared; he cared a lot.

"I think you should go home." He moved his head away and gave me a shocked look. "I just need some time. I have to sort through all of this." He kissed my forehead and gave me one last hug.

"Of course," He said and closed the door behind him. He didn't act annoyed or disappointed. He understood I needed space and he gave it to me. If it did happen with us, Jacob would make a good boyfriend.

Travis

By the time I finished making all of the appropriate calls it was close to noon and my stomach told me I needed to get something to eat. I headed to a local deli, which I had not been to since I was a teenager. When I walked in, I saw Maddy sitting at the counter reading a book and eating a sub. I couldn't believe my bad luck. I mentally debated whether I should stay or quickly turn around and bolt. I was starving and had been thinking about this sub the entire ride over, so I decided to stay. I wondered if I should apologize to her for the previous night's events. It hadn't happened the way I'd planned and I was feeling a little bad about it. Now that I was going to be here another week, I was probably going to see her again, so I figured I should just get this over with. I couldn't run out of every place if she was there.

As I approached her, she finally looked up from her book and realized I was walking toward her. She looked a little nervous, but I was sure I looked the same.

"Hi Maddy." I was determined to be nicer than I had been the night before. "Funny bumping into you here." I gave her a little smile to try and break the tension.

"Travis, what are you doing here?" She sounded surprised to see me.

"I'm hungry. I haven't been back in so long and wanted to see if the tuna sub was still as good as I remembered."

She smiled looking down at her half-eaten tuna sub. "I didn't think I would see you again before you left?" It was more of a question than a statement.

"I'm here for the rest of the week, actually. I decided

this morning." I left out the part about taking Sam back to Florida with me. Instead, I sat down in the empty seat next to her even though she didn't invite me to. "What are you reading?" I thought I would look interested.

"Oh, just some book I got from a friend of mine. Reading relaxes me," she said as if I didn't know her.

"Yeah, I remember."

Maddy looked a little embarrassed by my comment. She seemed to be remembering that I knew a lot more about her than her reading preferences. I knew that she was compassionate and funny, but stern and cutthroat when she needed to be. True Jersey girl. I also knew where she liked to be touched and that she moaned when we kissed. I realized I was smiling from thinking of that last memory and needed to quickly regain my composure.

"A week, really? What do you plan on doing for a week?" She was fishing and I knew it.

"I have to finish up with the lawyer for my parents and go through their things. Sam and I decided today that she would be moving back with me to Florida next week to finish out the school year. Looks like we're going to try and make this family thing work." So, I stretched the truth a little. I knew Sam wasn't happy with my decision this morning, I wasn't even sure if I was happy with it. But I wanted to show Maddy that I had manned up and taken responsibility. I wasn't sure why, but when I was around Maddy it felt like I had something to prove. I felt the need to show her that I was an adult now and willing to make sacrifices.

Maddy looked surprised by my admission and looked like she wanted to say something, but stopped. Instead she turned back to her book and said, "Well, that's good news, Travis. I'm glad that Sam will have you back in her life." I could tell that she didn't fully mean it, but I was willing to let it go at that. She obviously wanted to be done with our conversation and for me to leave.

"Well, it was nice seeing you. Maybe we can find

sometime this week to get together and catch up." I wanted to at least open the door.

"I'm not sure. I have work all week and end of year testing coming up for the kids." I had forgotten for a moment that Maddy was a schoolteacher and then realized she meant "kids" as in her students.

"Well, how about tonight?" Why was I asking this? Hadn't she already rejected me enough for one life? It was almost like I wanted to torture myself.

Or maybe the real reason I was asking her was because I loved the chase. I rarely had to chase women. Once they heard that I was an attorney, they saw the clothes and the car, they were all over me. Women in South Florida were very materialistic. But not Maddy. She didn't want anything to do with me, and that made me want her even more. It seemed to be human nature to want what you couldn't have, and I was experiencing that at this moment.

She looked up from her book right into my eyes. She was testing me to see if I was sincere. I gave her a little smile back and added, "Nothing like you think. I just want to catch up with an old friend." That sounded innocent enough. Maybe she would believe it. She did and agreed to meet me for drinks later on that evening. I didn't need her standing me up again, so I suggested drinks at her house. She was hesitant at first, but then when I suggested bringing Sam along she agreed. Now I knew that Sam would never go with me. Actually, I wasn't even going to ask her. But she was my "in" to see Maddy and it worked. I could always tell Maddy later that Sam was having a rough day or already had plans with one of her friends. I would figure it out.

We agreed on 5:00 p.m. for some cocktails and barbequing. It was a nice enough day and it seemed like a friendly plan. I said my good-byes, got my sub and left. I could feel Maddy's eyes following me all the way out of the deli as I walked to my car.

She intrigued me, and I was still drawn to her. I knew

she felt the same about me but was guarded, since I was only here for a short time. I had tonight to start something with her, but I needed to make sure that it was something I could walk away from. Given our past history, I figured it would be easy for me. She broke my heart once, and I mended it in a cement box. Even she couldn't get to it now.

* * *

As I drove up to Maddy's house it was around 4:45 p.m. I was early, but I couldn't mull around anymore. I was too anxious. I had already called Mr. Freeman and let him in on our plan. He was surprised but supportive, just like a good lawyer who only wants his cut.

I was dressed differently, more casually than I had looked yesterday. I figured it was a barbeque and faded jeans and T-shirt would be fine. I had concocted my story on why Sam was a no-show. When I got home earlier she ignored me, so I couldn't get her involved with my plan as a backup. She looked like she had a lot on her mind. She was still pissed at me for making her move to Florida, but then when her boyfriend called three times and she didn't take one call, I thought maybe it could be something else. Trouble in paradise I suspected. Who knew with teenagers, but it was a good story for Maddy. Sam had gotten into a fight with her boyfriend and was in no mood to hang out tonight. I figured it was partially true. Sam seemed to have something going on with Jacob, and she was in no mood to hang out with me tonight. It worked for me.

I had picked up some steaks and a bottle of wine on my way over. When I arrived, Maddy was waiting on the front porch. She had seen me pull up, and as I approached she looked skeptical.

"Where's Sam?" she immediately asked.

I knew that would be her first question so I told her the story that I had ready. She still looked skeptical and suggested that maybe she should call and talk to her. After a little coaxing, I convinced her that Sam just needed some space, that teenage girls were like that. Not like I knew from experience, but I had seen enough reality TV shows to know it was a solid case.

We settled out back, and Maddy made us some gin and tonics since it was still daylight. We both agreed it was too early for red wine.

We spent the next hour updating each other on the last ten years of our lives. I learned that she had graduated from the University of Rhode Island with her teaching degree. Her parents had died shortly after that, her mother of cancer and her father of a heart attack only a year after. It was a hard time for her. She inherited their house and lived here alone, although she sometimes thought of getting a roommate or a pet so that the house didn't feel so empty.

She was a teacher at the private high school, which was where she got to reconnect and become close with Sam. She learned that I worked my way through the University of Miami and went on to get an academic scholarship into their law school. In college, I met my best friend, Mike. I now worked with Mike for his father's law firm in Boca Raton. I told her about the clubs, restaurants and beaches. My life was definitely more exciting than hers, but I left out some of the more scandalous stories. I also left out any information about my past relationships or lack thereof. I found out that Maddy had dated a guy in college and he had asked her to marry him. To my surprise, she had said yes, but then when her parents died and she moved back home, their relationship fell apart. By the time we were all caught up, the sun was starting to set and I offered to fire up the grill.

I didn't realize how much I had missed Maddy. She was always the woman in the back of my mind that I still compared all women to, even my college girlfriend Beth. Beth and I were exactly the same breed. Driven, motivated by money, cutthroat. And not at all right for each other. I had met Beth in my first year of law school. She wanted to be a patent attorney. We dated all throughout law school, but in the end, we were both career driven and not ready for marriage. It ended right after graduation and we both went our separate ways. I wasn't certain why Beth couldn't see herself with me for the long haul, but I knew my reason—and she was sitting with me tonight.

I had always resented Maddy and how she had ended our relationship. I realized earlier today, when I decided everything else, that I needed closure with Maddy. I figured the only way to get it was to show her how it felt to be abandoned by the one you love. Basically, I would do to her what she did to me all those years ago. Not a mature way to look at it, but I thought I had been mature enough today to cover me the rest of my life.

I made the steaks to perfection, grilling was always something I enjoyed and was good at. We opened the bottle of wine I brought and sat down to eat. That's when Maddy decided to bring up Sam and the information that I had told her earlier at the deli.

"So, I know this is not my place to say," she started, and with that I knew she was going to pry into my decision to take Sam with me to Florida. She looked uncomfortable about saying anything at all but persisted nonetheless. "It's just that Sam and I have grown to be friends over the years, and I can't imagine her being okay with moving across the country and leaving all her friends."

"Well, Sam is a child and doesn't have much of a choice." I admittedly sounded a little defensive.

"She is not a child. She is a young woman, and she has the right to get some say in this decision. It is a pretty big move." She took a sip of her wine.

"Listen, I appreciate your concern for my sister, but she is my sister and I am responsible for her well-being now." I tried to be firm and believable. That got a little chuckle out of her.

"So now she is your sister? Was she your sister when she graduated eighth grade and you said you would show and you didn't? Was she your sister on Christmas when you didn't even call her, or all of her birthdays?" Okay, now she was getting a little out of line, and the alcohol was giving me the nerve to tell her so.

"There are reasons for all of that. I realize that I have not been the best brother. Sam pointed that out to me all on her own this morning. I don't need a lecture from you. The other option she wanted was to live in that house by herself. Do you think that's a good idea?" I knew her answer would be no and I wanted her to see my side of things. When she didn't answer, I went on. "Do you think it's fair for me to leave my life behind so that she can be near her friends?" Another question that I knew she would answer no. "The only viable option was to bring her back with me, given that she adamantly did not want to live with Aunt Alice." So maybe adamantly was a strong word to use considering that she probably would have said yes to Alice, knowing her fate was moving to Florida to be with me, but I left that detail out.

"You think that you are ready to be a father to a sixteen-year-old girl?" She looked me right in the eyes when she asked me this. I had asked her questions that I knew the answer was no and now it was her turn.

"Well, I am not her father; I am her brother, and we are both sort of adults." Maddy laughed at me. I had her warmed up and was pulling out the charm to get through this part of the conversation.

She shook her head in agreement "Two seconds ago, you called her a child, but you are right about one thing, you are sort of an adult." She laughed again and this time I joined in.

We had both realized that part of the conversation was over. I wasn't sure if Maddy would bring it up again at some later time, but for tonight it was over.

We finished off the first bottle of wine and did the

dishes that accumulated from dinner. It was nice spending time with Maddy in her home. It made me wonder what life would have been like if she hadn't cut me loose all those years ago. Then I remembered why I was there, shook my head to get out of the fantasy of life with Maddy, and offered to open another bottle of wine. I could tell that she was hesitant about a second bottle and what it might lead to, so I flashed my big white smile, and she gave in. Some things never changed.

We moved the evening into the living room. I noticed that she had an iPod in the corner on a Bose music station. I went over and scrolled through her music. She was still the same old Maddy from high school who loved classic rock like Bruce and classic love songs like Sinatra. I decided on Sinatra and joined her on the couch.

She looked a little uncomfortable when she heard the music start. "I know what you're trying to do, Travis. I'm not an idiot." She was holding her wine glass with both hands close to her chest, protecting herself.

"I just thought some music would be nice. You always had great taste in music." I sat next to her on the couch and inched in closer.

"Yeah, but bad taste in men." She giggled.

"You liked me," I teased.

She got a serious look on her face then, maybe the wine had gotten to her more than it had gotten to me. "No." She hesitated and then looked up from her glass. "I loved you." I could tell that she was embarrassed to say it but couldn't stop herself.

I slowly took her wine glass from her hand and placed both glasses down on the coffee table. I leaned in to kiss her, but she pulled away. "I don't think this is a good idea." She was being honest. I could tell by the angst on her face.

I was taken aback by her admission and wondered to myself what she had gone through all those years ago. I hesitated for a moment to try and collect my hazy thoughts. When I couldn't, I did the only thing that I wanted to do, I kissed her. At first the kiss was slow and soft, but it quickly turned into something more. As I quickened my pace and slipped my tongue in her mouth she let out a low moan and I knew I had her.

I had been with Maddy before, many years ago. I was a boy then, inexperienced and insecure. It was different now; I knew what I was doing. No longer did I need to fumble for her bra or guess where to touch her. I knew what women liked, and I figured that Maddy liked those same things. I was right.

I took my time now, caressed and kissed areas that I knew she would like. We were no longer teenagers, but we were exploring each other like it was our first time together.

I positioned myself on top of her on the couch. I could taste her sweet sweat as I kissed her neck. Just like I remembered from high school, our bodies were a perfect fit, even through clothes. As I started to unbutton her jeans she took a deep inhale and suddenly blocked me with her hand. She was rethinking how far we were going tonight, but after all this time I realized I needed her.

As much as I wanted it to be the same, it was different from the other women I had been with. I felt drawn to Maddy and wanted her more than anything. As we locked eyes, I could see that we were both debating how far we should take this, both wanting to experience the wave that we knew would come. I could feel her trembling beneath me and wondered if she could feel my heart beating quickly.

Her slight smile was meant to give me the go ahead, but instead it brought back a wave of memories. We had been here before lying on her couch, teasing each other, both wanting to take it all the way and get lost inside one another. But that was over ten years ago, when we were kids in love, and then she broke my heart. Suddenly, all of those bad memories and hurt came flooding back to me and the heat of the moment left me. I still had no answers from that night when she told me she no longer loved me, and suddenly that was all I could think about.

I quickly got up off the couch and grabbed my shirt that was lying on the floor. I didn't want to just leave, but she could see in my face that I was hurting. She asked me what was wrong, but I couldn't talk. I couldn't explain to her now that I was still holding on to all of that pain and heartache from when we were kids. I headed for the door and thanked her for dinner.

Before closing the door behind me, I glanced back to get one last look at her. She was now sitting up on the couch in only her jeans and bra, her eyes welling with tears, clearly upset with the way I was leaving. I had done to her what she had done to me, but I felt terrible about it. Had she felt this bad ten years ago? Was that what she meant when she said she couldn't go through this again? I couldn't think about that now. I didn't want to think about anything right now.

9 PLANS

Samantha

Ever hear of the saying "when it rains, it pours"? Well, that couldn't be truer for me at this very moment.

Yesterday was a rough day for me. I spent most of it crying in my room. I didn't want to talk to anyone. After I tried ignoring Travis all day, he came to my room and told me that he had already made all of the arrangements for me to go to Florida with him in six days. Six days? My new high school was called Shark River High School, and it was supposed to be good. He had a guest room that he said would fit my furniture if I wanted to move it down, which I quickly declined. He wasn't serious about this move, anyway, and I had all week to convince him to change his mind. Nothing was ever set in stone. You make your own fate, right?

It was Monday now and I had only six days before the date Travis had booked our tickets for Florida. That meant only six days to change my fate. I lay in bed all last night staring at my ceiling, trying to sort through the mess that had become my life.

On top of that I now had to deal with Lisa and Jacob in

I guess what you could call my personal life. I'd never really had much of a personal life. I'd had a couple of boyfriends in the last few years, but nothing serious and no one nearly as special to me as Jacob.

I sat in my bedroom trying to figure out how I was gonna deal with all of these different feelings. This made me miss my mom. I had always turned to her for advice and she gave it freely, even if it wasn't what I wanted to hear. I had to hold back tears as I imagined her sitting next to me with her hand on my back, reassuring me that everything would be all right. But she wasn't here, and I had to do this on my own.

The first task to tackle had to be the moving thing. If I wasn't successful in convincing my brother he was crazy moving me to Florida, then I wouldn't need to deal with the Jacob issue because I would be tens of thousands of miles away. I figured I could take one of two approaches. First, I could make his life miserable. Completely, undeniably terrible. I was a sixteen-year-old girl; I knew how to make an adult's life hell. Then he wouldn't want me to go with him and he would have to let me stay here. Or, my second option, I could run away. I knew that neither option was good, but desperate times called for desperate measures.

The problem with the runaway plan was that, even though I had a large inheritance from my parents, I was too young to touch it. Travis was the beneficiary, and so without him I had nothing. I had very little savings of my own, maybe a few hundred dollars I kept in an old cigar box in my closet. That wouldn't get me very far. I had a car but no license. Damn New Jersey and their seventeen-year-old driving age. If I got in trouble I would have to call for help, and that would lead me right back to Florida with Travis. This plan also left me without Jacob, unless he ran away with me, which I didn't think we were ready for yet. I didn't even know if I wanted that type of relationship with him right now.

That meant I had to go with the bitch plan. It was an okay plan, which I could definitely pull off, but I wasn't confident in its effectiveness. Travis already proved to be more resilient than I had initially thought, and I didn't want to underestimate his ability to put up with my crap. But for now, it was the only plan I had, so I had to go with it until I came up with something better.

I thought again about calling Lisa, since she was the best person to help me develop my bitch plan. She was by far the most vindictive person I knew. But then I remembered it was Monday and that meant everyone was in school but me. They had given me a leave of absence for my parents' funeral, but I hadn't thought about everyone else still being in school. I started thinking about what I would say to Lisa. She saw me walk out of the funeral hand in hand with Jacob, and she knew that we had arrived to my aunt's house late. I was still trying to figure out my feelings for him, but I knew that she had already figured out her feelings for him. She was obsessed. She was always asking about him if he wasn't with us, or worrying about what she looked like when she knew he was meeting us somewhere. I decided to call her after school was out. She would get suspicious if I didn't call her, given I hadn't spoken to her since Saturday. Maybe she wouldn't ask about Jacob and me. But I knew better.

At 3:00 p.m., I decided to text her rather than call, since it was more impersonal and she was less likely to give me the Spanish Inquisition. I started with something simple, knowing that Lisa would reply back within a few seconds. Sometimes I thought that if texting were a career, Lisa would easily make six figures.

Sam: hi school out yet?

Lisa: yeah headed home. It sucked as usual. How u feelin?

Sam: okay. Not sure if u heard but Travis is making me move to FL

Lisa: SHUT UP!! WTF?!?!

Lisa: who would I have heard from? Jake has been ignoring me all day :/

Uh oh. Jacob was ignoring Lisa, which meant that she probably knew something was up with us already. My best strategy was ignoring the last comment.

Sam: I guess he has some big brother fantasy to fulfill. I know sux right?

Lisa: I am coming over right now!

I knew she would be all about trying to help me figure out the best plan to stay home. Lisa loved gossip, even the bad kind. Even though she probably had questions about Jacob and me, this would take her mind off of it, at least for a while. She was definitely the one out of the two of us to overreact, so I needed to figure out my feelings for Jacob before I told Lisa anything.

I liked her because she was the type of person that always told you what was on her mind; you never had to guess about how she felt. She wasn't scared to speak up if she disagreed with you or give her opinion even if you didn't ask for it. Every girl had a friend like that. Someone you brought shopping because you knew she would tell you the truth about your butt looking fat in a pair of jeans. Lisa was that friend to me.

The funny part about us being friends was that neither of us liked hanging out with girls. We actually met through Jacob. I was a tomboy growing up and always had boyfriends. Not boyfriends, but boys that were friends. I liked playing baseball and kickball in the street and building forts out in the woods behind our house with the kids my neighborhood. The majority of my neighbors were boys close to my age. That was how I met Jacob. He used to live four houses down from me until his parents decided they wanted to upgrade to a bigger house about a ten-minute drive downtown. When Jacob moved, he met Lisa, who was his new neighbor.

Since Jacob and I were the same age, I used to go to his house after school to do homework. That was how I met

Lisa. I used to be jealous that they got to live so close together and I was all the way across town. They could hang out whenever they wanted and not include me, but they didn't. We became sort of like the three musketeers. In school, other girls were always so rude to me, I thought because the majority of my friends were boys and they were probably jealous. With Lisa, it was different. She didn't have many girlfriends because the other girls were flat out scared of her. She was brash, strong willed and a great athlete.

About a year ago, Lisa started crushing on Jacob and our three musketeer's situation made me feel uncomfortable. I knew it was going to be an issue the first time she told me. If she told him and he didn't like her, then all three of us couldn't hang out anymore. If she told him and he did like her, then I would be the third wheel. Luckily, I had built up a pretty tough skin throughout the years being friends with Lisa, and I told her both of these scenarios. I convinced her not to tell Jacob, figuring that eventually another boy would come along to steal her interest, and then the three musketeers would remain intact.

Lisa's interest in boys was much more diverse than mine. She dated a lot of boys, and they were all good-looking and popular. Lisa's personality also afforded her confidence to ask boys out, which apparently teenage boys loved. I guess it took the pressure and the fear of rejection off of them. Face it, teenage boys would go out with almost anyone in high school. After Lisa had broken up with her last boyfriend (she was always the dumper, not the dumpee), she told me that she still liked Jacob. This was just two weeks ago, one week before my parents' accident. That had to be why I was getting dirty looks from her at the funeral when she saw me holding Jacob's hand and when we left together. But knowing Lisa, she probably realized the next day that she had overreacted and that it was all very innocent, or at least I hoped that was what she thought.

I heard Lisa's car pull up. Both Lisa and Jacob had their licenses, but Lisa was the only one who had a new car. Her parents had bought it for her. I was the only one out of the three of us that was born later in the year. June, right before the grade cutoff date. So, I was one of the youngest in my class, which meant that I was even further away from eighteen and being of legal age to leave my brother's custody.

Lisa burst through the door in normal Lisa fashion, since she never knocked, and called my name. I was in my bedroom, and she was through my doorway about fifteen seconds later.

"OMG!" she said as she jumped onto my bed and sat Indian style across from me. She threw her purse on the floor. "You have to tell me everything that happened. How can he think he can take you back with him? Don't leave anything out!"

Lisa was also the type of girl that needed every detail. If I told a story, and she didn't think that I gave enough details, she would make me tell it all over again.

"So, I thought that we were going to have a discussion about where I would end up living, but it wasn't a discussion at all. He just told me what was going to happen," I said.

"Wait a second, back up." I told you she liked details. "So, he just started the conversation with 'Sam, you and I are moving to Florida, end of story.'"

"Well, not exactly."

"Okay, then start from the beginning. So, you went downstairs to talk to him. Where was he sitting?" Lisa started digging. By the way, she also watched a lot of Law and Order, so I always felt like I was being interrogated when telling a story.

"He was sitting at the kitchen table with a notepad in front of him, drinking his coffee," I said.

"A notepad? For what?"

"I thought at first that he might be working on a case or something. But then I realized that he had written down topics he wanted to discuss with me. He started by asking me what I wanted to do with the house, either buy it or sell it." I was getting riled up again just thinking about what had happened yesterday morning. "Then he wanted to know how I wanted to handle the money and if I wanted to live with Aunt Alice and take care of her." Okay, so maybe he didn't pose it quite that way, but it was my story to tell how I wanted.

"What do you mean take care of her? Like bathe her and do her cooking and cleaning?" Lisa looked disgusted.

"Yeah. Be like her live-in maid making sure that she doesn't fall down the stairs and die. Basically, like a full-time babysitter but for an old person." I wanted to make it sound like a full-time job, even though I knew that Aunt Alice was pretty self-sufficient. "So of course, I told him no, that I didn't want to live with her. I told him that I wanted to buy the house with the insurance money and live here by myself."

Lisa laughed at that one. "You told him that?"

"Yeah, sure, why not? It's what I want to do, and I don't think it's that bad of an idea." I thought she would be a little more supportive, but Lisa wasn't going to lie if she didn't agree with me.

"But that's crazy. You are only sixteen. He can't let you live here all by yourself. I think it's against the law, like child abandonment or something." I told you she watched a lot of Law & Order.

"Well, anyway, he thought about it for a while and said that I should live with him in Florida. He said that he was my guardian, and I had to do what he told me. Then he said he could make my life miserable if I fought him about it." Okay, I totally over exaggerated, since Travis never said any of those things, but I wanted Lisa on my side, so I needed to fib a little.

"So, why don't you just go live with your Aunt Alice?"

Lisa shrugged like she didn't understand why that was such a bad alternative.

"I don't want to live with her! I want to live in my house, in my room, with my things!" My voice cracked, since I was shrieking at this point and on the verge of tears again.

"Okay, Okay, calm down. Everything is going to be all right." Lisa had her arms out in front of her like I was some untamed animal out in the wild and ready to pounce on her. "Do you have a plan yet?"

This was when I told her about the bitch plan. Being a bitch herself, which she openly admitted, she appreciated the general basis of the plan but shared my concerns about its effectiveness.

"So, being a bitch isn't going to keep you in Jersey. You need to be more devious. What else could really get to him? I know you barely know the guy, but you must know some weakness he has? Think!" she commanded me.

After a moment, I realized what it was. I remembered the tension that I felt when I interrupted Maddy and Travis at the funeral and how shaken he looked as they were walking back to Alice's house after the funeral. I also remembered my mom telling me that when they broke up she wasn't sure what exactly happened, but that Travis seemed heartbroken. She said that it changed him, and that was when he left home and didn't look back.

"Well…" I started to tell Lisa about the only weakness of Travis's that I could think of. I told her about Maddy and the stories my mom had told me all those years ago and how Maddy would always ask me about Travis, even though she hadn't seen or talked to him in years. As I explained the situations that I'd witnessed yesterday and the stories from years ago, Lisa's eyes widened. I could tell that her brain was working up some devious plan.

"What?" I asked, excited and anxious to hear what she had to say. Lisa was much more devious than I was, which was why I knew I needed her help with this.

"I know how to keep you here." Lisa looked proud of herself. "It's so easy."

I was on the edge of my seat, and Lisa could tell, so she took her sweet old time to fill me in on her plan.

"You need to get Travis to fall in love with Maddy." She stated it so blankly that I couldn't believe I hadn't thought of the idea sooner. I felt like such an idiot. This was much better than the bitch plan.

"That's it?" I asked with a smile on my face. "That is brilliant. But how?"

"Well, first question is would Maddy ever move to Florida? Because you could do all this work getting them to fall in love and then she decides to go with you to Florida and your plan backfires." Lisa had a good point. I knew I kept her around for a reason.

"I don't think so, but I'm not really sure. I mean, I know that she owns the house she lives in now. She inherited it from her parents a few years back. She loves her job." I thought to myself a bit and then decided, "No. No way she would move to Florida, even for Travis."

"Okay, great. So, let's formulate a plan." Lisa had a big smile on her face.

We spent the next hour brainstorming ways to make Maddy and Travis fall in love. We could plant fake love notes to Maddy at her job. We could tell Travis that Maddy kept calling the house looking for him. We could make a romantic dinner reservation and invite them there separately so that they meet. They were all good ideas, and I would use them in one way or another. First, I needed to find out from Maddy how she felt about Travis. I also needed to find out what, or if anything, went on with them at the funeral.

After we came up with several different scenarios and agreed that time would tell us which plan to implement, Lisa turned the subject to Jacob, unfortunately. I had been dreading this topic all day in the back of my mind, but I knew it would come up eventually. It went differently than

I had imagined.

"So, I just want to say that I am really sorry about your parents and everything. I know I could have been more supportive, but I was so sad and didn't know how to face you and be strong for you." Lisa looked down at her hands. "I know that Jacob has been there for you, and I'm glad he was strong enough." Then she hesitated, but put it out there (I didn't expect anything less from Lisa). "I hate to ask you this because I know it's totally inappropriate and probably just me overreacting, which you know I do well, but is there something going on between you two?"

And there it was; she had asked me. Should I lie to her and preserve our friendship or tell her the truth and risk losing her? I decided I couldn't lose anyone else this week and if I did have to move to Florida, then it was no use telling her the truth anyway. If this plan worked and I stayed, then I would tell Lisa about me and Jacob.

I put on the most appalled looking face I could muster, "Are you kidding me? Are you really asking me that?" I knew I was a terrible actress. I never tried out for the drama club but I was sure they would kick me out right away.

"I know, I'm sorry. It's just that I could tell that he was looking at you differently during the funeral. He was probably just feeling sorry for you." She said rather bluntly.

I was a little insulted at the way she phrased that last part. He was probably just feeling sorry for me? I knew that ninety percent of the things that came out of Lisa's mouth were unfiltered, and she rarely thought before she said anything. That meant that most of the time what she said was interpreted wrong because of the inflection of one word or another, and I was hoping that this was one of those times. But no matter how insulted I felt, I needed to keep a straight face since I had, in fact, just lied to my best friend.

Travis

The morning after my night with Maddy I was starting to feel guilty about my intentions for going to her house. I had clearly wanted revenge for the pain that she'd caused me when we were teenagers, but I had also wanted to know what it would be like now that we were older and more experienced. It was better than I could have ever imagined, and that made me wonder what my life would have been like if I hadn't run away to college all those years ago. If I had stayed and fought for her. This was definitely not something that I had planned on happening and I guess I had a week to figure out what it meant.

Thinking of Maddy made me smile, which was unusual for me, since I wasn't the smiling type. I had spent the afternoon working, catching up on the case that I had left behind. Luckily, the trial date hadn't been set before I left for Jersey, and I found out this morning that the date was a solid five weeks away, which meant that as long as my boss didn't give me another case in the meantime, I had plenty of time to get ready and adjust to Sam living with me.

I knew that Sam had the week off, but I was a little shocked when I heard a strange girl enter the house and yell Sam's name. I was guessing that it was her friend, since Sam had called back right after, and the girl ran up the stairs to Sam's bedroom. They had been up there for a few hours, when I heard footsteps on the stairs and then the door close. I was guessing that Sam's friend had left but had no idea who she was since she didn't introduce herself.

I was guessing that Sam told her about the move to Florida. I didn't know how Sam was dealing with it, and I really didn't care much. I had made the decision and the arrangements, and she was coming whether either of us liked it or not.

As dinnertime approached, I went to the stairs to yell up and see Sam if she wanted anything, when someone rang the doorbell. I opened the door to find a skinny teenage boy wearing a Domino's hat, holding a pizza. "Here is your pizza, sir. That will be $11.83 plus tip." He smiled to show me a mouth full of metal braces. Sam came running down the stairs right as I took the pizza from the boy and handed the kid $15 and told him to keep the change. She turned and grabbed the pizza from my hands and headed back up to her room.

"Hey, I guess that means you don't want dinner," I called out after her.

"Nope," she yelled back down.

Then Sam came back down the steps. I thought maybe she had a change of heart and was going to offer me a slice, but instead she said, "I forgot to tell you that Maddy called for you today. Are you going out with her or something?"

Maddy called? How did I miss that? "Oh yeah? What did she say?" I tried to sound disinterested; the last thing I wanted was Sam knowing about Maddy and me.

"Not much, but I think she wants you to call her back. So, are you two dating?" Damn this girl was persistent. Couldn't she tell that I didn't answer her the first time?

"None of your business. Thanks for the message. Any pizza up there for me?"

"Maybe you should go out to dinner with Maddy," she said mockingly and turned to walk back up the stairs.

So Maddy had called for me today. I wondered what that meant. Wasn't she mad at me? Would she see me again after what happened last night? Should I call her back? Maybe the answer would come to me if I had a drink.

10 SECRETS & DISCOVERY

Samantha

Yesterday I started enacting my plan to stay in New Jersey by planting the seed about Maddy calling in Travis's mind. I wasn't sure if it worked, but I definitely could see a change in his demeanor when I mentioned her name. I began to think this plan had potential. Last night when Travis left, I texted Lisa to tell her that it was in motion, and she seemed excited and positive. I wasn't sure where Travis went, but hoped it was to meet Maddy somewhere. If not, then I would need to make some bigger moves today. I only had five days left before our booked flight to Florida. So if this plan was going to work, I really needed to step up my game.

As I contemplated my next move, my cell phone started to play "Hanginaround" by the Counting Crows, which meant that Jacob was calling me. It was already after 3:00 p.m., so I had slept most of the day away. Not good, considering my lack of time left to execute the plan. I was a little surprised when I hadn't talked to him all day yesterday, but I figured that Lisa had told him about our plan already. They were neighbors so she saw him more than I did, and since she was crushing on him I was sure she used our plan as an excuse to go talk to him.

I stared at my phone for a second, knowing that if I didn't answer soon it would go to voicemail. I had avoided his calls since our kiss. My head told me that it was a bad idea to continue this thing with Jacob, but the butterflies in my stomach made me answer.

"Hello?" I pretended I didn't know who was calling, even though he knew I could see from the caller ID it was him.

He played along. "Hey, Sam, it's Jacob."

"Oh, hey, where were you yesterday?" My defenses were falling down around me.

"I was at school, and then Lisa told me she was headed to your house. I figured I would let you two spend some time together. She came over after dinner last night to tell me about the plan you guys devised." I had a pang of jealousy, even though I had already figured Lisa would run to Jacob first chance she got.

"Yeah, so what do you think? You think it'll work?" I was interested in his point of view. Three minds were better than two, and I knew Jacob had a vested interest in seeing me stay.

"Well, it's much better than your bitch plan that Lisa told me about. Like you could really be bitchy enough to make someone leave you behind," he said with a mocking laugh.

"Hey, I can be a bitch when I want to be. And not everyone wants me around, especially Travis." I was defensive, which had been happening a lot lately.

"I don't know who wouldn't want you around." I could tell he was smiling as he said it.

"Lots of people." Now I was smiling, too.

"Well, not me that's for sure. So, when can I see you?"

His question took me a little off guard, although I wasn't sure why. I should have expected it.

"I really need to come up with my next move. I don't

have much time to get Travis and Maddy to fall in love." I was being honest with him, but also trying to avoid being with him again, afraid of what it might lead to. I had lied to Lisa, and I didn't want to tell Jacob because I knew it would hurt his feelings, but I didn't want us meeting up and that getting back to Lisa somehow.

"Well, I don't have much time to get you to fall in love with me either."

I sat on my bed looking at the phone. That was a punch to my gut that I wasn't prepared for. Not a bad punch, but it definitely took the breath out of my lungs for a few solid seconds. I didn't know how to respond, since Jacob had never said anything like that to me before. Actually, no one had ever said anything like that to me before. I hadn't really dated much, let alone gotten close to falling in love.

He must have thought I had hung up because he said, "You there?"

"Yeah, sorry. I'm here." I sounded a little stunned, because I was.

"Let me take you out tonight." It was more of a statement than a question.

"Like a date?" It sounded really immature, and Jacob giggled at me, but I was immature when it came to boys.

"Yeah, like a date."

"I don't think so, Jake." I felt bad for saying it, but I couldn't lead him on if I wanted to preserve my friendship with both him and Lisa.

"Why not? I know you like me. You can't hide it from me anymore. Like you said, we don't have much time." Jacob had never sounded so confident before and determined. I kind of liked it. I had never been pursued, and it made me blush. Good thing I was alone in my room.

After a few seconds, I let go of my inhibitions. "Okay, but I don't want to go out in public." I needed a reason for this fast, since I didn't want to hurt his feelings or tell him about my lie to Lisa. "People look at me differently now that they know my parents died. They stare. I feel uncomfortable." That was believable enough. The truth was I hadn't really been out since my parents' death other than the funeral, and I hadn't liked all of the fake sympathy and sad faces there.

"Okay, no problem. I'll pick you up at six. I am going to pick up food on the way, so don't order Domino's." He knew me all too well.

I agreed to be here, Domino's free, at six. I asked him where we were going, and he told me it was a surprise. I didn't like surprises, and he knew it, but he was trying to be mysterious so I let him.

In the meantime, I still needed to come up with the next step to get Travis and Maddy together. Since drastic times called for drastic measures I picked up my cell again, but this time I called Maddy.

Travis

I found myself sitting at a restaurant bar waiting for Maddy. She had called unexpectedly this afternoon asking if I would meet her for dinner. I hadn't called her back yesterday after Sam gave me the message, and I didn't go to her house last night, even after a handful of beers told me to. I had to keep my mind focused on getting Sam to Florida with me by the end of the week, and I had to plan the strategy for my case that now had a court date five weeks away. I couldn't let my feelings for Maddy, if I had them, get in the way. But I had answered the phone this afternoon and couldn't turn her down.

I hadn't seen her come in, but the next thing I knew she was sitting beside me ordering a glass of the house cabernet. She looked over at me from the corner of her eye to see if I had noticed her, which I had. It was hard to miss Maddy, especially when she was sitting right next to you wearing an intoxicating perfume.

"Hey." What else could I say?

"Hey, yourself," she replied.

"So, what's up? How've you been?" I knew it seemed like an odd question, since I'd just seen her a couple of days ago, but I wasn't sure why she called or what she wanted. So, I decided to tread lightly.

Maddy was dressed in a blue silk top and white pants. She looked great, and I got nervous just thinking about what was underneath.

"I've been fine, thanks. I just thought we could meet up and talk about what happened the other day." She hesitated, and it was obvious the topic made her uncomfortable. "The night ended so quickly, I just wanted to make sure you were okay."

She was interested in seeing if I was okay? That seemed odd to me. I was the one who left her. Did my quick departure send her the wrong signal? Was she the one feeling guilty?

"I'm fine, thanks." I felt like I was about to lose the upper hand, so I needed to reclaim it fast. "Sorry about leaving so quickly the other night. I just realized it was a mistake and didn't want the situation to turn uncomfortable." Maybe it was a rude way to gain back control, but it seemed to work.

Maddy looked confused and a little disappointed. "You think it was a mistake?"

Typical girl response. Even if Maddy agreed that it was a mistake she would never admit it. Girls were like that. They never wanted to come off too desperate or slutty.

"Not if you don't," I said with a smile. "I enjoyed myself."

I wasn't sure what Maddy was thinking or if she was buying my charm, but she smiled. The next thing she said caught me completely off guard. "Listen, Travis, I just don't think it's a good idea to get back into a relationship. I mean, I have my life and you have yours. The other night was nice, but I just don't think it's a good idea."

She must have reacted to my confused look because after she made this statement her expression also turned confused. Then she added, "You did want to start something up with me again, didn't you?"

My reply was brief but to the point. "Um, no. What made you think that?"

"Well, it just seemed that you were pursuing me, and I didn't want you to get the wrong idea from the other night. "She hesitated, clearly embarrassed by the fact that she had jumped to the wrong conclusion. "Oh my gosh, I am such an idiot." She put her hand to her forehead and started shaking her head and nervous laughter followed. "I thought I saw something in your eyes the other night when you stopped. That's a total relief."

I laughed with her to ease her embarrassment, but the entire situation was still a little unbelievable to me. So, what if I didn't want to start a relationship with Maddy? So what if I was just trying to get revenge for all of those years ago when she dumped me? She didn't know that, and now she was the one telling me that she didn't want a relationship. She was dumping me all over again (technically she wasn't dumping me since we weren't actually together).

I started to get insulted and angry about what was going down here. She clearly didn't seem to have any feelings for me, at least not enough to want a relationship. If I was truly going to get my revenge, then I needed to get her to fall for me. I hadn't planned on being so malicious. I originally just wanted to sleep with her and then leave, but I couldn't even do that. The situation evolved and now I needed to take it to the next level and follow through with it this time. I had time, at least four more days, to work my magic and then leave. We would see how she felt after that.

I suggested that we finish our drinks and have dinner to mend fences. Luckily Maddy agreed, which I figured she would, since she basically just gave me the "I just want to be friends" speech. During dinner, I laid on the charm. I had her talking and laughing. I could tell she was having a good time. Later that night she was having an even better time. We barely made it out of the restaurant before we were all over each other like teenagers. I had her pinned up against her car and I could feel the heat radiating off of her as it travelled all the way down my body. We were both busting out of our clothes, when we realized that we were still in the middle of the restaurant's parking lot.

"Let's go to the lake," she breathed.

The lake was another one of our places growing up, besides the airport. We would go there to make love under the big willow tree. It was a nice enough night out, and I almost just stripped her down to nothing in a public parking lot, so I guessed the lake was a good enough place. Plus, the lake was only five minutes away, and Maddy's house was a twenty-minute drive.

When we got to the lake, it was just how I remembered it: big willow tree on the banks off to the left and a small broken wooden dock on the right. I left the car headlights on since it was pitch black out. Maddy grabbed a blanket from her trunk, and we headed over to the base of the tree.

As she laid down the blanket, a flood of memories came back to me. This was where I had lost my virginity all those years ago, same place with the same girl. Although, Maddy was no longer a girl now, she was a woman. I could see that she was experiencing the same memories by the faraway look in her eyes and the smile on her face. When she saw that I was staring at her, she slowly took her shirt off and dropped it on the ground. Next, she removed her pants, and she was left in nothing but her bra and panties. I could tell that it was my turn so I took off my clothes and was left standing there in my boxers. As I approached her, the cold breeze hit our skin and we shivered.

We pressed against each other, slowly making our way down to the ground to that spot under the tree, finally removing the last bit of clothing. Her need tonight was different than the other day. The other night was more about urgency and excitement, which scared the shit out of me and had me running the moment we got too close. Tonight, was more about discovery and desire. We moved in perfect motion as we let our hands and lips move over each other. I traced kisses around her breasts, licking and biting her nipples until they were hard. I moved down her stomach to the place I needed the most. When I got to her soft folds, she was so ready for me, but I couldn't let her have me that easily. Even after all these years I wanted her to know what she was missing. I let my tongue do the work as she was begging me for more. Her breathing started accelerating, and her body was shuttering. When she crumbled underneath me, I could taste her pleasure.

Allowing her to regain control, I made my way back up to her mouth. I let her taste herself on my tongue, watching her with excited eyes the entire kiss. We were once again teasing each other, and I couldn't take it anymore. I needed to be inside her. I reached for my jeans only a few feet away and grabbed the condom I kept in my wallet. After securing it on, I slipped inside of her, slowly taking in her warmth. She was so tight that with each deepening thrust I felt the pleasure building. I knew that I wasn't going to last much longer with her body clasping around me. As I came, she was experiencing her second, and this time we moaned and shuttered together.

Tonight I found myself lying under the willow tree, holding Maddy, thinking about the years past when I loved her. I'd been devoted to her. She was practically my religion. I could easily feel that way about her again if I let myself. But Maddy had changed me when she broke my heart, and I wasn't the same sentimental fool I'd once been. I was tougher, stronger, and I had her to thank for that. I loved being with Maddy, but I had a life back in Florida, and I wasn't ready to walk away from it all. I had to pull myself out of the past and move forward. I decided while I lay next to Maddy that I would have to tell her all of this. But not now.

11 TRUTH

Samantha

It was quickly approaching 6:00 p.m. and Jacob would be here soon. What did one wear on a "date" with your best friend? At least that's what I was calling it, even though I didn't know where we were headed. I decided to dress weather appropriate and wear comfortable shoes. Who was I trying to impress? Jacob? The idea of us going on a date was still hard for me to grasp, but it was also hard for me to get that kiss out of my mind. There was something there, and I needed to see what it meant. If my plan worked and Travis let me stay here, at least until the end of the school year, then I would have the entire summer to be with Jacob and figure things out. If not, then I only had four days left. I wondered why he'd waited so long to tell me how he felt. Although, I wasn't sure how it would've worked out if it had happened sooner, especially with Lisa in the mix.

I decided on my favorite purple top from Express and dark jeans. These were clothes that Jacob had seen before, and I remembered that he commented on how much he liked my purple shirt when I got it. It had some sparkles on it, and I dressed it up with a long dangle necklace I got for six dollars at a kiosk in the mall. My jeans were tight and accentuated my curves. I put on a pair of my favorite sandals and grabbed a gray cardigan in case it got cold.

I was finishing up my makeup when the doorbell rang. Unlike Lisa, Jacob didn't like to barge into my house even though I told him several times to just come in. He said that he thought it was disrespectful to my parents. I guess he was still trying to keep some sort of normalcy.

When I opened the door, I could tell that Jacob had gone all out in getting ready. He was freshly shaven with his hair slicked back, and he smelled really good. He had on a dark blue long-sleeved collared shirt that had been nicely pressed and dark jeans with black newly polished shoes. He smiled at me while we looked each other over. His teeth looked so white compared to the rest of him. He looked beautiful. I knew you weren't supposed to say that about a guy and I would never tell him that to his face, but he was really beautiful.

I smiled back at him and then all of the sudden got really nervous. My heart started pounding, my palms got sweaty, and I could feel the blood rush to my cheeks. So much for playing it cool and keeping it friendly. I thought Jacob sensed my change in demeanor because he quickly looked down and his smile got even wider, if that were possible.

He reached out for my hand and said, "Hi." The informality and closeness of the simple word made me giggle. Probably nerves contributed to that as well. I took his hand, even though I feared he would notice how hot mine was, but to my surprise and relief his hand was just as clammy. I guess we were both nervous. We were headed into uncharted waters, and neither of us wanted to make the wrong move and kill the friendship entirely.

"Hi. So where are we going? I hope I'm dressed okay." So maybe I was fishing for a compliment here.

"You look beautiful," he said.

I pressured him. "So…where are we going?"

"It's a surprise," he said

"You know I hate surprises." I sounded a little childish, but it was true. I liked to know exactly what I was doing and where I was going so I could prepare myself. I always said the wrong thing when I was surprised.

"I know." He looked like he was enjoying torturing me. Wait, he was flirting! I had never seen Jacob flirt with a girl, and I had never been the recipient before.

I locked up the house behind me, since Travis had already left to meet Maddy for dinner. I knew this, not because he told me before he left, but because I had suggested it earlier when I called her to tell her that Travis couldn't stop talking about her and how infatuated he was with her. Okay, so I knew it was wrong to lie and mess with someone's life, and risky since Maddy could tell Travis exactly what I said, but I didn't have much time. And for now, I couldn't think about the success or failure of my plan, I needed to focus on my date with Jacob.

When I got into Jacob's fathers truck that he must've borrowed, I noticed that there was a bag in the back with a loaf of bread sticking out. "So where are we going? And why are we taking your dad's truck instead of your car?" I asked again.

"I thought we would go watch a movie," he said.

"But you brought a bag full of food and a loaf of French bread. Not exactly popcorn and candy."

"We're not going to the movie theatre. We're going to the drive-in theater in Manalapan." He sounded very proud of his romantic idea. I knew exactly where he was referring to. I'd been to the outdoor drive-in years ago with Lisa and her older sister. I was only a kid then, but I remembered it being pretty big and the cars were parked far enough apart where you could carry on a conversation. And even though there was a concession stand there, it looked like Jacob had picked up a real meal for us on his way over, which I thought was sweet. He was really trying to make this a romantic date.

Suddenly I remembered hearing about the drive-in from some kids at school saying it was a great make-out spot since there was still a sense of privacy. I was hoping that wasn't Jacob's intention. I thought about the type of person Jacob was and decided that he wasn't planning a private make-out session. He probably just thought it'd be a nice idea, given that I didn't want to go out in public. Jacob thought I didn't want to get the weird looks from people who knew my parents had just died, when the truth of the matter was I didn't want to run into Lisa. Since Lisa really liked Jacob and I convinced her it would hurt our friendship if she shared her feelings with him, I didn't think she would like the fact that I was on a date with Jacob right now.

As we pulled into the theatre I saw on the screen that we were going to be watching a 7:00 p.m. showing of The Notebook. Boys always thought it was a good idea to bring girls to chick flicks on a date, but truly it was a terrible idea. Chick flicks didn't put us in a romantic mood, they made us sad and self-conscious, since we ended up crying at the end and ruining our makeup. For me it was worse, since I'm Irish and fair skinned, so I also got lovely red blotches all over my face. I wasn't a good crier like Demi Moore in Ghost. I made a mental note to be deep in conversation when the sad parts came on the screen. While I was thinking of it, I figured I'd better also make sure we were deep in conversation during the love scenes. No need to make myself feel any more nervous.

Jacob had brought Brie cheese, prosciutto, and some fancy olive oil that he served with the bread to start. The next course was shrimp cocktail that he had packed on ice. And finally, we finished with strawberries and whipped cream. To drink, he'd stolen a bottle of wine from his parents, a twist top, and we drank it in some red plastic cups. I was glad that there was no one checking IDs here because the wine helped me relax.

As we ate and watched the movie, Jacob would touch my hand or brush my cheek with his thumb (even though I knew I didn't have anything on my face like he claimed). At first I felt weird about the closeness, but after a few times I found myself hoping he would do it again. It was nice being on a date with Jacob. He was funny, but a different kind of funny. He was flirty funny, and I liked this side of him. He would tease me about how fast I ate, and he would tell me I was a sap when I would get teary eyed during the sad parts of the movie. Each jab he would deliver with a smile, and I knew he meant it as flirting. Near the end of the movie when we were finished with our food and almost half the bottle of wine, Jacob pulled me next to him and put his arm around me. We sat like that for a few minutes, when I instinctively put my head on his shoulder. It was nice having him there comforting me. I had been through a lot these last couple of weeks, and the new feelings for Jacob were a nice change.

Then it came to the part of the movie when Alley chose Noah, and Jacob leaned over and kissed me. It wasn't a rough or hurried kiss; it was slow and I could feel the butterflies in my stomach doing cartwheels. I was starting to feel a rush of heat all over when the kiss became more passionate. I found myself running my fingers through his hair and trying to get closer to him. Then out of nowhere my mind clicked on, and I realized I was in public making out with my best friend. All of the sudden I got nervous and embarrassed. I had been caught up in the moment but now I was afraid people were staring at me. I pulled away from Jacob, breathless. He looked just as disoriented as I had felt and surprised that I had pulled away.

I started to search around to see if anyone had noticed us, but they were all still watching the movie, or making out in their own car. I even saw one older man sleeping while his wife tried to wake him up. So, I guess no one cared about my indiscretion with Jacob. When I turned to him I could tell that he was coming back to reality.

"What's the matter?" he asked in a whisper.

"I just think we got a little carried away." I was clearly stating the obvious, in my opinion.

Jacob chuckled at me. He cupped my face in his hands, like he had done the first time we kissed, and kissed me quickly on the lips. "I think you're right." He repositioned himself and looked uncomfortable.

"Are you okay?" I asked naively. The movie was over and the credits were rolling.

Jacob looked embarrassed and replied, "Yeah, I'm fine. I just need a couple of minutes." I followed his eyes down his body since he was clearly trying to imply something. When I realized what it was, I looked away and tried not to laugh, as my cheeks were blushing. I wasn't sure how I felt about being able to generate that reaction from him. It had never happened to me before, and even though I was embarrassed I was a little intrigued. It meant that Jacob did like me and I turned him on. We were nowhere ready for that step, but it still made me feel a bit better about myself.

I suggested that maybe he should take me home. I had a wonderful time, and I knew that if I stayed with Jacob any longer we could end up back in this situation, which I wanted to avoid for now.

As we pulled up to my house I was distracted by my thoughts of a goodnight kiss. Given that Jacob and I had already kissed twice before, I knew one was coming. I needed to keep my wits about me and not let it get out of hand like it had at the movies.

Jacob walked me to the porch holding my hand the entire way. When we got to the door, he kissed my hand first, and then he leaned in and gave me a short kiss. I smiled and thanked him for a great night as I closed the front door slowly. I stood leaning against it and heard Jacob's truck start and back out the driveway, recapping the wonderful evening in my mind. Then, out of nowhere, I felt the door being pushed open and I fell on the floor in the foyer.

"Hey!" I yelled. I turned and saw it was Lisa. Oh no! I wondered what she had seen. Clearly enough to get her so mad that she just threw me on the floor. "What is wrong with you?" I shouted, even though I probably figured it out already.

"I just saw you kissing Jacob. Our Jacob. My Jacob!" Lisa was in a rage, and I knew I didn't want to take her on when she was like this.

"Listen, it's not what you think." A guilty person always started out with that line. "Jacob wanted to take me out to get my mind off things, so we went to the movies and it was The Notebook and he brought wine and I didn't want to hurt you but I know I should've told you the truth." It was one long run-on sentence, and I said it desperately and with pain in my voice. I knew that I had just potentially ruined my friendship with both Lisa and Jacob in one night. I could lose Lisa forever, since I lied to her and she found out. And after that kiss with Jacob in the car, we could never be just friends again.

I felt desperate. I was sure Lisa could tell by my voice and the tears that were streaming down my face. I could see the anger calm down in her eyes, but she was still really mad.

"I can't believe you would do this to me. You convinced me not to tell Jacob how I felt so that you could have him all to yourself! I bet that was your plan all along. Well, you know what? He doesn't love you; he just feels sorry for you that your parents died." They were hurtful words, and she meant them to be. Lisa knew how to go for the jugular, which was why I had enlisted her in the Travis/Maddy plan. It was one thing to be on the same side with Lisa, but I knew better than to cross her. She held grudges and didn't forgive easily.

I had really hurt her. I took in everything she said to me with tears in my eyes and replied with the only response I could, "I'm sorry."

With that, Lisa turned around and walked out of my house, probably forever.

My only concern now was the backlash from what just happened. I knew Lisa would try to get revenge on me, so the first thing I did was text Jacob. He had to know what just happened, since most likely his house would be the first one she went to. He texted me back not to worry and that he would talk to her if she came over. I told him that she had feelings for him, too, and about my role in deterring her from confessing to him. Not with much detail since it was via text, but I was sure he got the idea. I felt a little better as I lifted myself up off the foyer floor. I had landed there when Lisa busted through the door, and I had stayed there throughout our confrontation for fear of what would happen if I got up.

Then I heard a car coming up the driveway, or so I thought, and I realized that I'd never heard Lisa's car pull away, or at least I didn't remember hearing it. I looked out the side window next to the front door and saw Travis standing in the front walkway. It was too late. I was too late. There was Lisa telling Travis all about the plan we had devised just yesterday to help me stay here in Jersey. I could tell that Travis was angry with what Lisa was telling him but that he also knew not to mess with a scorned teenage girl, so he let her get out her entire story before directing her home.

I knew that I was in deep trouble as Travis's eyes met mine through the window after Lisa had driven away. I ran up the stairs like the scared little girl I was and locked the bedroom door behind me. The effects of the wine from earlier were definitely gone, and my joy from the night with Jacob and fear from my confrontation with Lisa had quickly turned into sheer panic. I could hear Travis come in the front door and put his keys on the counter. I heard the closet in the hall open and close and figured he had taken off his jacket and hung it up. He was torturing me, or I was torturing myself, either way I was being tortured.

I heard a light tap on my door. I didn't respond. Then I heard Travis say, "Sam, I know you're in there. We need to talk, but it can wait until morning. I want to know what you have to say for yourself."

With that, Travis walked away and went to his own room down the hall. I heard him getting ready for bed for the next few minutes and then only silence. I was lying on my bed, still fully clothed, wondering what I was going to do. How had this night turned from the best night of my life to the worst so quickly? I knew that my friendship with Lisa was permanently damaged. More importantly, I wasn't sure how Travis was going to react to the news of my setup. I'd never really seen him angry before and was worried about what his reaction would be. Not like he could punish me anymore than he already had with making me move to Florida. Was he going to yell at me and try to hurt me with words like Lisa had done? I guess I had all night to think about it.

If his strategy was torture by guilt, then maybe Travis was a more formidable opponent then I initially gave him credit for.

Travis

I knew as soon as my head hit the pillow that I was going to have a hard time falling asleep. I should've been exhausted after the night I had, but I couldn't stop all of the thoughts running through my mind. Sam's friend had been angry over something and clearly she was trying to hurt Sam. So was she telling me the truth? Had Sam tried to orchestrate a relationship between Maddy and me? Had she been the real reason that Maddy and I had ended up together? How far back had it gone? The girl tonight didn't mention anything about the funeral, so had Maddy shown up to the funeral on her own or had Sam asked her to come, knowing that seeing her again might make me want to stay here?

I knew Sam thought that I was angry with her, which was why she was hiding from me in her room. But was I? No. I couldn't blame Sam for trying to find reasons to stay. This was her home, with her friends and the only life she knew. Was I doing the wrong thing taking her away from them?

As I lay in bed staring up at the ceiling, I felt a heavy weight bear down on my chest. I grabbed my chest and rubbed right where the weight felt like it was pressing. I didn't think that I was having a heart attack, but it was a strange feeling I'd never had before. Responsibility. It had just dawned on me that I had to answer all of these questions before we left for Florida.

I hadn't realized it, but lately I hadn't had a lot of confidence in my decisions. Usually I made decisions easily with no problem at all. People who hesitated showed signs of weakness. When you were a lawyer you needed to be confident in your decisions, precise; you had to know that you were making the right choice for your client. But lately the decisions that I was making were not affecting a nameless client I couldn't care less about. These decisions were affecting my own life.

I had thought the decision to move Sam to Florida was in her best interest, that I was doing what my mother would have wanted. Well, maybe it wasn't really that at all. To be honest with myself, I had to admit that the decision to take Sam back to Florida was the best decision for me. It would relieve the guilt I felt for not calling my mom back countless times, for missing every holiday, for being a bad son. I would have total control over Sam to make sure that she didn't get into any trouble. But now that I thought more about it, she was more likely to rebel if I moved her to Florida than if I left her here. And she seemed to have a relationship with that Jacob boy. But I needed to keep my job, to make money. I had worked really hard at the firm to get where I was, and I wouldn't leave it all behind because Sam wanted to be with her boyfriend. I knew that

I would be able to get a job here or in the city, or even open my own practice, but that would mean I would have to decide what to do about Maddy.

Maddy. She was another wrench in my plan. Even if Sam had prematurely pushed us together, I knew myself, and I would have chased after her just for the sheer pleasure of the game. If that shrieking girl tonight was telling the truth, then Sam had just done me a favor speeding up the process. The problem was that I really had feelings for Maddy; I might even still love her. I'd never really loved anyone other than her. So, would I be willing to throw away the career I'd spent the last ten years building for her, for a life here? It would be a small life but still potentially a full life. It would be full of family compared to my life now, which was full of money, work, and friends. Actually, I really only had one friend because when you were successful people were always talking about you behind your back or resenting your success. Friends were hard to find and Mike was truly the only one I had.

Thinking about all of these things started to give me a headache. I turned over on my side hoping that would help me fall asleep. It didn't work. I turned to look at the clock and it read 2:13 a.m., which meant that I had been contemplating all of these situations and scenarios for close to three hours.

I got up to get a glass of water from the kitchen. As I walked down the hallway on my way back to my room, I caught a glimpse of an old picture of my parents that was in a wooden frame on the foyer table. It was hidden behind pictures of my sister "throughout the years." I picked it up and studied it. The smile on my father's face, the whimsical expression in my mother's eyes. This picture had been taken at the beach before my parents had been married, before either my sister or I were born. They looked happy, young, and stress-free.

Then I remembered my childhood growing up in this

house. My parents' arguments, my father's drinking, all of the memories I had hidden in the back of my mind...the reasons that I had moved away. I wondered...what if they hadn't chosen the small life, the life with the family and the one they loved at that moment? What if they had chosen a life better for themselves that led to success and a different kind of happiness? One that was not filled with the heavy weight of responsibility bearing down on your chest. I looked up in the mirror at my own reflection and realized I had made my decision. Now I had to figure out a way to tell Sam...and Maddy.

12 MOVING FORWARD

Travis

I decided that I was going to tell Sam this morning. Why wait? Last night I also decided that we were going to need to leave as soon as possible. Once I told both Sam and Maddy, neither of them were going to react well, and I figured that the faster we moved on, the easier it would ultimately be for them...and me.

Even though I hadn't slept well the night before, I was still up at seven. The weight of the decision was off my shoulders, but it had been replaced with the weight of telling Sam the news. I brewed a pot of coffee, hoping the aroma would wake her up and coax her to come downstairs. Once again, I was wrong. She was probably still afraid I was going to be mad at her from the previous night's events and fearful that I would make her leave for Florida today. Well, she was half right.

When I heard the hum of music come from her room around 8:30, I decided to go upstairs and take charge. I knocked on her door and the music level turned up a bit, so I knocked a second time but this time louder.

"Hey, Sam," I yelled over the music. "I need to talk to

you. I'm not angry about last night if that's what you think." I heard the music slowly lower in volume and footsteps approaching the door. As Sam opened the door slightly, she turned around and started walking away from me.

She went into defense mode. "I don't know what Lisa said to you last night, but she was mad at me, so I'm sure the majority of what she said was a lie." So, that was the crazy girl's name. Good to know. As I noted the friend's name for the future, I realized that Sam looked like she'd been crying. If I wanted this to go smoothly and to not get hit with a baseball bat again, which my side was still healing from by the way, then I needed to put on my charming lawyer "I care about you and your feelings" persona. This won over clients in a heartbeat most of the time.

"Have you been crying?" I asked her. "Sam, tell me what's happening with you, because after last night I'm really confused, and I'm sure there's a good explanation." I had charm when I needed it. And when I laid it on, I laid it on thick.

Sam sat on her bed and looked up at me with red-rimmed eyes. Her forehead was wrinkled like she was trying to decide if I was for real and she should spill her guts or if I was totally playing her. I guess she went for the first choice since she started to share with me what was going on with her. I wasn't sure if it was because she trusted me or because she didn't have much of a choice and thought that confiding in me might help her case for staying.

"Well, I know you don't know, but Lisa, Jacob, and I have been best friends since we were little kids." Wasn't she still a kid? I thought to myself. I nodded, acknowledging her statement. "And, well, lately Lisa has had feelings for Jake, but Lisa has feelings for lots of boys and they usually only last a month or so." She looked pleadingly at me like she wanted me to agree with her, even though I had no idea who this Lisa girl was other than my lovely conversation with her last night.

"Okay," I said slowly, not wanting to be rude but trying to coax her to speed up her story.

"Well, since Mom and Dad died, everything has been so horrible around here. I've felt so empty and alone. And I've had to deal with you coming back, no offense." She gave me a half smile.

"None taken." And I flicked my hand to signal her to continue.

"Well, something happened between me and Jake last night, and Lisa saw it, and she totally flipped out on me." Sam's voice escalated and she started to speak more urgently. "I mean, it was nothing big. We just kissed, but Lisa saw and had a conniption. She says she hates me and never wants to see me again. What am I supposed to do?"

Sam looked at me with hurt in her eyes. She seemed more concerned about losing her friend than what her friend had told me last night. I didn't know what to say to her. What did I know about teenage girl relationships? Jacob must have been the boy I thought was her boyfriend. I started to get uncomfortable realizing that Sam was talking to me about their relationship.

"Wow" was all I could say. "I don't know Sam, but I'm sure she'll get over it." Then I paused and found myself saying something an absentee brother didn't typically care about, "All you did was kiss this Jacob kid, right?"

Sam let out a mini scream and stormed out of the room. Clearly that wasn't what she was expecting to hear. I quickly realized that we hadn't discussed the real reason I was in her room, so I chased after her down the stairs into the kitchen. Fast on her heels, it was my turn to talk.

"Listen, I know you have got a lot going on with your friends, but Lisa did tell me something last night that I need to talk to you about." Sam turned to me, and I saw on her face the realization that I hadn't forgotten about the real issue at hand and that her little teenage drama didn't deter me from this subject. "Lisa told me that you lied to Maddy and me to try and get us to, um…how do I put this nicely? Get together." I waited for her response.

"Well, what exactly did Lisa tell you I did?" She was fishing for information, not willing to say more than she needed to.

"Her exact words were kind of harsh, and she called you some interesting words that I think were curses. She said that you lied when telling me that Maddy had called for me that night and that you set it up so that we would go to the bar and meet up. She also said that you were hoping I would get all fucked up in the head over Maddy and stay here so that you could stay here." I stopped there, waiting for her response.

"Okay, so maybe I did. I don't see the harm in it. I just wanted you to rekindle the love you two used to share, and then maybe we would all win and I would get to stay here." It sounded innocent enough, but I knew that her intention was purely selfish. I couldn't blame her. There were worse things she could've done to me to make me stay. Like call my boss and gotten me fired, or break both my legs in a hit and run accident. I was lucky that Sam wasn't that vicious or creative.

"I see." I hated it when people said I see. It was like they were patronizing me, but for some reason it seemed to fit in this circumstance. "Well, you succeeded at one part. Maddy and I did sort of rekindle something from our past, but it made me realize that it was my past and there was a reason I left this town." I could see something dawning in Sam's eyes, and I needed to look down at my hands to get the rest out. "I left here to escape this small town and small town life. I didn't want to be with Maddy all of those years ago because I was afraid that I would be stuck with her forever." Okay, small lie on that point. I loved Maddy back then and would have done anything to marry her, but she left me and broke my heart, so I had the right to remember things a little differently in the retelling.

"I wanted big things for myself, and guess what? I got them all." I was trying to convince Sam I was doing this for her best interest. "I want those same big things for you, and you can't get them when you're stuck here. We're going to Florida tomorrow. You might want to spend the rest of the day packing up essentials you want to take. You can take two big suitcases with the majority of your clothes and shoes, and we can ship the rest of your things." I rambled this part out fast, since I didn't want her vile shriek that I knew would follow to drown out any of the important points.

I was right. As soon as I finished talking Sam shrieked at the top of her lungs like someone was burning her alive. She then ran upstairs with tears streaming down her face, yelling about how much she hated me. I followed her upstairs and stood at her locked door that she had just slammed two seconds earlier. Before the blaring music started, I yelled through the door how we were leaving on the noon flight out of Newark tomorrow whether she packed her stuff or not. She could wear the same clothes every day for the rest of her life for all I cared.

As I walked back downstairs I shook my head and said out loud to no one, "One down, one to go."

Samantha

I fell on my bed crying, barely able to collect my thoughts. I couldn't believe Travis was doing this. Tomorrow was Thursday; we weren't supposed to leave until Saturday. It was what Lisa told him last night that made him make this decision. That bitch. I didn't care anymore that she hated me because I hated her.

I needed to see Jacob. I turned the music down and called him. I was still crying almost uncontrollably, and it was going to be hard for me to tell him what just happened. Instead, when Jacob answered the phone I composed myself as much as possible and told him I needed to talk to him as soon as possible, but that it couldn't be at my house. We agreed to meet in the park by the wooden benches. I had to sneak out of the house, which was pretty easy since there was a lattice outside my window. I had used it to sneak out several times before.

I rode my bike to the park. By the time I got there, I could see Jacob was already sitting on the bench by himself with no one else around. I picked this area of the park because it was secluded and I rarely saw anyone here. I was not in the mood to be around people and I knew this place would give us privacy.

Jacob looked stressed. Apparently, I hadn't masked my crying well enough on the phone.

As I walked up to meet him he got up off the bench and gave me a hug. He was so warm. I squeezed him as hard as I could. I never wanted to let go.

"I know what happened after I dropped you off last night," he said. "I already got a nasty email from Lisa basically telling me to go to hell."

"What?" I was still congested from crying, and I must have looked terrible. We separated but were still holding hands.

"Yeah, she also told me you said you didn't really like me." He laughed. "I guess she thinks I don't know her at all. I know she's a liar, especially when she's angry." His mouth turned into a huge smile showing all of his beautiful white teeth. I smiled back. "Do you believe how big of a bitch she is? Trying to make me mad at you. Who does she think she is?"

At that, I decided it was best for us to sit down. I always heard you should sit someone down before telling them bad news. "Well, she told Travis about 'the plan' last night, and now he is making us leave tomorrow." Tears started to stream down my face as I told him.

Jacob let go of my hands and looked away. When he looked back I could tell he was also on the verge of tears. "Florida isn't that far. There's only one year of school left.

We can still be together. I love you."

Those last three words hit me like a ton of bricks and my emotions took over. I could no longer hold back my sobs. I fell into Jacob's chest and sobbed like I did when I lost my parents. I was so alone then, and now I wasn't alone anymore. I had someone who loved me and who I loved back. After I was done crying, I realized that I'd left a big wet stain of tears on his shirt.

"I'm so sorry. I got your shirt all wet," I said, as I lifted my head.

"It's okay, it'll dry." His hands had moved from my waist to my shoulders. "I love you," he said again, waiting for a response.

I didn't know what to say. I did love Jacob, but this was all so new to me and happening so fast. I had just lost the two most important people in my life and now I was moving away. While half of my life was crumbling apart, the other half was just starting. I was a different person from the one I was last week. "I love you, too," I whispered and kissed him gently. We sat on the bench in the park for another hour just holding hands and thinking.

After our long silence, I had to accept my fate. "I need to go home and pack some stuff. I really think Travis is serious about leaving tomorrow, and I don't want to get stuck having nothing, just in case he doesn't change his mind."

"How do you plan on changing his mind?" Jacob looked serious again. He was struggling with the fact that I was leaving tomorrow. I was struggling with it, too, but I was clinging to my one chance.

"I don't. I'm hoping Maddy can. She's my only chance." I gave Jacob one final kiss and headed home.

When I got home, Travis was gone. I figured he went to tell Maddy we were leaving tomorrow. My one last chance was happening right at that moment.

Travis

I heard Sam leave about an hour ago, down the lattice outside her window. She must have forgotten that her room used to be my room and that lattice had also been my escape route. I figured she wasn't running away because when I picked the lock on her door to check her room, all of her stuff was still there. I assumed she was going to see Jacob. Given that today was her last day to see him, I let her go. Besides, I had other things on my mind.

I called Maddy at her house to see if she had some time to see me.

"I think we need to talk about last night." That was all I told her on the phone. Luckily, she agreed and said that I could come over.

As I drove to Maddy's house, I went over in my head what I was going to say to her. First, I was thinking that I should lie and tell her that last night I had too much wine and made an awful mistake. But we hadn't really had all that much to drink, and I didn't want her to know I was lying because she might read too much into it. I thought about telling her that I was leaving tomorrow for Samantha's best interest. About how I thought Sam was getting too close to this boy, Jacob, and the best thing would be to leave immediately so that it would be less difficult for her. It was partially true. The truth was I didn't really care whether or not Sam got too close to Jacob because it might emotionally damage her; I cared more because I thought it would cause issues for me once we got to Florida. I didn't think I could take her attitude about the situation or her potential attempts to run away back to Jersey.

Or, I could go with the total truth, which would be harder for me to rationalize since I was having some trouble with it myself. The total truth was that if we stayed any longer I might be the one who didn't want to leave, and then I would get stuck in this old life that I had fled from all those years ago. I wasn't the settling down type and I didn't want to start that now while I was in the prime of my career.

I figured that the actual truth was too risky, since I might collapse into the temptation of her, so I decided to go with option number two: make Maddy think that I was leaving with such short notice for Sam's sake. If she didn't believe me, then I could just walk away and that would be the end of it. If she did believe me, I ultimately became the hero and might be able to salvage some relationship with her.

As I drove up to Maddy's house, I saw her sitting on the front porch swing. The swing had been around for as long as I could remember and I couldn't believe she was taking the risk of sitting on it. She was wearing khaki shorts and a white top. She looked stressed and nervous. I figured she knew what was coming. She was a smart girl, and we'd been through this once before, except now the tables were turned.

"Hey. It's good to see you," I said as I approached her. I grabbed one of the chain links that was holding up the swing and looked up to the roof. It looked like the swing was holding on for dear life, and I didn't want to tempt fate by sitting and adding even more weight. "Are you sure you should be sitting on this old swing? It looks like it could fall at any moment."

"It's okay. I had a contractor work on it a few years ago, and they reinforced the roof." She didn't move off the swing.

"Maybe we should go inside?" I suggested.

"No, that's okay. I think we should say what needs to be said here." So, she did know what was coming. I prepared the story in my head about looking after the best interest of Sam. "I'm leaving to go back to Florida tomorrow morning with Sam." That was all I could get out.

Maddy sighed and gazed down at her hands that were holding a glass of lemonade. "I knew it."

"Well, there is this boy that she has just started seeing, and I think it would be best for me to stop it before anything really starts up with them. It'll be harder for her to leave if she thinks that she's in love."

Maddy had a sly smile on her face as she glanced up at me. "Wow, I didn't realize how considerate of a brother you had become. It's good to hear that you finally care about what's best for Sam."

"Yeah, well, I have to start sometime. I am her legal guardian now. "

"Too bad I don't believe a word you just said."

"What?" It looked like she saw right through my story. Soon would be the time for me to walk off and never see her again. "Are you calling me a liar?"

"Oh no. I am calling you a great bullshitter. I don't think you care at all about Sam or what's best for her right now. I think Travis only cares about himself, which is a shame because she's a wonderful young woman." Maddy stood up and I saw that she was going to end it before I even had the chance.

"If you knew anything about Sam you would know that she's known Jacob since they were in grade school, so my best guess would be that she's already in love with him. She may have loved him all of these years and never figured it out until just now." Maddy took a small pause to either gauge my reaction or gather her thoughts. I didn't move. "I knew you weren't going to move back here and stay with me. I knew that we weren't going to have a happily ever after because we had our chance and we threw it away. But I was hoping that you would give Sam her chance at love. But now she's probably going to end up just like you, bitter and alone." At that point Maddy turned around to walk into her house. When she reached the door, she stopped and turned back around to look at me. I was still standing there completely shocked at what she had just said. Technically, my plan had me storming out before she could convince me to stay, but somehow she had turned the tables.

"Don't kill her spirit, Travis. She's the best thing that could happen to you right now. Please remember that and try to become the man that I always knew you were." As quickly as she said those words, she was through the door, and I heard it lock behind her.

As I drove home, I realized I was still in shock. I was thinking about everything that Maddy had said to me. The problem was that I still loved Maddy, after everything I told myself and as much as I tried to be a jerk, she still was the only woman I had ever loved, and our second chance was gone.

But that was all behind me now. It was time to move forward.

13 HEADING SOUTH

Samantha

When I got home from the park, Travis wasn't there, so I went straight to my room to start packing some of my things.

Almost ten minutes later, I heard Travis return from wherever he had gone and then a knock on my door. A little glimmer of hope passed through my mind. Maybe Travis had gone to see Maddy and changed his mind. Maybe we were staying.

I opened the door, then went to take a seat on my bed, leaving it open for him to enter if he wanted.

"Where did you go?" I asked hoping for the best possible answer.

"I could ask you the same question." I guess he knew the climb down the lattice trick. Not surprising.

"You could, but we both know you don't care enough to ask it."

Travis walked into my room and leaned up against my dresser. I could tell he was nervous about being in my room even though I had sort of invited him in. The dresser was close enough to the door where he could still make a quick exit if needed.

"Listen, we need to talk," he said. "We are going to Florida tomorrow."

I glared at him with the most piercing eyes I could muster and saw him flinch a little. I didn't say anything in response to him. My hopes were crushed at that very moment. Travis wasn't going to change his mind and I was all out of ideas to make him.

"I have UPS stopping by the house today at 4:00 p.m. to pick up boxes that you want to ship down south. I notice that you haven't really started to pack yet." He looked at his watch as if he were counting down the minutes to the end of my world as I knew it. "It's just after noon. I recommend you get started. I bought some boxes. They're outside the door just here." Travis pointed to the wall where the boxes would be on the other side in the hallway.

I started to cry. Not sobbing like I had before, but more of a pathetic single teardrop down my cheek. I was honestly done. I had nothing left in me.

"Are you sure we have to go?" My final plea.

"Yes. Listen, Sam, this is the best thing for you right now. You may not believe me, but Florida is a great place to live. And we'll be able to reconnect. Get back some of the time that we lost." He sounded sincere, but I knew he was only saying these things to get me to stop crying and comply with the packing.

"Please leave," I asked in a barely audible voice. It was all I could do to stop myself from attacking him and going completely postal.

Travis didn't argue with me. He simply turned to the door and walked out. He left the door open so that I could get the boxes and packing materials he'd left in the hallway. I walked up to my full-length mirror and evaluated how I got to this moment. I decided to turn the mirror around, since I didn't want to think about it anymore.

I spent the rest of the afternoon packing up the

essentials I wanted to take with me. I figured the more I left here the better. I knew I wouldn't stay in Florida long. I figured that this was only a temporary roadblock.

I called Jacob and told him that Travis was for real, and we were leaving tomorrow. He asked if he could stop by and see me tonight, and I smiled. At least I would be able to spend my last night here with Jake.

Then I texted Lisa. I didn't want to talk to her yet because I was still fuming mad at her for telling Travis my plan and causing us to leave prematurely. But I knew that if I didn't tell her that I was leaving I would regret it. I didn't get a response, but at least I tried.

Travis

I hated to see women cry, but I got through my sister's little outburst unscarred. I figured she wasn't going to be happy, but I needed to get her packing. I was hoping that she wouldn't use all of the boxes because it was going to be expensive to ship them all to Florida, and I wasn't sure where I was going to put them. I lived in a three-bedroom apartment with my best friend Mike. It wasn't tiny, but it also wasn't a house. I hadn't spoken to Mike since I left so he had no idea that Sam was going to be moving into our third bedroom, which we now used as an office. Our apartment was a decent size, but very expensive because it was right on the Intercoastal. I closed my eyes and thought about how great it would be to be outside on the patio right now watching the boats go by. It would all work out fine. It was only a year.

Luckily, Sam only had two boxes that she had the UPS guy take. And one gigantic suitcase to check on the plane.

"Is this all you're bringing?" I asked her, thinking normal girls would've packed five times what she was bringing.

"Yeah. I figured I could come back for a couple of weeks this summer and visit with Aunt Alice so I can bring the rest back then." It sounded reasonable, although I wasn't stupid enough to ignore the hint of rebellion in her tone.

After the UPS guy picked up everything, and it looked like the drama for the night had passed, I yelled upstairs to Sam that I was ordering Chinese food for dinner, and it would be here in forty-five minutes.

I poured myself a glass of vodka on the rocks and sat on the couch to watch some television. I thought about what it would be like to be back in Florida. Different from what it was like here. Here everything was so quiet and relaxed. If I were in Florida right now I would still be at work. Then I would meet Mike out at the bar for a couple of drinks. We would go out to the club, pick up a couple of girls and bring them back to our place. I had a great life. That would change with Sam coming to live with me. We also had been known to do the recreational drug from time to time. I couldn't do that with a sixteen-year-old girl living with me. I couldn't even bring girls home anymore. Maybe I hadn't thought this through all too well. And what would Mike say? He'd think I was crazy and maybe even threaten to move out. That might be best, since with too much whisky and ecstasy Mike had a bad history of hitting on anything that walked.

I poured myself another drink as I thought about the environment in which I lived my life and would be bringing Sam into. Maybe my mom was right, maybe this was the best thing for me. It would get me to slow down a little. I would definitely need to think about the Mike situation, though. I didn't really trust him.

Samantha

We were eating the Chinese food at the kitchen table. I wasn't sure why I decided to eat with my brother, but I was trying to make something out of a terrible situation.

"What's the matter?" I asked him. He looked like he

was thinking about something that was bothering him. I didn't really care, but I had to break the silence.

"I want to tell you that it's different in Florida. I'm different in Florida." He was looking at his lo mien with troubled eyes.

"What do you mean you're different?" I asked.

"I work a lot, almost sixty hours a week. And when we get back I have a deposition that's due, and it will take up the majority of my time."

"Okay. So?"

"Well, I didn't want you to think that it would be like this. I won't be able to eat dinner with you or go to any school events or anything." He was saying this like I cared.

"That's fine by me." I paused, feeling like there was more to it. "Is that all?"

"Yeah. For the most part," he replied halfheartedly. "Well, I also have a roommate. He's my best friend from college. Mike. "

"Oh." I didn't know how to react to the news that my brother had a roommate. He had never mentioned this before, which was surprising. "Does he know I'm coming to live with you?" It seemed like a logical question.

"Actually, I haven't told him yet." Travis took another egg roll and shoved it into his mouth so that he didn't have to say anything else.

I was shocked and a little insulted. "You didn't tell him! How's he going to react? I mean, you are going to tell him before we show up tomorrow, aren't you?" I was almost yelling.

"Well, I would call him now but he's probably still at work. He works with me at the law firm." Travis was shrugging this information off like it wasn't important.

"I don't understand." I was struggling to comprehend this information. "What will he do when he finds out that your sister is coming to live with you? I mean, is he going to be nice to me?"

Travis laughed. "He might be too nice."

"What's that supposed to mean?"

"Well, he drinks some, and I'm not sure how he'll react." Travis took another bite of his egg roll. "If he has a problem with it he can move back to his parents' house. But that will never happen, because it's not cool to bring a girl back to your parents' house."

I was disgusted at his comment about women. "Do you have a lot of women over?" I was afraid to hear the answer.

"Sometimes, but now with you there I'm sure it will be less. I mean, we don't want you to feel uncomfortable." He said 'we' like he was talking about him and Mike. If Mike knew about me I would have believed him.

I felt really uncomfortable all of the sudden, like I was about to move from my home that I loved and go live with two drunken, horny strangers. Oh, wait, I was. Fabulous.

I no longer had an appetite. I had to get up and leave fast.

"I'm going to hang out with Jake tonight," I said as I got up to clear my plate.

"I don't know if that's such a good idea," Travis said.

"Well, I don't think it's such a good idea to move to Florida when I don't know anybody, your drunken perverted roommate has no idea that I am coming, and you work all the time. But you don't listen to me, so I think I'm going to hang out with Jake tonight. You can let him in the front door or I can make him climb up the lattice." I stood in the doorway and shot my brother the piercing look I had been perfecting all week. "You choose, since you seem to decide everything else for me." And I stormed out of the kitchen.

In retrospect, it was a bad idea to eat dinner with my brother. I thought if I tried to get along with him, then maybe I wouldn't be in Florida long, but clearly, I was going to have a harder time with Travis than I'd initially thought.

When I got to my room, Jacob was lying on my bed

reading my People magazine.

"Hey, you. What are you doing here?" I was so excited to see him and glad he didn't use the front door, since Travis might not have let him in. I jumped on the bed next to him and grabbed my People magazine playfully from his hands.

"So, it looks like you didn't pack much," Jacob said, as he got off the bed and walked around my room surveying the items left.

"Well, I don't plan on staying in Florida long. Travis can't keep me there against my will forever, right?" I said, following Jacob with my eyes.

He sat next to me again and took my hand. "Listen, Sam. I don't want you to do anything stupid because you want to get back here. I mean, nothing is going to change. I'm still going to be here whenever you come back." Then he looked up at me "Or maybe I can come visit you in Florida. We can go to the beach and surf or just collect shells." I could see the happiness in his eyes as he envisioned "vacationing" with me in Florida.

I leaned over and kissed him. His lips were soft and warm, just as I remembered.

"That sounds good," I whispered. "I won't do anything that you wouldn't expect me to do."

"That's what I'm afraid of," he said and laughed lightly.

He was holding my hand and rubbing my fingers, looking intently at them like they were going to disappear at any moment.

"What?" I asked, already knowing the answer.

"This is the last night I'm going to see you for a while."

I sat up on the bed. "Listen to me, Jake. This is only temporary." I took my other hand and lifted his chin so that he was looking me in the eyes. "I love you. I must have loved you forever and just didn't know it. I'm not going to lose you now."

I could see the tears starting in Jacob's eyes, so I kissed him again. This time he kissed me back strong and deep. "I love you, too," he whispered in my ear.

Then we lay in bed and just held each other. No talking, no thinking, nothing but Jacob and me.

After about twenty minutes of nothing, I asked him, "What are you thinking about?"

I wasn't sure what he was going to say. I was trying really hard not to think, but sometimes I couldn't help it. I was thinking about what life would be like in Florida. Living with a brother I barely knew, who admittedly wouldn't be around much, and another man who was his roommate and best friend. I found it interesting that Mike was Travis's best friend and I had never heard his name before. Not like I was ever close to Travis, but I thought that I would at least have heard his name. And the comment that Travis made about him like he wasn't the most trustworthy person. Could I handle myself around someone like that?

Then I started thinking sadder thoughts. About how much I would miss Jake. About how much I loved him. My eyes were closed to him for all these years and now that they were finally opened I was leaving.

"I was just wondering why we didn't do this years ago. We lost all that time." Jacob was holding me close to him, talking into the top of my head. I could feel his hot breath on my hair, and I moved closer to him. I took a deep breath and smelled his sweet scent.

"What are you doing?" he asked me, pulling back.

"I am breathing you in. You smell so good."

He pulled me closer.

I'd thought that it would be a good idea to spend my last night here with Jacob, and now I was rethinking that. This would only cause heartache for both of us. But it was worth it, at least for me.

"You know, I have secretly loved you for over two years," Jacob said.

"Shut up!" I hit his chest with the palm of my hand playfully. "You're just saying that."

"Um, no." He paused. "Honestly, I have loved you all this time. I tried to tell you once."

"You did not." I was wracking my brain, trying to think of a time when he was at all romantic, "When?"

"We were at Justin Grayson's party freshman year. I asked you to dance, and you said yes. On the dance floor I tried to tell you three different times, but each time I chickened out."

"Well, it's a good thing."

"Why?" He looked down at me with questioning eyes.

"Freshmen year I had a huge crush on Justin Grayson. That was the only reason I went to that party." I laughed knowing that would make Jacob jealous.

"You did?" He looked confused. "But you danced with me…"

"Well, honestly, you were the only one who asked me to dance that night." I giggled into his shirt.

Jacob powerfully moved his body on top of mine on the bed. I suddenly felt very vulnerable. "And I will be the only one you dance with from here on out," he whispered in my ear, and I smiled shyly. Jacob had my hands pinned above my head. I was in no position to argue, even if it was all in good fun.

"Want to dance?" He smiled at me, waiting for my response. He let go of my hands and got off the bed heading toward the stereo.

"What? Dance? Now?" All of the sudden I was more nervous than when I was pinned on the bed. "I don't think that's a good idea. Travis will hear us, and he'll make you go home."

"You blast music all the time. What will make Travis think this is any different?"

Okay, he had a point. I hated to dance. It was honestly the only reason I hated going to dances in middle school, because I was afraid a boy would ask me to dance. That night at Justin's freshman year party I even felt vulnerable when Jake and I were dancing. He said he tried to tell me how he felt three times, and the truth was I remembered them all. I'd been so afraid that if he said his feelings for me out loud it would ruin our friendship. So, I avoided him, and when we were dancing I made sure to change the subject each time he looked like he was about to say something. Back then I did like Justin Grayson. Jacob was just a friend. I really did think it was good nothing happened that night, because now I was appreciating him so much more.

"I hate to dance," I stated flatly, hoping Jake would get the hint.

He didn't. He started going through my CDs and chose Garth Brooks. He put the CD in and skipped to "The River." He walked over to the bed and reached out for my hand. I let his hand suspend there a couple of seconds before I reluctantly grabbed it and stood next to him.

He wrapped his arms around me. "I know you love this song," he said.

"So you think that this song will make me dance with you?"

"Don't look now, but you already are." He smiled and kissed me softly on the neck.

We were dancing in my room to my favorite song.

"How do you do it?" I whispered into Jacob's ear.

"Do what?" he asked, while still kissing my neck.

"Make me forget about everything that's about to happen and just live in this moment?"

Jacob pulled back to look me in the eyes. "It's not easy. I know you're leaving tomorrow, but I can only hope that you will love me even when you go and experience a new life." Jacob looked down to the floor before he said the next thing. "I don't want to end up like Maddy. Years from now still in love with you, not being able to move on with my life."

That hit me hard. I didn't realize Jacob thought Maddy was pathetic for still loving Travis after all this time.

I stopped dancing and took Jake's face with both

hands. "Listen to me. I'm not like my brother. I'm leaving because I have no other choice. If I could stay I would."

Jacob walked away, pulling his face out of my hands. "I know," he said as he sat down on my bed. He gestured for me to join him.

"I don't want to lose you, but I don't want to hold you back. It's taken me years to finally admit to you how I feel and now you're leaving. It is my fault." Jacob grabbed my hands and stared at them like they might disappear again. I guess to him they would.

"Stop," I said, begging. "I just want to enjoy you here and now." I felt a tear stream down my face. I didn't want to cry anymore but couldn't help it.

That was when Jacob leaned over and kissed me like he had never kissed me before. It was slow, and I could feel his breath quicken as he breathed me in. His hands roamed from my hands to my waist, and eventually up my back. I had goose bumps all over.

He started to lay me down on the bed and rolled on top of me again, but this time not in a playful way like before. And his arms weren't pinning me down; they were exploring my entire body. Jake was breathing heavily now, and we were moving like we had in the car at the drive-in movie. Except this time I didn't want him to stop.

Our lips broke apart and he took off his shirt. I lifted my shoulders off the bed with him still straddling me and removed my shirt. Jacob's eyes took me in, and I could feel his excitement on top of me. This time I wasn't embarrassed, I was excited. This was my last night with Jacob for a long time, and I wanted it to be memorable.

It was the first time for both of us, but he was gentler than I expected. I had been to second base before, but it wasn't anything like being with Jacob right now. As he moved down my body he slowly slid off my sweatpants. He followed by removing his jeans, grabbing a condom out of his pocket before throwing them on the floor.

"Are you sure?" He hesitated before going any further,

looking deep into my eyes.

"I'm sure," I said with a smile on my face. And I was. I was more than ready and couldn't contain myself any longer.

It was different than I thought it would be. At first it was a little painful, but after a few minutes the heat and warmth of his body took over, and we found our rhythm. When it was over, Jacob and I lay in my bed spooning, and I didn't want the moment to end.

I must have dozed off, because it was 9:30 p.m. the next time I looked at the clock. Exactly twelve hours and I would be off to Florida. I was starting to get scared. Scared that life as I knew it today would be gone forever after tomorrow. I had to focus on this moment with Jacob, making it last as long as possible. I tried hard not to fall back to sleep, but the events of the day took over, and my eyelids got heavy.

Jacob woke me at 11:00 p.m. when he said he had to go. He had a curfew and didn't want to get in trouble, just in case he was allowed to visit me in Florida. He didn't want his parents to have a reason to say no. We kissed one last time, both professing our love with tears in our eyes, before he climbed down the lattice and drove away. I stood at the window for several minutes crying over the life I was leaving. Nothing would ever be the same again.

PART 1

14 ARRIVING

Samantha

Even though I had left my house and gotten on the plane today, it all still seemed like a blur. Like maybe I was just going on a vacation. I didn't know how to comprehend that I might not ever live in my house again. Before I left the house this morning, I walked through each room, trying not to think about the next time I would be back. As I walked through my parents' room, I dusted off the pictures they had on their dresser with my fingers and straightened their covers. I knew they would never be back, but it comforted me to see the room neat and the bed perfect. I made sure all the lights were shut off and the water was shut off. I checked the AC unit and did one last walk through my room to make sure I had the essentials.

I stared at my bed remembering last night. I had made my bed this morning not knowing when I would sleep in it again, but hoping it would be in just a few months. Travis might let me come back for the summer and stay with Aunt Alice if I was good, but I had no guarantees. It didn't seem like Travis was being rational.

I managed to sleep almost the entire three-hour flight from Newark Airport to Ft. Lauderdale. I had been up so late the night before thinking about Jacob that I was exhausted by the time the flight attendants were going through the safety presentation. Luckily, Travis let me be and didn't try to talk to me or bother me at all. We remained silent during the entire airport experience through getting off the plane, picking up the bags from the luggage carousel, and the car ride to Travis's apartment.

Travis had parked his car at the airport, probably thinking his trip to New Jersey was going to be shorter than it ended up being. He drove a black Lexus sedan, which looked expensive. As I got into the car I saw all of the gadgets. The GPS system lit up as soon as he started the car and welcomed him back. I suddenly realized my brother had more money than I'd thought. I wondered what his apartment was like. I was hoping that it was as nice and big as his car so that I could stay as far away from him as possible.

We took the highway to Travis's apartment, which was about thirty minutes from the airport. I realized almost immediately that we were in a different world than what I was used to. There were palm trees lining the highway and the sound barriers had swans and fish expertly carved into them. Also, the other cars on the highway were even nicer than Travis's. We were passed by three Bentleys and two Ferraris. I was so amazed that I almost said something out loud, but when I looked over at Travis, he didn't even seem to notice. I decided not to say anything and continued to give him the silent treatment.

We pulled up to Travis's "apartment," which looked more like Trump Tower than an apartment building. I had only seen Trump Tower once on a class trip to New York City when I was twelve, but if I remembered correctly, it looked a lot like this place. The outside of the towering building was covered in reflective glass and full of large balconies, it must have been twenty stories high. I could see the ocean as we pulled through the security gates. I was guessing that the little mechanism on the front windshield of the Lexus opened up the gates. I was trying not to stare at the ocean and look so amazed, but I wasn't doing a good job. When Travis looked over at me and chuckled, I quickly remembered to close my mouth and look forward.

The parking garage was underground and all the spots were numbered. We pulled into spot 1218(a), next to a silver Porsche. I wasn't sure what model Porsche it was, but it looked like a race car, and it looked expensive.

Travis saw me looking at the car and told me it was his roommate, Mike's, car. I had almost forgotten about Mike, since I'd just found out about him the other day. Travis's best friend. I hardly knew anything about him, but by looking at his car I could tell he was probably the more successful of the two.

We took an elevator to the twelfth floor and walked to apartment number 1218, the same number as the parking spot, which made sense. Travis took out his key, and we both walked inside.

"Welcome to your new home," he said.

Hearing that made my stomach turn, but I tried to shake it off. I was still in a haze, not able to believe that we were actually here.

Travis's apartment was fairly large, and the walls were painted a faint gray color. The floors were white marble with lines of gray that matched the walls. There was a small foyer as I walked in, and the kitchen was immediately to my right. There were stainless steel appliances and black granite countertops. It was definitely a step up from the 1990 white fridge and tile counters we had in Jersey and the old rickety wood floors that echoed with every step.

As I walked into the living room that was directly in front of the kitchen, I saw huge floor-to-ceiling windows that showed the view of the ocean. It was a beautiful view, and I saw that Travis had a large balcony similar to the ones I saw when we first pulled up.

Then I stopped in my tracks. There was a man sleeping on the couch. The flat screen TV hanging on the wall was on, and it looked like he might have been wearing his clothes from the night before.

I turned and whispered down the hallway after my brother, "There's a man sleeping on your couch."

Travis had already set one of my suitcases down outside the door that was probably going to be my room. He walked back into the living room and looked at the couch with a sly smile. "That's Mike," he said. "Looks like he had a rough night." Travis laughed and kicked the man on the couch. "Get up!" he yelled as he continued to kick the man.

The man stirred and then opened his eyes, squinting and covering his face as if the daylight blinded him. "Hey, man, you're back." He sounded groggy and still drunk. I could smell the whisky and cigarettes from where I was standing.

"Yeah, I left you a message on your cell yesterday that I was coming back and bringing my sister to stay with us for a while." Travis sounded frustrated, but not quite angry. It sounded to me like Mike forgot a lot of things.

As soon as Mike heard that Travis's sister was there, he bolted up on the couch and turned to look at me. Even though he was clearly a mess, he wasn't bad looking. He had black hair and light blue eyes. He wasn't clean-shaven, but I couldn't tell if it was on purpose or if he was just dirty.

I smiled and gave him a little wave. "Nice to meet you."

He looked disappointed and waved back. "Hey," he said and lay back down. "Can you give me just a few more hours?"

Travis got frustrated and rolled Mike off the couch. I tried to hold in my laughter.

"Mike, you can sleep in your room." Travis held his nose and said, "Dude, you stink. Take a shower."

Mike looked insulted but not enough for a rebuttal. He slowly got up, smelled his armpits, nodded in agreement and walked down the hall.

Travis turned to me and held his hand out gesturing for me to follow Mike down the hall.

We stopped at the first door on the right, straight across from the bathroom, as Mike continued on to the next door down. Travis pointed to the bathroom and said that I would be sharing it with Mike. I was shocked and got a minor twinge of nausea in my gut. I had just seen Mike, and he was nasty, so I was betting the bathroom was worse.

There was no way I was sharing a bathroom with Mike. "Where is your bathroom?"

"In my room," he said, pointing toward the last room at the end of the hall.

"Okay, then I will take that room," I said blankly. "It's not in your best interest to have that man sharing a bathroom with a sixteen-year-old girl. Trust me." I was trying to imply that the creep I just met on the couch might try to sneak a peek at me while I was in the shower, but I didn't know if all of that came across.

"Hell, no," Travis said, his tone unyielding. He leaned over and opened the door we were standing next to. "This is your room." And that was the end of that.

As I turned to take a look at the room that Travis called "mine," the first thing I noticed was how small it was. It was literally one step until I was at the bed. There was a full-sized bed and a single nightstand, which covered the entire back wall. The far side wall had a small square window, which gave me a view of the ocean, and a small dresser. Right in front of me was a small desk. All of the furniture was white and the bedspread was a depressing light gray. The closet was the full length of the wall closest to the door and not a bad size. It was probably half the size of the room.

"Are you kidding me with this room? It looks like a

prison cell." I couldn't believe that he was going to make me live here.

"I know it's small, but I had my assistant measure and get you this bed and matching furniture the other day. We can get a TV to hang on the wall. It should work out." Travis paused and finished with, "It's only for another year, right?"

I was still in shock at the setup of the room. I couldn't help feeling like I was being punished for being alive. My eyes started welling up with tears, as much as I tried to stop it I just couldn't help but cry.

"Really, it's not that bad," Travis said and turned to walk out. "I'll get your other bag and leave it at the door. Just try to get used to it, please." He was back less than thirty seconds later with my final suitcase. I was still standing in the same place he had left me with tears slowly trickling down my face.

"I'm going to let you settle in. I'll order dinner in about an hour." He turned and left the room.

I turned around and sat on the bed, still with tears in my eyes, and the haze of the day hovering around my head. I sat there for about twenty minutes until the realization hit me. I was never going to be the same Sam that I had been just two short weeks ago. If I was going to make it through this experience I needed to build a wall up to protect the girl I once was so I wouldn't lose her forever. I would see her again in a year. I took a deep breath and decided I would start to unpack before calling Jacob. I needed to calm down a little before talking to him. I didn't want to upset him, too.

Travis

We had arrived in Florida and things were not off to a good start. Mike was drunk and passed out on the couch in the living room when we got here, Samantha hated her room, and I was starting to get a headache. I knew when I woke up this morning it wouldn't be a good day, and I was right. On a scale of one to ten, ten being the best day and one being the worst day, today was a negative three. Of course, these past two weeks had run the gamut on the scale of best to worst with my parents' death coming in at a one and being with Maddy a ten. I needed to focus on getting my life back to normal. Up until two weeks ago, my life usually ranked at a comfortable eight.

I sat down on my bed, thinking things over. I noticed that Natalie, our cleaning lady, had been in to change my sheets and had given me fresh towels in the bathroom. I took advantage of both, first by taking a shower and then by resting before I had to face Samantha again.

After the shower and nap, I was ready for a drink and to get back into some semblance of my normal life. When I headed out into the living room I realized that Mike was up and thankfully showered.

"Hey, man," I said as I walked into the kitchen to see if we had tonic and limes.

"Hey, Trav," he said and sat up on the couch. The TV was back on, and he was watching football. "Sorry about this afternoon, man. I totally forgot that you were coming back today."

I poured myself a Tanqueray and tonic and took a long sip. "That's okay. You had to meet my sister sometime and you definitely left an impression." I laughed as I joined him in the living room and sat next to him on the couch. Mike and I had only one couch, and we each had a side that we typically sat on.

Mike was watching the game, but I could tell that he had something to say. I knew him pretty well.

"So, what are you going to do now?" he asked.

I had been expecting this. "I'm not sure," I said, and shook my head as I said it.

"I have known you for a long time and there is no way you are going to be able to take care of a sixteen-year-old girl. Hell, the girl I was with last night was only four years older than her."

I scowled at Mike, realizing how close to a pedophile he actually was. "I know, but I had no other choice." I wanted to tell Mike about my mother's letter, about seeing Maddy again, and everything else that happened this last week, but guys just didn't talk like that. Instead, I drank. "You can think of it this way, she's old enough to take care of herself. I don't see much changing."

Trying to convince myself it was all going to stay the same, I said, "Why don't we go to Morton's tonight for Power Hour and forget about all this crap right now?"

"Sure, man, I'm in." And with that, Mike and I were off the couch getting our keys.

I had to tell Sam, so I knocked on her door and listened to see if I could hear her. She was talking on the phone, I assumed to her new boyfriend, so I said through the door, "Mike and I are going out tonight. I left the take-out menu on the counter in the kitchen for you with some money. They deliver." I didn't wait for a response from her.

I took out the Sal's Pizza menu from the kitchen drawer, knowing she was a fan of pizza, and threw it on the counter with a twenty-dollar bill. And then I was off, back to my old life, trying to convince myself with every drink that not much would change.

Samantha

I heard Travis say something through the door about take-out, but honestly, I didn't really listen because I was too focused on my conversation with Jacob. I heard the front door close and thought little of it. I was trying to be positive for Jacob, but I knew he could see right through me. I teased him about how I slept on the flight because someone had tired me out the night before, which made him laugh and lighten up a little. I told him about the scenery and the apartment, promising to text him pictures of my room as soon as I was settled in. We ended with an "I love you."

After hanging up, I sat on my bed staring at my phone, thinking of how far away Jacob was. I had only been in my "new life" for a few hours, and I already felt lonely and lost. How was I going to survive in this life, even if only for a year?

I had almost finished unpacking my things when my stomach growled. Realizing I hadn't eaten all day, I headed out into the living room. It really was a gorgeous apartment. I understood now why Travis didn't want to leave it behind. I quickly realized no one was here, I was all alone. I saw the take-out menu and the twenty-dollar bill on the counter. It was Italian, so I ordered my favorite food, pizza. I ordered a cheese pizza for delivery. I got the full address to the apartment from a pile of mail on the counter and then headed back to my room to finish settling in.

Since I was going back home for the summer, or at least I was hoping, I hadn't packed too many things. It was good, too, because the closet wasn't really that big, and I only had one dresser. The furniture was pretty nice, and I could see that whoever decorated must've been a woman. The comforter was light gray with the outline of large yellow flowers and the sheets were a matching pale yellow. The wood finish on the furniture was painted white, neutral but still sort of girly.

After I was done unpacking, the pizza still wasn't here, so I decided to call Jacob again. I didn't want to bother him, but I was feeling really lonely.

Unfortunately, he didn't answer his phone. I checked the clock, and it was a little past six, so maybe he was having dinner with his parents. I knew that my parents never let me bring my cell phone to the table. Then I imagined him sitting around the dinner table with his family and thought about how I would never eat dinner with my parents again. For the first time I envied Jacob.

He still had his family and his regular life. Here I was transplanted into this tiny room in this lavish apartment in a different state. I was supposed to start at a school in a few days, with kids I had never seen before, in a town I had never heard of. I had an emptiness in the pit of my stomach that I knew would never go away.

I walked out of my bedroom to take a look around the apartment. I was assuming that Travis and Mike would be out all night so I wanted to take the opportunity to snoop around. If I was going to be living here, then I needed to learn my surroundings. Of course, I first started with Travis's room. Because Travis hadn't really ever lived with a girl, he was unaware of our innate ability to snoop, so he didn't lock his door. I knew I had to take advantage of this situation while I had the chance.

Travis's room was neat but clearly that of a bachelor. Black and white bedspread, black wood furniture, and a large flat screen TV hanging on the wall. His room seemed clean, so I was guessing they must have a housekeeper. I noticed his bathroom to my left and had to go in. My mom used to always say that if you want to really learn about someone you should look through their medicine cabinet. It seemed like a good place to start.

The bathroom was also very neat, not what I was expecting of a man's bathroom, but he hadn't been here in a week. It had a standing shower with white marble backing and floors. He had a very fancy sink with an impractical water spout. I opened the cabinet next to the sink but he had only standard stuff, mouthwash, toothbrush, toothpaste, razor, after-shave, cologne, and a huge bottle of Advil. There was also a prescription bottle full of little white pills. I read the label but didn't recognize the name. When I opened the top drawer, I shockingly found a big box of condoms. I slammed the door and ran out of his room. I felt like I had crossed a line and was really grossed out. My snooping trip was over, at least for now.

The doorbell rang, and my pizza was finally here. I ate it in my room and watched videos on my laptop since I didn't have a TV. Travis and Mike woke me up when they got in around 4:00 a.m. I rolled my eyes, put the pillow over my ears and thought out loud, "You've got to be kidding me."

15 REALIZATION

Travis

The next few days were a blur. Mike and I had gone out Thursday night, the day Sam and I had arrived back home, and I'd never really stopped. I had to convince myself that my life wasn't going to change now that Sam was living with us. I also kept thinking about Maddy. I had so many feelings that I didn't want to explore. I knew that Natalie delivered groceries every Friday morning and cleaned up around the house, so I wasn't too worried about Sam. I was in denial about her needing anything and figured that she was old enough to be self-sufficient. I seemed to be right because on the few rare occasions that I did see her that first weekend she was always clean and didn't look like she was starving.

To thwart any hangover, I made sure that I had a constant buzz. I didn't have to start back at work until Monday so I took advantage of Friday and Saturday to try and kill any of the feelings that had been dredged up since my parent's death. But I still found myself thinking about Maddy when I was alone, even when I was totally wasted. I just couldn't stop the thoughts from creeping into my mind. Between the loss of my parents, the responsibility of Sam, and walking away from Maddy, these past couple of weeks were stressing me out. Good thing I knew how to drown my feelings with alcohol. I both thanked and resented my father for that.

The truth was I had a very different life growing up than Sam had. The saying that parents make all of their mistakes with their first child was true in my case. When I was born my parents were struggling in their marriage and barely making it through each day. I was always on the food assistance program at school, and we had only enough money for frozen food, fast food, or meatloaf. To this day I still can't think about eating meatloaf without gagging.

My father spent the majority of our family's money on booze. He was belligerent and drunk most of the time. He blamed my mother for everything that was wrong in his life and yelled at her constantly. Most nights were so bad that I had to do my homework hiding in the tub with the shower curtain closed so that my father didn't drag me into the middle of one of his tirades. The worst part was that my mother took the abuse, like it was her punishment for choosing him as a husband. If she ever thought about leaving him, she never showed it or attempted to. My father never hit us, but sometimes I wished he had. The verbal abuse was bad, so bad that my neighbors once called the cops because they thought he was beating us. But my father was a cop, so that didn't work. True blue and all that crap. No matter what he did, he was always a cop, until one day he crossed the line. Not with my mother and me, but on the job.

If you asked Sam, our father swerved his police car to avoid hitting a deer, but the truth was he was driving home drunk from a bar and fell asleep behind the wheel. He saw the deer—he probably saw three deer, swerved, and ran into a telephone poll. Since he was heavily intoxicated, he hadn't remembered to put his seatbelt on and smashed through the windshield. He had irreparably damaged his right hand that day and would never be able to fire a weapon again. The funny part of the story, in my opinion, was that he was so blitzed he didn't even realize how hurt he was and walked almost half a mile down the road for help. Again, if you asked Sam it was adrenaline that made him walk that far, bleeding the whole way. When we were younger I didn't have the heart to tell her the truth.

I only knew the truth because I'd heard my mother yelling at him one night. After my father had lost his job, he just got worse with the drinking. He went on disability and sat around the house all day getting drunk. These were the little facts that Sam didn't know about our parents. When my mother got pregnant with Sam, my father straightened up, proclaiming that he wouldn't make the same mistakes twice. That always made me resent Sam and was one of the main reasons I wanted to get as far away from them as possible.

But the reality was that Sam didn't know any of that. I had decided years ago not to tell her, and I was going to stick with that. I figured one of us was already so fucked up in the head, no need for both of us to be there, especially now that Mom and Dad were gone.

I turned to look at the nightstand clock, and it was a total blur. Whenever I was hung over I had trouble focusing my eyes. I decided the way to fix this was to get a beer from the mini fridge I kept in my nightstand. After the first chug I refocused my eyes and read the time: 12:42. I knew it had to be p.m. because the sun was shining in through the creases of my window blinds. I pinched my lips together and thought really hard; I figured it was Saturday. I replayed the events of the last two days in my mind, remembering most of them.

Thursday Mike and I had started at Morton's and then ended up at a restaurant nightclub called Bova. I couldn't remember what time it was when we got home, but it must've been late since I didn't get up on Friday until around four in the afternoon. I had some cold pizza from what Sam had ordered the night before, with a beer. After a quick shower I was ready to start all over again. Mike and I went to downtown Delray Beach to a club called Union where we met a group of beautiful young women who were there celebrating a bachelorette party. I thought Mike brought one of them home, and I was hoping it wasn't the bride to be. He'd been known for doing that before.

With that memory, I quickly looked around my room for any traces of a strange girl. None. Then I vaguely remembered telling one of the girls that I was involved with another woman and trying to figure it out. Why would I say that? I mean, I know the logical reason. I was drunk. We all do crazy things when we're drunk. But maybe it was the most honest thing I said to that girl all night.

I rolled out of bed feet first, and the room was suddenly spinning. I slowly stood and eased myself to the bathroom to take a few Advil and a much needed shower. When I was done, I headed out to the kitchen to see if there was anything to eat.

To my surprise, Sam was sitting in the living room watching TV. I hadn't seen much of her these last few days, mostly because I hadn't been home, but every time I was home she was always in her room. Granted, it was usually four in the morning and she was probably sleeping, but I was fending off a hangover and incapable of thinking rationally.

"Hey, stranger." I tried to keep it light, figuring she was still not too happy with me.

"Hey," she said back without even a glance in my direction.

I sat next to her on the couch.

"You reek of booze," she said with a disgusted look on her face.

I grabbed my shirt and smelled it. I had just showered and put on a clean shirt, so I knew it couldn't be that bad.

"I do not."

She still had the disgusted look on her face when she turned back to the television.

"Come on, I just showered. I can't smell that bad."

"You seriously stink like beer and whiskey," she said, as she moved to the farthest end of the couch away from me.

"Hmmmmm," I said, considering her claim and smelling my arm. I drank so much this weekend it was probably seeping through my pores. "I guess I should switch to vodka. They say that doesn't smell," I said, laughing at myself. I didn't think she was amused.

"You're a mess," she said blankly.

"Well, you're not much of a prize either." With that, I decided it was time for another drink. I thought I might just go with vodka. If I did smell like beer and whiskey, I needed to fix that. I didn't want to show up to work smelling like I had been on a bender.

"You're pouring yourself another drink?" She looked over at me with judgment in her eyes.

"Yeah. You got a problem with that? It's my first one today." I neglected to mention the beer I had in my bedroom when I woke up.

"I think you have a serious problem," she said, not a hint of real concern in her tone.

"Yeah, well, you wouldn't know anything about having a serious problem." I didn't want to bring up Dad, but she really had no idea who she was talking to about this subject. The truth was I'd always wondered if alcoholism was genetic, because if it was, then I was a walking time bomb. "Let's just drop it." And I poured myself a drink.

"Are you going out again tonight?" she asked.

"Ummm, yeah." I sort of laughed as I answered because it seemed like such an absurd question. It was Saturday night; of course I was going out.

"Well, I'm getting sick of pizza and sitting around this apartment. I thought maybe you could take me to the grocery store to buy food." She had her arms crossed on her chest and looked at me with piercing eyes.

"I don't go grocery shopping. Natalie buys our food and drops it off. She should have dropped off food yesterday morning," I said as I checked the fridge.

"Yeah, I met Natalie, but all she buys is coffee, creamer, bread, milk, and eggs."

"So, have an egg sandwich." I was getting frustrated with her attitude. It wasn't like I was leaving her with nothing. I guess she didn't like my answer because she huffed and left the room slamming her bedroom door behind her.

Right after Sam's door almost fell off the hinges, I heard Mike come out of his room. He was a hot mess. "What the hell was that?" he asked, as he scratched his head and rubbed his eyes. I could tell he was having a hard time focusing and needed a beer like I did.

I grabbed one out of the fridge and tossed it in his direction. "Heads up! This will do the trick."

He snatched it out of the air, popped it open and took a swig. "Thanks."

"My sister's not that happy about our drinking binges, but who cares. Where do you want to go tonight?"

"Oh, I'm not sure. We can't stay out too late again, because we have my father's barbeque tomorrow."

Damn! I had forgotten all about my boss's barbeque tomorrow. Mike's father, Mitch, was also my boss and a partner at the firm that Mike and I worked for, Wallace & Shipley. I met Mike my freshman year at UM. He was a goofy, wild kid, and I was shy and withdrawn. We realized quickly that our opposite personalities made us fast friends. I had gotten into UM on an academic scholarship, and Mike had gotten in because his father was a large financial contributor to the school, what most people would call a booster. Mike and I had lived together since our sophomore year and both decided to go to law school together. I decided to get into law because I liked the idea of power, money, and the lifestyle it had to offer. Mike went into law because his father expected him to. What I'd figured out over the years was that rich people are different than normal people. They didn't do what made them happy. They did what was expected of them. Not for their parents' love and admiration, but for their trust funds. Or at least that was Mike's deal.

I was lucky that Mitch had offered me a job right out of law school because I was Mike's best friend, but after that he didn't do me any favors. The idea of a luxurious lawyer lifestyle was soon gone. I worked long hours and the little time I did have to myself I spent going out with Mike to meet women. Only after I won my fifteenth case did I get a raise and start making the money I thought I deserved. Mike wasn't as good of a lawyer as I was, but I didn't think his father expected him to be. Mitch was my mentor; he took me under his wing and taught me how to be a damn good lawyer and as cunning as they come. I could walk into a deposition with a witness and leave an hour later having gotten them to spill all their secrets. I made the firm, and Mitch, a lot of money and got them a lot of new business. In South Florida, there was a law firm on every corner, but none with the reputation of Wallace & Shipley, and I liked being a part of that.

When my parents died, Mike and Mitch were the only two I told. Mitch was very understanding, and when I had to stay longer than expected he was the one who told me to take as much time as I needed.

Every spring, Mitch had a corporate barbeque at his house and invited all the lawyers at the firm and their families. It was a pretty big deal, and you didn't miss it. Every year I went solo and spent the majority of my time hanging out with Mitch and Mike. But this year was clearly different.

What was I going to do with Sam? I couldn't bring her. She might have a fit and tell my co-workers about my drinking or even worse, Maddy. She definitely couldn't be trusted to behave herself, especially after her little fit in the living room five minutes ago.

"You know my Dad is expecting to meet Sam, right?" Mike said rather plainly. He'd found an old bag of chips that were hidden in the cabinet and was snacking on them.

My panic stricken face made Mike realize he said something I wasn't expecting.

"Really man? You come home with a sixteen-year-old sister we didn't even know existed. You had to figure my parents would want to meet her." Mike was right, but I hadn't even thought about it. The last thing I needed was Mitch meeting Samantha.

"I don't think it's a good idea." I was shaking my head, trying to figure out what I was going to do. "I need to come up with a story to tell your Dad and I need you to back me up."

"Sure, no problem, but I'm in no condition right now to come up with a viable lie to tell my father." He was hanging his head over the sink looking like he was really regretting eating those chips.

Once Mike got his sea legs back, we decided to go out to Rocco's Tacos and come up with some ideas over a few margaritas. In retrospect, Rocco's wasn't the kind of place you went to think up a plan. It was brightly decorated with star-shaped light fixtures, old ugly Mexican tribal masks on the walls, and a bar the length of the restaurant. The music was loud, and it was always busy with people lined up at the bar waiting for their free shot of tequila served by Rocco himself, poured straight into your mouth.

After a few shots, Mike had come up with some less than stellar ideas. One of them involved handcuffing Sam to the couch, which I thought was a bit extreme, knowing she would somehow get to her phone and call the cops on me. He also suggested that we say she had a cold. Ultimately, I didn't agree with that excuse in case Esther, Mike's mom, heard that Sam was sick and wanted to go check on her. I couldn't risk that.

A few hours later, maybe more, I decided it was best to

keep it simple. She had a headache. I heard women use that one all the time to get out of things. And it was only temporary, so I didn't need to stay home with her, and she could still go to school on Monday. I wasn't sure why it took me an hour to think of this excuse; maybe it was all the cocktails I'd had.

At around eight we decided to call it a night.

Samantha

I was in my room when I heard Travis and Mike leave for what I was assuming to be the night. I was hoping that he had left money for food, but after I was such a bitch to him earlier I doubted it. It was my third day in Florida and I still hadn't left the apartment. I was feeling trapped here. I didn't have a license or a car or even a bicycle. I had already talked to Jacob three times today so I couldn't call him again. I was starting to become needy, which wasn't good for a new relationship. I missed him, and I could tell that he missed me, too, but talking to him every waking moment was not doing either of us any good.

I started up my laptop and logged into my Facebook account. There weren't many updates from my friends since last I checked, but Jacob had sent me a private message to let me know he was thinking of me. I used to be the girl that made fun of all my friends in love, but now I was head over heels and I missed him. After checking some friends pages I decided to go through my pictures. There were so many of my parents and me at my school, my softball games, Christmas, my birthday. There were a lot of me and Jacob and Lisa. I hadn't talked to Lisa since I left home and was starting to seriously doubt if I would ever talk to her again. I realized how much I missed her. Don't get me wrong, it was great talking to Jacob, but it was totally different talking with a girl. I could tell Lisa anything and she would never judge me or lie to me. I could really use her opinion about my relationship with

Jacob, but I knew that would never happen. I'd lied to her, and she was really hurt by Jacob and me. I'd probably lost her forever.

I started wondering what the kids would be like at my new school. Did they have a softball team? Were they any good? I thought it would be a good idea to look up the school online and try to find different clubs and things on their website. While searching, I actually found a New Student Club where you could sign up and get another student who volunteered to show you around the school and make sure you found all your classes on time. I decided to join.

By the time I had done all of my school research, I realized it was already eight o'clock and I should probably get something to eat. As I walked into the kitchen to see if Travis had left money, the front door opened and Travis and Mike stumbled in. I checked the clock again to make sure it was as early as I thought. They hadn't been home before 3:00 a.m. since we got here. They were clearly drunk, and I couldn't even imagine how they had gotten home.

"What are you doing home so early? Run out of mickies to slip to innocent girls?"

"How'd you guess?" Mike said, laughing as he literally stumbled to the couch, tripping over my shoes, the barstool, and the coffee table in the process. He was so disgusting I couldn't believe how any woman would ever want to be with him unless they were drugged.

I turned back around to look at Travis, and he was slumped over the counter not looking too good.

"Are you okay?" I asked, even though I knew he wasn't. He really did have a serious drinking problem. I knew it wasn't my place to point it out, but I couldn't stop myself. "You have issues, you know that, right?"

As soon as I said that Travis's face turned red with anger. I must have touched on a nerve.

"We went over that this afternoon. You need to keep

your nose out of my business. You have no idea what you're talking about," Travis said through gritted teeth while still slumped over the counter.

He was right. I didn't know much about his life other than what I had experienced over these last few weeks. But from what I saw, he was a useless, angry drunk who offered nothing to society. He was spiraling out of control, and I wasn't going to take his crap anymore.

"You haven't been sober since we stepped foot in this apartment! I have no idea what I'm doing here or why you brought me back here. How do you even hold down a job? You are the most irresponsible, selfish person I've ever met, and I'm embarrassed to share the same bloodline with you. You don't care about me. You just feel guilty for being such a terrible son to Mom and Dad. They were great people and they spawned a son like you. You are a shame to our family, and I'm glad that I barely know you because you aren't worth getting to know. You're just wasting the air of all the other people who deserve to live!" I was frantically yelling. I couldn't take it anymore. All of my feelings that had been compiling over the last three days poured out of me in the direction of my good for nothing brother.

Travis just stood there looking at me without saying a word, waiting for me to finish. I knew Mike was behind me somewhere, but during my tirade he had stopped moving and was probably staring at me in shock. I heard him slowly move down the hall and his bedroom door close.

After we were alone in the living room, Travis stood silent for a few moments before he said, "Are you done?"

I slowly nodded my head yes. I had said all there was to say. I knew this was probably going to get me sent to boarding school where I would never see Jacob again, but I didn't care. It had to be said.

Travis slowly walked to his room but didn't shut the door. I was left standing in the living room alone. A few moments later, Travis was back with an old yellowed paper clipping. He threw it on the counter in front of me.

"You think our parents were such wonderful individuals. You have no idea." He pointed down to the paper. "Read it."

I was still silent, in shock, and confused by what he was trying to show me.

He moved toward me and opened up the folded article, laying it out in front of me on the counter. "Read it!" he yelled.

As I looked down, I saw that the headline read "Local Cop Fired for Drunk Driving While on Duty." Then I saw the picture, it was our father. I looked up at Travis with disbelieving eyes.

His face was blank almost like he didn't want to confirm it for me, but then I saw him slightly shake his head yes. "Read the whole thing. Our saintly father wasn't such a saint when I was the only child in the family." He paused, looking down at the ground before continuing on. "You have no idea what my life was like when I was growing up. Dad was no saint; he was the real drunk. You think that I'm a drunk because I go on a bender after my parents die. My father used to drink all day and all night, and then he would yell at my mother for hours. He would yell that our house wasn't clean enough, that she didn't support him enough, and that she didn't love him enough. And let's not even go into how he treated me. If Mom wasn't good enough, the woman he chose, imagine the things he would say to me, the child he never wanted. The accident they made too early in life. But it was all okay because he 'never really meant it,' Mom would say. He doesn't know what he's saying, she would cry. He has to work out his inner demons. Well, what about my inner demons? How many times could I cry myself to sleep at night? You have no idea what it was like for any of us back then."

I was still standing in the kitchen, my legs barely

holding me up. I couldn't process everything that Travis was telling me. My face must have displayed my desperation because Travis continued on.

"You think you know everything. Mom got knocked up with you, and Dad straightened up after she threatened to abort you. He got sober, and he apologized to her over and over again. But where was my apology? Once he even said it was good for me, that it gave me a thick skin. I was just a kid!" He was so angry that each syllable was accentuated with spit. I could see the tears starting to well up in his eyes as the memories of what he'd lived through all those years ago were coming back to him. "Your memories are full of birthdays and laughter, mine are full of crying and yelling. So, you have no idea what you're talking about when you tell me that I have issues, let alone a drinking problem." He turned to walk out of the room, but quickly turned back around. "I have a lot of problems, and you don't know about any of them, so never again pretend like you do. You think I'm such a horrible person. Too bad our parents aren't around anymore for you to thank them for making me this way." With that he left the room.

Suddenly I was the one that didn't feel so good. I hadn't eaten anything all day, but I felt like I was going to throw up. The room started to spin so I ran to the kitchen sink and splashed water on my face. I felt like my entire life had been a lie. How had my parents kept this from me for all those years? They'd always seemed so happy. I knew my Mom was internally tortured by her relationship, or lack thereof, with Travis, but I had no idea the past that they had shared. I grabbed the article, read the headline again and looked at the picture of the crashed police car. Tears started streaming down my face as I thought of the hurt I just saw in my brother's eyes. I said some terrible things to him. I still believed them all, but now I felt guilty for saying them out loud.

Travis had more inner demons than I had realized. I

was on information overload. I needed to retreat to my room and read the entire article to see if what my brother had said was true. What if it was?

16 REVELATIONS

Travis

I woke up on Sunday morning full of regret and a major hangover. The barbeque at Mitch's started at noon today and it was already 10:00 a.m.

I got up and went directly to the bathroom to throw up. After ten minutes, I was feeling well enough to get in the shower and wash off some of the guilt I was feeling for telling Sam about what had happened to me as a kid. No one knew about it except my parents and Maddy. And now Sam, the one person I swore I would never tell. Obviously, quite a few drinks mixed with some goading from a younger sibling are a bad combination. I knew the right thing to do was talk to her about it, but instead I grabbed a beer.

Samantha

I heard Travis get up and start his shower. I had been lying awake in bed for over an hour, still trying to process the events of last night.

I had come back to my room with the article and read

the entire thing about twenty times. It did in fact say that my father was the cop that had wrecked the car and that there would be an internal investigation based on some tests that were administered at the accident site. It was reported that my father had failed a Breathalyzer at the scene of the crash and was taken away in an ambulance after injuring his right hand.

I spent the rest of the night online trying to look up any records of potential arrests or domestic abuse complaints that involved either of my parents but couldn't find anything. I did find the newspaper article online so I knew that it was real and not fabricated by Travis. It was printed in the Cranberry Press on November 21, 1990. This had all happened just before Thanksgiving when Travis was just a boy.

I had trouble sleeping after learning about the disturbing life my brother had grown up with. I couldn't even imagine it, since I had only known love and compassion from the people that my brother grew to hate.

I had a dream about the night my parents were killed. I was usually a vivid dreamer, but this was the first dream I had since my parents' death. In the dream, my parents, Travis, and I were sitting in my father's old police car. The front end was smashed and the windshield was broken, but we were still driving down the road like nothing was wrong. The hole in the windshield was large enough for a person to fit through, but my father was still in the front seat. He was in his old uniform, and my mother was in her favorite pink dress in the passenger seat. I was in the back behind her and Travis was sitting next to me, but it wasn't the man I knew now, it was Travis as a little boy. It was raining like the night they were killed, and my father had a can of beer in his right hand, which was a bloody mess. He took a long sip of the beer and then passed it on to my mother who did the same. Then she leaned back and passed the beer can to Travis, who was now the grown up Travis. They were all laughing and swaying back and forth.

I was yelling at my Dad to pay attention, but no one was responding to me. It was like they couldn't hear me. As we were coming up to the intersection I could see the truck coming straight for us. I knew it would run the red light and kill us all. I was screaming to all of them to stop and I was crying. Then I woke up.

My sheets were drenched in sweat. The dream felt so real that when I woke up I jumped out of bed, still trying to get away from the truck. Once I realized I had been dreaming, I lay back down but couldn't fall back to sleep. I just lay there the rest of the night wondering how different my life was from how Travis's had been.

I had to talk to him and explain that I didn't know. I was hoping that this could be a turning point for us. Maybe a turning point for him. I had realized last night that I no longer hated my brother; I felt bad for him. He had become the person he hated the most in this world: our father. He didn't realize it, but he was a drunk, and if he didn't turn his life around fast he was going to end up just like our father. Dead.

Travis

By eleven thirty I started to feel human enough to put on some clothes and comb my hair. I knew that Mike was going to want to leave any minute, so I had to get moving. A quick rinse of mouthwash to combat the beer and I was ready.

I walked out to the living room and into the kitchen. Mike was already there with a cup of black coffee waiting for me.

"You rock," I said to him as I took a slow sip. I needed to keep this down since I had been throwing up all morning.

Just as I was starting to feel better, Sam came down the hallway and into the kitchen. She was still in her sweatpants. "Are you going somewhere? I haven't seen

you up and showered before 3:00 p.m. since we got here."
I could tell that she was still angry with me about last night
so I let that sly remark roll off my back.

"I have a barbeque at my boss's house today." I took
another sip of coffee before pouring it down the sink.
Mike and I needed to hurry if we were going to get there
on time. I turned to Mike. "You ready?"

Suddenly Sam caught me off guard. "Why is Mike
going with you?"

"I told you already, Mike and I work at the same firm."
I left out that Mike's father was my boss. I didn't like
calling that out in front of him.

"Mike is a lawyer, too?" she asked disbelievingly. She
looked over at Mike who wasn't even paying attention to
her but focused on something on his phone. "I didn't
realize that they let just anybody be a lawyer. Can he even
read?"

"Hey!" That got Mike's attention, and he looked up
from his phone.

I put my hand out toward Mike to let him know that I
could handle her. "I know it doesn't look like it, but Mike
is a pretty good lawyer." Probably not the raving review he
was looking for, but I was too hung over to lie.

"Would you mind if I went with you? I promise I won't
embarrass you or say anything bad," she pleaded.

I wasn't expecting her to ask to go. I thought she
caught that when I jerked my head back and scoffed at her
request. "Yeah, right. Not in a million years."

"What happens when they ask about me? Have you
thought about that? You can't keep me locked up here
forever." She was right, but I had a plan for that.

"If anyone asks, you have a headache." And with that I
grabbed my keys and walked out. I couldn't risk sticking
around and letting her plead her case.

As we drove to Mitch's house, my head was spinning,
but at least my stomach had stopped retching. We arrived
just in time to be fashionably late but not get ourselves

fired.

Last year, Mike and I got in trouble for showing up to the barbeque two hours late and wasted out of our minds. The next day Mitch had threatened to fire us both if we didn't get our shit together. We were not going to make that mistake again. At least we weren't going to show up wasted. What happened over the course of a long afternoon was yet to be seen.

We were in Mike's car. Even though I took my keys, this was Mike's house so he always drove here. As we pulled up to the house I could see that the big iron gate was open and there were already at least ten cars in the driveway. Luckily, Mike had his own garage to the left of the main house, next to the guesthouse. We pulled up and parked next to a black Cadillac SUV with blacked out windows and giant chrome rims. I knew that was Mitch's company car.

We walked up to the front door of the house, which was made of dark wood and etched glass windows. We didn't knock or ring the doorbell, we just walked right in.

I remembered the first time I was at this house. Mike and I were still in college, and I had been invited over for Thanksgiving dinner. It was the biggest house I'd ever stepped foot in.

The floors were marble tile and there were two curved stairways on either side of the foyer leading to the upstairs. Straight through you could see a huge living room. The entire back wall of the house was one big sliding glass door with a perfect view to the backyard. Today the door was open and being used as the main entry to the barbeque area. The living room furniture was all white and there were huge paintings on the walls. The first time I was here Mitch told me that they were Jackson Pollack's. I was impressed. To the left of the living room was the kitchen with large white cabinets and light gray soapstone countertops.

I broke away from Mike, who was headed to the

backyard, and went into the kitchen. I knew that Esther was probably in there cooking up something she had gotten out of Martha Stewart's cookbook. Also, because the kitchen opened up to the family room where there was a seventy-two-inch flat screen television, which I knew would have some sporting event on. I was right on both counts.

Esther Wallace was a short, thin woman who looked like she would break in half if you hugged her too hard. She had on a bright blue blouse and white slacks. She wore bright blue eyeliner and pink lipstick. Her straight hair was bleached blonde and shoulder length, and her skin was so tan it looked like she lived at the beach. She was in her late fifties but didn't have a wrinkle on her face, even though she was smiling from ear to ear.

I'd always liked Esther. She was a true southerner, loved to entertain, and always welcomed guests with open arms. She had a thick Mississippi accent. "Travis!" she shrieked when she saw me walking toward the kitchen. She gave me a huge hug, but I just loosely embraced her back, mindful of her small frame.

"It's good to see you Esther," I whispered into her ear.

She released me from the embrace but still held on to my shoulders as she leaned back and examined my face. "How are you doin', honey?" she said with concern in her voice.

"I'm fine," I pleaded, but Esther looked skeptical. "Really, I'm doing fine. I'll be okay."

As a mother, she probably wanted me to be more broken up with the death of my parents, but I could only fake so much emotion.

She craned her neck around to look behind me. "And where is this sister of yours I never knew about but can't wait to meet?" When she realized I was alone, her eyebrows shot up as she waited for me to respond. I hesitated, and she asked again, prodding me for a response this time. "Travis, where is your sister?"

"She stayed back at the apartment. She has a terrible headache." I looked her in the eyes, hoping she couldn't see through my lie.

Thankfully, after a long pause, she seemed to accept my response. "Oh, well, that's too bad, honey. After all the heartache and stress you two have been through these past couple of weeks it's probably understandable. I just would've loved to meet her." She finally released my shoulders and turned back toward the kitchen to check on whatever she was baking. "We will have to have you both over for dinner when she feels better."

"Sure, that sounds great," I lied.

I excused myself and headed over into the family room to see what the other guys were watching on TV. Mitch had the Ultimate Sports Package from Dish Network, so they were watching rugby. It wasn't a sport I watched all that often and I didn't really understand the game, so I simply said hello to a few of my co-workers and went outside the large sliding door to find Mitch.

The backyard was probably as big as the entire first floor of the house. There was a large paver patio with a pool and spa straight ahead. To the right was an outdoor living room fully equipped with a fireplace, covered seating area with an L-shaped couch, and another huge flat screen television with sports on. I could see several of my co-workers lounging around the television in deep conversation, probably about work. To the far left, there was a large countertop area with a built-in grill. I could see Mike standing next to Mitch at the grill. Once they saw me Mitch waved me over.

I started heading in the direction of the grill but was cut off. Charles Shipley, the other partner at the firm, was standing in front of me with his wife, Mallory. Charles was a tall, slimly built, white-haired man with a solid frame and chiseled face. When you looked at him you could almost smell his money. His wife, Mallory, on the other hand, was a short woman who dressed more subtly. I hadn't seen her in a while and noticed that she had lost a lot of weight. Her skin was pale and her eyes sunken in. She wore a light pink sundress that was hiding her small frame. I'd heard a while back that she'd been diagnosed with brain cancer and was undergoing chemotherapy. I instinctively gave her a sympathetic smile.

"Mrs. Shipley, it's so good to see you," I said, as I leaned over and gave her a light kiss on the cheek. I turned to Charles and shook his outstretched hand. "Charles, how are you?"

He nodded. "Good, thank you, Travis. I see this year you're on time and looking good." If he only knew that I was battling the bile in my stomach.

My reaction must have given me away because Mallory Shipley gave a faint laugh. She must have to battle this feeling all the time on chemo.

"Thank you, sir." I desperately needed something to eat to soak up the acid in my stomach. I glanced over at Mitch and Mike at the grill and caught them watching us.

Charles turned in their direction, and Mitch gave him a little wave. "I won't keep you from Mitch, he has some things to discuss with you," he said with a sly smile. "We just wanted to get a chance to tell you how sorry we were to hear about your parents." He started to look around the backyard. "And we were hoping to meet your sister Samantha. I'm assuming she's here with you?" It was more of a question than a statement.

I scratched my head and looked around the backyard. I wasn't sure why I was looking around for Sam when I knew she wasn't there, but Charles made me nervous. "No, sir, she didn't come with us today. She stayed home with a headache." I tried to look as disappointed as he did.

"Oh no," Mallory Shipley said. "I was really hoping to meet her. I know that you and she have been through a lot, and I just wanted to extend my deepest sympathies." She had so much compassion in her eyes, and I could tell that her recent illness had given her a better understanding of death. "You know family is so important, especially in times like these. Your family's story has been such a motivation for us to reconnect and bring our family back together. I shared your story with…" Charles quickly grabbed her hand and cut her off. Mallory looked startled, not expecting him to interrupt her. With a slight smile and tears in her eyes she conceded to him. "You're right. Now's not the right time for that."

I smiled back, not understanding what she meant or why Charles felt the need to stop her admission. Who had she told our story to? Were the Shipley's having family problems?

Before I had enough time to really think about what just happened, Charles interjected, "Maybe you should take some more time off. Take your sister on vacation. Someplace you used to go as children." He was trying to be compassionate, not a trait he showed often. He smiled and looked longingly at his wife. "We used to take our boat off the coast of South Carolina." He paused remembering his own past. "It was wonderful. If Mallory were…" He didn't finish.

I immediately thought of that picture from "my" room in my parents' house. I didn't want to remember right now, so I pushed it to the back of my mind.

I realized there wasn't anything left to say, and the silence between us was making me uncomfortable. "If you both would excuse me, I'm starving and there are hot dogs calling my name." They both nodded at me and let me pass.

I walked up to the grill and shook Mitch's hand. Mitch Wallace always had a strong handshake. It was very intimidating, which I was sure was its purpose. "Good to see you, sir," I said.

"Travis, good to see you, too." Mitch was tall, probably six foot two with salt and pepper hair. He had an impeccable posture and always wore clothing made by Ralph Lauren or Gucci. Today he had on a navy blue

Ralph Lauren polo shirt with a red polo player emblem and khaki shorts. He reminded me of Mitt Romney, without the Hollywood smile. Mitch rarely smiled. He was all business. He owned his own firm and had more money than I would ever see in three lifetimes.

I could smell the food on the grill, and my stomach grumbled loudly. Both Mitch and Mike looked at me amused.

Mike laughed. "Travis obviously hasn't eaten yet today. Load him up with some good stuff, Dad."

Mitch filled my plate and handed the tongs to Mike. "Watch the grill for me son." I nervously glanced at Mike, wondering what he had told his father about my trip to New Jersey, my parents' funeral, Samantha, and Maddy. Usually I kept all of my secrets to myself, but this past weekend I had been so heavily intoxicated that I spilled my guts to Mike. In theory, you should be able to trust your best friend, but I knew Mike and he was an open book with his parents. He could never keep anything from them, even when they asked him about the partying, women, and drugs. It had always been an issue with us, because there were certain things you didn't want your boss knowing. But Mitch never judged me or Mike, however, he did make it clear that if we ever got into any legal trouble, our careers at Wallace & Shipley would be over.

As we walked away, I saw a faint smile on Mike's face and knew that I was in for the ninth degree. Shipley had made a comment earlier about how Mitch wanted to talk to me, so I was hoping it was more work related than about my personal life.

"What's up, Mitch?" I was in the middle of eating, so I figured if I took a bite right as he asked me a question it would give me more time to think of a response. Especially if they were questions I didn't want to answer.

Even though Mitch had been supportive when I called him to ask for more time off last week, I knew he wasn't happy that I had missed so much work. Cases were piling up on my desk, and that was not acceptable. "Are you going to tell me the truth about what's going on with you, or are you going to make me guess?"

I slowly chewed and swallowed my bite of hot dog. "Mitch, I'm fine. Nothing is going on. I'm getting back on track." Even I didn't believe myself.

"Don't blow smoke up my ass, Travis," he scolded.

"I'm sorry, Mitch. I shouldn't have stayed away for so long. It was harder than I thought getting..." I paused, "everything settled."

"From what it sounds like, you don't have much of anything settled." Mitch seemed concerned now, and we took a seat on a couple of lounge chairs. He placed his hand on my shoulder as I focused on the food on my plate so that I didn't have to look him in the eyes. "From what I hear, you're taking your parents' death really hard. Now I know that this was a big loss for you and I'm truly sorry, but to go out on drinking binges every night and neglecting your new responsibility of being a brother is just not acceptable." I quickly looked at Mike realizing that he had thrown me under the bus. Of course, he probably left out the fact that he was on those binges with me. Mike shrugged like he didn't know what his father was talking about and Mitch caught me looking at him.

"Don't blame Mike. He's just concerned about your well-being like we all are." I couldn't tell if Mitch was really concerned about my well-being or the well-being of the current caseload I was carrying for his firm. Mitch and Esther Wallace were always great to me and treated me like one of the family, but the reality was that I wasn't their son. If push came to shove, I always knew they would turn their backs on me.

"Listen, Mitch, I appreciate your concern, but I'm fine. I had a few bad days, but after today everything will get back to normal." I threw a glare in Mike's direction. He took a swig of his beer and walked away. "I know Mike's not happy about Sam coming to live with us, but what else was I supposed to do with her? She's my sister, and I am her legal guardian now."

"Travis, we all understand that, and we'll all adjust to your new circumstance. It may take Mikey some time, but I can't afford to have you out drinking at all hours of the day and night. I need you focused on work, now more than ever. There's a new partnership up for grabs, and Charles and I are looking at a few candidates, one of them being you." Mitch had finally shown his true colors. He wanted to make sure that I would still be able to contribute as much to the firm as I had before my parents' death and the arrival of my sister. I glanced over to Charles, who was watching Mitch and me. He gave me a small nod and then returned his attention back to his wife.

I had known that a partnership was up for grabs after Jordan Glassman, the previous partner, had left to start his own practice about a month ago. I just always assumed that Mike would get the job since that was what Mitch had dreamed about since the day we graduated from law school. We all knew that Mike wasn't a good enough lawyer to be partner, but we all assumed it was the natural progression of the firm.

"I thought Mike was next in line to take over for Jordan," I said bluntly. I was never one to mince words and it was a quality that Mitch said he admired.

Mitch shook his head. "No, no, no, no, Travis. We are looking at both you and Mike, so now is not the time to get distracted." He was basically telling me to figure out a way to send Sam back to New Jersey. I knew it. That was the way things worked here. You had to draw your own conclusions from Mitch's vague innuendos.

I nodded to communicate that I understood what he was implying. "I hear you."

"There's this new case I'm working that I would like your input on. We're representing Victor Nunez. Ever hear of him?" Mitch knew that I had heard of Victor Nunez. Everyone in South Florida had heard of him. He was a

Cuban national who had ties to the drug cartel. I knew that our firm had represented him in the past, but usually Mitch was the only one who worked his cases, and he never talked about the cases with anyone.

"Really? Me?" I was honestly shocked.

"Of course, Travis. You are one of the best lawyers I have." Mitch put his hand on my shoulder and leaned in closer to me. "I'm not as young as I used to be and Esther has been on my back to take some time off to travel. If I want flexibility with my schedule, I have to bring someone in on the Nunez case." He paused. "I think that someone is you."

I nodded, not exactly sure what to say next.

"The only thing is that Victor needs to know he can trust you. He's very…" Mitch was searching for the right word, "protective of his privacy."

This was a big deal and I knew it. In order for me to be brought into the Nunez case, I needed to get back on my game.

"Do you understand?" Mitch asked.

I nodded that I did.

"Good," was all Mitch said before getting up and walking back to the grill.

I stayed on the chaise lounge and finished the rest of my plate. I was too hung over to process the conversation I'd just had with Mitch.

Mike walked over and sat down next to me. He handed me a beer. "Here you go man. You look like you could use it." Honestly, the thought of drinking a beer made me actually vomit in my mouth a little, but after that queasiness went away I thought what the hell and took a swig.

"Seriously man, if you were that pissed about Sam coming to live with us you could've just told me directly. We did spend the last three days together non-stop." I was only half mad at Mike. I knew that I had put him in a bad situation, springing Sam on him without even asking, but I figured he would yell at me in a drunken stupor, not go tell his Mommy and Daddy.

"Sorry, dude. I had meant to say something to you about it, but we were having fun, and I didn't want to ruin it. But you should have given me some more notice that I was going to have to share my space. I mean, she isn't using your bathroom, she's using mine." He had a point.

"But still, to go tell you parents. Not right, man." I shook my head and took another swig of beer. I knew I would forgive Mike. I always forgave him for running his mouth to his parents. When something went wrong or he felt guilty about something he always ran home. He was the total opposite of me, which was probably why we got along so well.

I decided not to tell Mike about what Mitch and I had talked about. The last thing I wanted right now was Mike resenting me, and I knew he would. We didn't talk again; we just sat there for a while.

Could I really compete with Mike for a partnership at Mitch's firm? Was Mitch really going to bring me in on the Nunez case, or was that just a carrot he dangled so I would straighten up my act? Either way, the message came through loud and clear. I needed to figure out what I was going to do with Sam or else my professional life would be in just as much turmoil as my personal life.

17 NEW BEGINNINGS, NEW PROBLEMS

Samantha

When Travis and Mike left for the barbeque I was so distraught about what was going on, I needed to talk to Jacob. He was the only one left in my life that I could count on. The only person that I knew cared about me and that I could share this information with. Thankfully, he answered after two rings.

"Hello," Jake's voice was good to hear.

"Hi, Jake." I tried to sound strong, like I hadn't been crying, but at the sound of his voice I broke down. I realized how alone I had felt these last few days. The sobs came out in loud gruff coughs.

"What's wrong, Sam? What is it?" Jake sounded scared, and I realized he had no idea what went on last night.

"I'm sorry. Everything's fine," I choked out. "It's just that I feel so alone. I need to tell you what happened last night."

With that, I poured out every heartbreaking detail. Travis coming home drunk, and me getting on his case.

How he had screamed at me and told me about our parents and his childhood. The truth about my father's car crash all those years ago, and why he'd been on disability. I talked so fast and was crying the entire time. I didn't pause while telling the story, except for when Jake had to interrupt because he couldn't understand me through all the tears. I told him about the newspaper article and how I had researched it online and found out it was true. I told him about the dream I had and asked him what he thought it meant. When he didn't respond immediately with an answer, I told him how Travis had left me that day to go to a barbeque at his boss's house. I told him how I hadn't really left the house much or eaten a home-cooked meal. How Travis and Mike both hated me and how difficult it was to live in a house where you are severely unwanted.

When I finally finished, I realized I'd been talking nonstop for close to an hour. "I'm so sorry to spring all of this on you, Jake." I knew we were still early in our "relationship" and I was probably coming off as more trouble than I was worth. I decided to tell him that.

"Oh, stop it, Sam. I know you too well to think you're needy." Jacob was always the voice of reason. "You have gone through a lot these last few weeks." He went quiet briefly and I could tell I had upset him. "I wish I could be there for you."

I smiled, finally feeling loved for the first time all weekend. "You are here for me. Even though I can't touch you right now, just listening helps."

We sat in silence for a few moments. I was thinking about how much I missed him.

"I want to come down to visit you," he said.

I immediately got excited at the thought of seeing him. I needed a friend here, and I missed him so much. But then I quickly realized that Travis would freak out if he knew. Not for any other reason but to be a jerk.

"I don't think Travis will let you stay here."

"Why not?" Jake sounded insulted.

"It has nothing to do with you. Trust me. He just hates me so much and won't allow me to do anything that makes me happy." After last night's revelation, I had a better understanding of the hatred my brother had for me. Not that I agreed with it, but at least I understood it better.

Jacob sighed, knowing I was right. "Can't you work on him?"

"What?" I didn't quite understand what he meant.

"Butter him up a little. Don't fight with him anymore. Help him around the house. You know."

Even while Jacob was explaining what he meant, I knew it wouldn't work. What was I going to do to butter Travis up? Cleaning wouldn't help; he already had a housekeeper. Cooking wouldn't help; he wasn't home enough to eat here. I guess I could completely stay out of his hair and try to become self-sufficient. I wasn't sure how I was going to do that with no car, but I could at least stop picking fights.

"I'll try." And I was going to try. "Let's aim for Memorial Day weekend. That gives me some time."

We agreed on Memorial Day as a target. Jake was going to talk to his parents and research how much a flight would cost. I told him I would keep him updated on my progress. We ended the call with "I love you" and then hung up.

I lay in bed for a while, thinking about how to work on Travis. I decided the best thing to do was stay out of his hair completely. I looked up the nearest grocery store and realized it was very close, close enough to walk to. I had cash that I had brought with me from home, so I thought it would be a good idea to get myself some food. This way I didn't need to bother Travis for anything. Surprisingly, it only took me thirty minutes to get there, shop, and come back home. It felt good to finally get out of the apartment and get some fresh air. I knew that I would have to do this at least a few times a week.

My self-sufficiency plan was off to a good start. At least

it was until Travis and Mike came home. Once they walked through the door my plan fell apart.

Travis

Needless to say, after the barbeque Mike and I decided to go out for a drink before heading home. I knew I had to clean up my act if I was going to keep my job, but that could start tomorrow. Tonight, I could still have some fun.

We started at Bru's Room and then headed to Cabana El Rey. After three caipirinhas (a Brazilian cocktail made with rum, sugar, and limes) I wasn't sure where we ended up. I remembered getting into Mike's Porsche and speeding home down A1A. Probably not the best idea, but we somehow made it home. Mike carried me into the elevator and through the front door. The room was spinning, and I rushed to the kitchen sink. I hoped I made it there before getting sick all over the kitchen.

I heard Mike in the background laughing and yelling at how gross I was. I stumbled to the couch where I crashed. I didn't even remember my head hitting the pillow.

Samantha

I was lying in bed searching through Pinterest for some outfit ideas, when I heard what I figured was Travis and Mike barging through the front door. All I could hear from my room was Mike laughing like a bumbling idiot and yelling at Travis that he was gross and would have to clean that up in the morning.

My plan had been to stay locked in my room and not bother Travis, but I had to see what was going on.

When I stepped into the living room, the scene in front of me was horrific. The front door was still wide open and Travis was passed out on the couch facedown. There was a hideous smell coming from the kitchen, and when I walked in I gagged at the sight of vomit all over the floor, kitchen sink, and running down the kitchen cabinets. I quickly covered my mouth with my hand, just in case my gags turned into my own vomit.

I glanced back at the living room where I saw Mike sitting on the recliner. Travis was still passed out on the couch, and a fleeting thought ran through my head: maybe he was dead.

I ran over to the couch and checked my brother's neck for a pulse.

"Don't worry, honey, he's not dead." Mike was drunk and the words slurred together. He was slumped back in the recliner and had turned his head in my direction. His gaze gave me the chills and I had to shake off the feeling.

I understood from the beginning that Mike was a womanizer, but this was the first time I had actually seen him drunk, and it creeped me out. He was staring at me like he was going to attack me at any moment. Then, thankfully, he looked away.

I focused my attention back on Travis. I turned his head to the side so that he could breathe. He had dried vomit around his mouth and I could see some on his shirt collar. If I hadn't come out here to see what was going on he could have suffocated.

I walked over to the front door and closed it. Then I headed back down the hall to the bathroom. I grabbed some rubber gloves from under the sink and wet a washcloth that I got from the hallway closet. I stopped in my room and grabbed my wastebasket that was lined with a bag. I went back out into the living room and cleaned off Travis's face. I placed the wastebasket next to him, just in case he woke up in the middle of the night and needed to throw up again.

The whole time I was doing this I could feel Mike's eyes burning a hole in the back of my head. Once I had finished with Travis I turned around to look at him. I still hadn't said anything since they had gotten home. He was really making me uncomfortable with the way he was staring at me. What looked like longing on his face before had now turned into anger.

"What?" I decided to break my silence.

"Why are you doing all that?" he said with distaste in his voice.

I looked back at Travis. The truth was I didn't know why I was helping my brother. I felt bad for him after hearing the story last night and seeing him lying there on the couch defenseless.

"I don't know. Someone has to." When I looked back at Mike he looked away.

"You know we were fine when you weren't here. He's passed out on the couch before and was fine. You aren't his mother." Mike's words were cold, clear, and explained a lot. I had suspected that Mike hated me, but I just realized that I was wrong, he was jealous. I decided not to say anything else.

I got up and went to the kitchen. I tiptoed through the mess and got paper towels and cleaning supplies from under the vomit filled sink. I spent the next two hours cleaning the kitchen. While I was cleaning, I randomly felt a chill run down my spine, and when I looked out into the living room I saw Mike staring at me. I tried my best to ignore him and keep working. When I finished with the countertops and cabinets, I went to the hallway closet and got the mop out from where Natalie had stored it. When I walked back into the living room, Mike was gone. I didn't see him pass me in the hallway, which meant he must have left through the front door.

I didn't think much of it and finished up the floors. After I was done, I poured Travis a large glass of water and left it on the coffee table in front of him with the bottle of Advil from the kitchen. If he woke up in the middle of the night he might be thirsty.

I stood in front of my brother and stared at him, lying lifeless on the couch. I knew he was breathing but couldn't tell, since he was lying on his stomach. I tried to think about what he had to deal with growing up. Had he done this for our father when he was a young boy? Had he watched our mother do it? How many times did he have to deal with a scene like this? It was my first, and I was hoping it would be my last, but I doubted that. I had a bad feeling that from now on my life would be filled with nights like this. Taking care of my older brother.

I headed back to my room more mixed up emotionally than ever. I really wanted to hate Travis, but seeing how pathetic he really was just made me feel sorry for him.

I had to start school tomorrow. I decided that I had done enough for one night.

18 THE PLAN

Samantha

I had my alarm set for 6:00 a.m. I wasn't sure what time Mike needed the bathroom, so I decided the earlier the better for me, since I figured he would sleep in from being so drunk the night before. It was a good bet because when I opened the door to my room to survey the apartment it looked like Mike's door was closed and the bathroom was open. I realized I didn't even know if he was home or not.

I walked out into the living room to find Travis still on the couch. Instead of lying on his stomach he had moved over on his side and was hugging the couch cushion. I shook my head and focused my attention on getting ready for the day ahead of me.

I didn't know much about my new school. I knew it was the local high school, ineptly named Boca Raton High School, and that their mascot was a shark. It was a public school, which meant there was no school uniform or dress code. I had done some research online about classes and how to get there. There was a bus stop right around the corner that I could walk to, which meant I didn't need to bother Travis for a ride.

My plan was to stay as far away from Travis as possible. I needed to prove to him that I was independent and self-sufficient. If I could do that, then I might be able to convince him to let Jacob visit as long as we stayed out of his way.

I knew I had to be out of the apartment by 7:15 to make it to the bus stop on time. I had finished getting ready by seven o'clock, and I was so nervous that I couldn't sit still and watch the clock. I decided to leave early. The sun was already shining, and it would be good to get some fresh air. Plus, walking outside might take away some of these nervous jitters.

As I left the house at 7:05 a.m., I glanced back in the living room to see that Travis was still passed out in the same position, hugging to the couch cushion. I thought about waking him, since I knew he had work, but then realized that I needed to stick to the plan. As little interaction as possible. So I left to walk to the bus stop.

Travis

I woke up with several problems. First, I had a terrible hangover and the worst taste in my mouth. Second, I had Samantha's wastebasket next to my head and a glass of water with Advil on the coffee table. Third, the kitchen was spotless, when I vaguely remembered throwing up everywhere last night. Finally, I dreamt all night about Maddy. I woke up three different times thinking that she was lying next to me, only realizing this morning that it was the couch cushion I was holding.

I knew that Mike hadn't cleaned the kitchen or gotten me water. He was just as wasted as I was last night, and he wouldn't clean up my puke in a million years. I had known him too long and we'd been through this too many times for me to think differently. That meant that Samantha had to have done it.

I sat up slowly from the couch and grabbed my

throbbing head. I reached for the water and downed the entire glass with three Advil. I knew that my sister had seen me in a terrible condition last night. It was probably the first time she'd had to take care of someone when they were drunk. I felt ashamed and embarrassed.

I got up and walked to my room. I paused at Sam's door and thought about knocking but didn't. Instead, I started my morning ritual. After taking a super hot shower, I brushed my teeth to get rid of the nasty stale vomit taste and got dressed for work. It was Monday and my first official day back in the office.

All throughout my morning routine I couldn't stop thinking about my dream of Maddy. Usually when I was that drunk I didn't dream, one of the positives about alcohol. I hadn't actually spoken to Maddy since I left, other than through text. I wanted to leave it all behind me, but when I got home I felt differently. I went out with Mike as usual and I bought drinks for beautiful women, but I didn't want to be with any of them. I didn't even want them to be near me. I just wanted to keep drinking to make the memories of the last couple of weeks disappear. But it was backfiring, the more I drank, the more I thought about Maddy. Now I was even dreaming about her. What was wrong with me?

I had texted her two days ago, to tell her that we were settling in and not to worry about Sam. I really just needed an excuse to reach out to her, and Sam was my neutral ground. She replied back that it was good getting to know me again and she knew I had a special future ahead of me. My heart sank when I read it. I wasn't sure what I was expecting her to write, but maybe something that showed some more emotion. I would've even been happy to see she'd written that her heart was broken and she thought I was a bastard for leaving.

I shook my thoughts away and realized that I needed to focus on the reality that was in front of me. I needed to get back to work and get my head on straight per Mitch's instruction.

When I was ready to leave for the office, I noticed that Sam's door was still closed, so I knocked. She didn't answer so I opened it slowly to check and see if she was in there. Her room was empty. I closed the door and headed down the hall to look for her in the living room. She wasn't there either. I knew that today was her first day of school; I'd had my assistant enroll her while we were still in Jersey. I figured she would nag me about taking her, but I guessed I was wrong. She must have already gone.

When I got into the office that morning, Mitch was waiting for me. He was literally sitting in my office at my desk. It was 9:15 by the time I made it in. Not too late, but I also knew I wasn't looking my best.

"Good morning, Mitch," I said with a smile, trying to hide the fact that my head was about to split in two. "How are you today?"

I could tell that Mitch wasn't buying my act, but he smiled back at me and played along. "I'm good, thanks. How are you today, Travis?"

"I'm good, thanks. Outstanding, actually." It was an oversell and I knew it.

"Outstanding?" Mitch questioned as he got out of my chair and gestured for me to take a seat.

"Yes. Sorry I'm late, but it was Sam's first day of school." It wasn't a lie, even though Sam had already been out of the house by the time I left, but Mitch didn't know that.

"Oh, yes. That's right." Mitch paused and brought out his phone. "It has nothing to do with the fact that you were passed out on the couch last night." He handed his phone over to me, and I saw an image of myself lying face down on the couch.

I wrinkled my brow, about to deny the picture when I realized it was open in his text messages and had been sent to him by Mike. I decided to shake my head and apologize instead.

"I'm sorry Mitch. It was my last night, I promise," I pleaded.

Mitch took a seat across from me in one of my sling back leather guest chairs. "I know, Travis." And just as I thought he was going to fire me, he pointed to a file that was on the top of my desk. "That's the Victor Nunez case file. I was hoping we could go over it this morning since I'm having lunch with him today and thought you could join us."

"Really?" I wasn't sure why, after everything, Mitch still wanted me on this case, but I was happy I still had a job. "Of course. Just give me an hour to review it, and I'll be in your office to discuss the details before lunch."

"Sounds good." Mitch turned and headed for the door. He stopped in the doorway and turned back around. "Did you get Sam to school all right this morning?"

"Sure did," I said with a smile.

He nodded in approval and walked out.

I sunk into my chair and opened up the file. It was an awfully thick file, and I only had an hour to review it.

Samantha

As I was walking to the bus stop, I got a text from Jacob. He had gotten permission from his parents to visit Memorial Day weekend, and he'd already bought his ticket. What was he thinking? He had already bought his ticket? But I hadn't had enough time to enact my plan. I felt the butterflies in my stomach when I read the last sentence: "I told them that I would sleep on the couch the entire trip and they believed me ;)." I knew what the wink meant. It meant that he expected to sleep in my bed when he was here. Maybe we could get a hotel room instead, but who would rent out a room to a couple of teenagers? Memorial Day weekend was approaching quickly, and if I wanted Travis to agree to Jacob's visit I needed to tell him about it. The worst thing that could happen right now would be for Travis to find out about Jacob's trip before I had the chance to tell him. Or at least I thought that would be the worst thing that could happen.

Travis

It was around 6:00 p.m. and the sun was still shining outside my office window, leaving a line of yellow sunlight on my desk. I still couldn't get Maddy's face out of my head while reading through the five case files that I had on my desk. The thickest and most recent Nunez file was on top. The lunch had gone well today, better than expected. I had gotten through most of the file and had a pretty thorough meeting with Mitch beforehand. I was mostly at the lunch to meet Victor and was surprised when he asked me so many personal questions. He wanted to know where I went to college, if I was married, if I had a family and if I had worked on any other cases that were similar to his. I told him as much as I could without breaking client confidentiality and that the rest, was respectfully, none of his business.

I was a little shocked when he gave me his condolences on my parents' death and asked how Samantha was adjusting to her new life in Florida. Given the business he was in, I figured he already knew about my personal life, but didn't think he would come out and say it. It felt almost like a threat. I thanked him for his kindness and told him she was doing just fine. I moved quickly off the topic of my family and got back to discussing business. When you're new to a client you need to earn their trust and that takes time. Today's lunch was only the first of many that I would need to attend in order to earn Victor Nunez's trust. It was not something a man like him gave out easily.

I hadn't gotten anything done the last hour of the day except stare out the window. I had the Nunez file open in front of me, but when I looked at it I just read the same sentence over and over. I realized I was no longer being productive, so I called Mike to see what he was up to. He was headed out to dinner with a girl that he picked up the day before, so I decided to head to the local pub for a beer and some dinner.

While at the pub I still couldn't get Maddy out of my mind. A few drinks in, I decided it would be a good idea to text her and see what she was up to. In retrospect, drunk texting was never a good idea, but at that moment it seemed like a great idea.

I tried to sound as casual as possible.

[Travis] Hey, it's Travis. I was just eating dinner at a pub thinking of when you almost stood me up. What are you up to?

I didn't hear anything back, which took the wind out of my sails. Maybe she was out to dinner or working late grading papers. I ordered another drink and tried to pretend that I wasn't secretly agonizing as to why she didn't respond. Then suddenly my phone vibrated on the bar notifying me I had received a text.

[Maddy] Hi, it is good to hear from you. How's Sam and the transition going for her?

Why would she ask about Sam the first chance she got? Wasn't she interested in how I was doing? What did I care about Samantha's transition? Clearly, I couldn't text that to Maddy, so I lied.

[Travis] She's okay. You never answered me about what you were up to tonight…

[Maddy] I am sitting at home listening to music, drinking wine, and finishing up some work.

Just as I suspected earlier, her phone was probably in her purse or on the kitchen table and she didn't even notice my first text.

[Maddy] I almost didn't text you back

Okay, there went that theory.

[Travis] Why not?

[Maddy] I just don't think we should keep in touch. It's

better this way. I don't even know when I'm going to see you again, the last time it was ten years

How was I supposed to respond to her? Did I want a relationship with Maddy or was I just torturing the two of us? Memorial Day weekend was approaching and we could visit so that I could see her.

[Travis] I was thinking about bringing Sam home for Memorial Day

[Maddy] Isn't Jacob visiting you that weekend? Why would you come back here?

What was she talking about? I had to think for a minute about who Jacob was. Then I remembered the boy from the funeral. Damn that girl.

[Travis] This is the first I've heard of it

[Maddy] hmmm…I just saw Jacob and he said he already bought the ticket. He's really excited about it. Don't get mad at her for not telling you. She's a teenager.

This meant that Sam had been planning this behind my back. So her boyfriend was just going to show up at my house, and she thought I wouldn't even notice? I started to get angry and asked the bartender for the check. I left cash so I didn't have to wait any longer and stormed out to my car.

I checked my phone again after feeling it vibrate with a text. It was Maddy, but I was too angry to read it. I decided that I didn't want to hear from her again, so I blocked her number.

"Samantha!" I yelled as I entered the apartment ten minutes later. I didn't know what time it was and I didn't care. I knew Mike wasn't home yet because his car wasn't in his spot. And that was better, since I didn't want him hearing me yell at my sister. It would just give him another bit of ammunition to use against me with Mitch.

Sam ran out from her room like something was on fire. She looked shocked and a little bit annoyed. "What?! What's going on?"

"Is your boyfriend coming here Memorial Day

weekend?" I asked in a crazy calm voice. My hands were shaking with anger and Sam looked scared. "Think about your answer very carefully before you lie to me."

She did. I could see her brain working, searching for some response that would calm me down. But she made the wrong choice. "I have no idea what you're talking about."

"Then why did Maddy tell me tonight that Jacob told her he already bought his ticket?"

She looked shocked. "You talked to Maddy? What else did she say?" Sam asked desperately.

"Is there any more I should know?" I asked. "And I can talk to whomever I want."

"No nothing." I couldn't tell if she was lying to me.

"So did he buy a ticket to come here Memorial Day weekend?" I persisted.

"He told me he bought his ticket this morning." She looked down while she said it, knowing she was in trouble.

I banged my fist on the kitchen counter, "Damn it, Sam! Just go to your room so I can think for a minute." She slowly turned and walked to her room.

Samantha

I couldn't believe that Travis found out about Jacob before I had a chance to show him how I was trying to change or at least tell (ask) him myself. I sat on the bed and cursed myself for not thinking he would keep in touch with Maddy. I really thought once we'd left Jersey that he would cut himself off from her. I didn't even think to tell Jake not to mention it to her.

I sunk my face into my pillow and screamed. After letting out all of my frustrations on the pillow, I wiped the tears from my eyes and grabbed my phone from the nightstand. I needed to call Jake and tell him what just happened. But what was I going to say? "My brother is an asshole and he won't let us be together. Why did you tell

Maddy before I had the chance to tell Travis?" I was too upset to talk to him now. I didn't want to say anything I might regret, like blaming him for this happening.

I didn't know what I was going to do now to convince Travis to let Jacob visit, but I had to think of something. I lay in bed all night trying to come up with another strategy.

19 MISCOMMUNICATION

Travis

The next morning I got to the office early, a little after eight. I hadn't slept well again because I kept dreaming about Maddy. This dream was different than the last one. This time Maddy was out on a date but not with me. I was sitting in the back of the movie theatre watching her share popcorn with another man, giggling and snuggling with him. I was just sitting there watching them. I didn't approach them or throw something at them; I just sat there staring. I didn't know what that meant, but I woke up feeling a deep sense of loss and loneliness.

When I stepped into my office, once again, my chair was already occupied. This time by Mike. I checked my watch making sure it was as early as I thought it was.

"Hey, Mike, what are you doing here so early? And in my office?" I asked, not sure what was going on.

"I just wanted to see how you were doing with your case load and catching up on things since getting back." I looked down at the files on my desk and realized that the Nunez file was open.

"Are you reading through my cases?" I asked,

confused. Mike had never interfered with my cases before.

Mike quickly looked down at the folder he'd forgotten to close. "You left that open." He moved out from behind my desk and walked past me through the door.

I knew he was lying but wasn't sure why. I walked over to my desk and moved around my folders to see if there was anything else of importance either open or missing. Nothing that I could see. All of my other cases were insignificant. I flipped through the Nunez file, but everything looked as I had left it. I wasn't sure what Mike was up to, but it didn't feel right. I was trying to decide if I should tell Mitch, when all of the sudden Mitch was at my door.

"Is everything okay, Travis?" Mitch had a puzzled look on his face.

I quickly decided not to mention that Mike had been in my office going through the Nunez file. "Yes. Good, thanks," I replied with a smile.

"What can I help you with, Mitch?"

"I thought we could meet about the Nunez case this afternoon if you have some time."

The truth was I didn't have time, but you can't say no when your boss wants to meet with you. Especially since I was being considered for partner. "Sure, no problem."

I had ordered a salad for lunch from the café downstairs in our office building. It was the first healthy meal I'd eaten in a while. I ate at my desk so that I could finish prepping for my two o'clock meeting with Mitch.

I was in front of Mitch's office at 1:55 and could hear more than one voice behind the door. When I knocked, I heard their voices hush and then someone answered the door.

It was Mike. He didn't look surprised to see me, even though I was surprised to see him. "Hey, Travis, I was just finishing up with my father."

He walked by me out the door. "No worries, man. I'm a few minutes early."

Mitch was sitting behind his desk. His office, unlike mine, was very large, close to one thousand square feet. He had a conference table on one end of the room with two flat screen TV's hanging on the wall. His desk was on the other end of the office, placed in front of a wall of windows. The desk was large in stature and ornate in design. It looked more like the United States President's desk than a law firm partner. The wall next to the door was full of built-in bookshelves, which housed some of Mitch's antique book collections, as well as all his law books. I remembered being intimidated the first time I had stepped into this office, but by now I was used to it. I had been in hundreds of meetings here, and I expected this meeting to be just like all the others.

"Sorry to interrupt your meeting with Mike." I apologized when I walked in and took my regular seat at the conference table.

"That's okay, Mike is just having a bit of a personal crisis right now," Mitch said as he walked over and sat at the head of the conference table.

"A personal crisis?" I knew that meant with me. Mike didn't have much else of a personal life. "Does this have anything to do with me or my sister? I can go talk to him if you want."

Mitch was already shaking his head no before I finished speaking. "No, it's fine. Mikey is just a little sensitive. It will work itself out."

Mitch started readjusting his paperwork on the table and continued talking, "Do you know why I called this meeting Travis?"

I was confused by the question. I thought I had known. "To talk about the Victor Nunez case, sir." I tried to sound certain in my response, but even I could catch the hint of question in my voice.

"Well, yes and no," Mitch said, finally finishing with his papers, folding his hands in front of him, and looking up at me.

"I'm sorry, sir. I don't quite understand what you mean."

"Victor and I have a very close relationship." He stressed the word close. "Victor is a special client of mine, and I need to know if you are on board with representing him."

I didn't say anything, since I still wasn't sure what Mitch was getting at.

"I'll be blunt with you, Travis. Sometimes you are going to have to look the other way with Victor's business dealings. Not everything he does is one hundred percent by the book." Mitch had gotten right to the point with me.

"I understand, sir." I had heard the stories about Victor Nunez, what he did for a living, and his ties to drug related incidents. I figured that not all of his business dealings were legitimate. When you're a lawyer, sometimes the less you know about your clients the better.

"Good, and you are okay with participating in his defense?" Mitch asked.

"Yes, sir. I only want to know the facts about the case. I won't get involved in anything else." I needed to assure him I was on board.

"Good to hear." He pointed to the door, the direction that Mike had just left. "I want you to know that Mike came to me today, just before this meeting, to talk to me about this case. He is concerned that you aren't ready for this yet."

I'd figured Mike was in here talking with Mitch about this case, especially after I'd caught him at my desk this morning going through my files. I had a choice to make now, did I tell Mitch I caught Mike going through my files or did I take it up with him directly? I decided that I wasn't like Mike. If I had something to talk to him about, I would talk to him directly.

"With all due respect, sir, I don't think Mike knows what the fuck he's talking about." The secret in getting ahead in an office full of testosterone was being aggressive.

"If you don't mind, I would like to take it up with Mike offline. I can handle this case, and I am the right person for the partnership."

Mitch smiled. "Okay, then let's not waste any more time."

Samantha

I had to call Jacob today and let him know that our Memorial Day plans might be ruined. I waited a day to calm down, but also because I was secretly hoping Travis might wake up this morning and change his mind. It didn't happen.

I wasn't allowed to have my phone on in class. I learned the hard way yesterday, my first day, when I got a text from Jacob in the middle of study hall. The study hall teacher, whose name I still couldn't remember, took my phone away the entire day. Schools in Florida were different than back home. The rest of the day I decided to keep my head down and try my best to blend in. Maybe I could make it through this next year by becoming invisible. It seemed like a plan that would work at school and at home.

I decided to skip the New Student Club that met after school. After I didn't have my phone the entire first day, I wasn't in the mood to meet anyone, and today I was so stressed about what to tell Jacob I couldn't socialize.

I waited until my walk home from the bus stop before I called him. Unfortunately, he didn't answer so I had to leave him a message.

"Hey, Jake, I just wanted to call and tell you that I have some bad news about Memorial Day weekend. It's not set in stone yet, but you probably shouldn't talk to Maddy about it anymore. She told Travis before I had the chance, and he's pretty mad. Don't blame her, she didn't know. But now I need to do some damage control. I still want you to come, but we might not be able to stay here. We will figure something out. I love you and miss you and will call you later tonight."

When I hung up I realized the battery was low. I didn't have my phone off in school, but on silent just in case I needed it. Damn, the new IOS update was draining my battery.

I had to get home and charge it just in case Jacob called me back before Travis got home. I quickened my pace away from the bus stop.

Travis

I was fuming at Mike. I couldn't believe that he would go through my files in my office and then tell Mitch that I couldn't handle the case. I knew he was pissed at me about the Sam situation, and he probably figured that since Mitch had asked me to second chair on the Nunez case I was up for partner. But to go and tell Mitch I wasn't ready? Who was he to pull a stunt like that?

Now that I was on this case, I knew I would be working late nights. I texted Sam to tell her not to expect to see me around much for the next couple of days, since I would practically be living in the office. Then I texted Mike and asked to meet him.

He didn't respond back to me until almost 11:00 p.m. I was still in the office sipping a glass a brandy when I saw the text. "Meet me at Bru's in thirty minutes." I replied that I would be there.

When I walked into the bar, I found Mike sitting alone chatting with the bartender. He must have gone home to shower and change because he wasn't in the suit he'd worn to the office today, like I was, and his hair was wet. I sat beside him and didn't say a word. I ordered a beer.

Mike looked over at me. "So, what's eating you?" He was pretending like he didn't know.

I got my beer and took a swig. When I finally looked over at him, I realized he looked tired. His eyes were hazy and red, and his hair was wet and uncombed.

"Let's start with why you were in my office this morning going through my case files," I stated.

"What are you talking about?" Typical Mike, he always started with denial.

"Mike, I know that you went through the Nunez file. I also know I locked my office door before I left last night, so either you have a key to my office or you broke in. Either way, you shouldn't have been in there." I couldn't even look at him I was so disappointed.

I paused, allowing him time to respond, but he didn't. He just took another sip of his drink.

"I also know that you went to your father today and told him that you didn't think I could handle my cases, specifically the Nunez case. Why would you do that?"

Again, he didn't answer.

"I'm sure you also know that I'm up for partner." I finally looked at him and he looked back at me. "Are you jealous of me?"

With that comment, Mike started laughing obnoxiously loud. He started drawing attention to both of us, and I suddenly felt self-conscious and grabbed his arm to make him stop.

He took that as a combative movement and ripped my hand off of his arm. He got up and threw a fifty- dollar bill on the bar. "I have never been jealous of you, ever." And Mike left.

20 LOST

Travis

I had stayed at the bar that night until closing at 2:00 a.m., thinking about what Mike had said. I wasn't drunk but felt buzzed. I still didn't understand the sudden change in character for Mike. This was the same guy that I hung out with every night this past week. The same guy who took me with him to his family gatherings and someone I considered a brother.

I had to be in the office by eight that next morning and didn't get much sleep. When I left for work, I didn't see Sam or Mike, which was fine by me. I didn't really need the stress of either of them right now. It was Wednesday and I had a day full of meetings, which meant another late night at the office. I left a note for Sam on the kitchen counter with two twenty-dollar bills. I would eventually have to talk to her again, but I wasn't ready. Right now, I needed to work. That was what my life was like before my parents' death, and it was what I needed to get back to. It would help me get through this time with Sam, and it would help me get over Maddy. It had worked for me before, and it would work for me again.

When I got home Wednesday night, it was close to eleven, and the money and note I had left Sam was still on the kitchen counter. I guess she didn't want it. I thought about how stubborn she was being. Maybe she thought I would eventually cave about her boyfriend coming to visit, but I didn't see that happening anytime soon. I paused at her door, trying to decide if I should knock and find out what she did for dinner, but when I heard nothing but silence behind the door, I figured she was sleeping and kept walking.

I did the same routine on Thursday morning and still didn't see Sam. I knocked on her door in the morning and didn't get a response, so I opened it and checked her room, her bed was made and she wasn't there. I decided to text her that I would be home from work early today and I wanted to talk. It had been long enough, and we needed to get on better terms if this was going to work. I checked my phone at lunch, but there was nothing from Sam. I had several missed calls, all from the same unknown number, but figured it was probably just a telemarketer. Something didn't feel right.

When I got off the elevator shortly after 5:00 p.m., I saw a familiar teenage boy sitting at my front door. It took a few minutes, but then it struck me all at once. Jacob. And I immediately knew something was wrong.

As I walked over to him, he stood up looking stressed and worried. The questioning look on my face must have told him I didn't know why he was here.

"Hi, sir, I'm Jacob. Sam's boyfriend." He looked very worried.

"What's wrong?" I barely let him finish talking.

"I haven't heard from Samantha in a few days. I got a voice message from her on Tuesday, but then nothing. When I call her, it goes to voice mail, which means her phone is off." He was talking so fast I could barely understand him. "I tried to get Maddy to call you, but we couldn't get through to you either." I remembered the last time Maddy had texted me I blocked her number. I hadn't wanted to talk to her again.

My heart started to speed up and pound out of my chest. I grabbed the keys from my front pocket and fumbled putting them in the door, not realizing that my hands were shaking. I hadn't seen or talked to Sam since Tuesday. It was Thursday, which meant that I hadn't seen her in two days. I finally got the door open and ran into the apartment. It was empty, like it had been when I left this morning.

I searched through every room, even flinging open Sam's closet to make sure she wasn't just hiding. Jacob was following me around screaming questions in the background, but I couldn't focus on him. I couldn't focus on anything. I had known something wasn't right this morning. I'd had a gut feeling. But I hadn't followed my gut, because I needed to work. And all day, I had known something was wrong, but I tried to ignore it, thinking maybe I was overreacting.

I finally sat down on the couch with my head in my hands, trying to think through the events of this week and how I had missed even noticing that Sam wasn't here. I couldn't think clearly and was beginning to shake. I could feel my whole body moving back and forth and realized that it was Jacob next to me with his hands on my shoulders trying to get my attention.

I finally cleared my head and hit his arms away. "I haven't seen or talked to her since Tuesday," I said, finally admitting what I had just realized only a few moments ago. "Actually, I didn't even see her Tuesday. The last time I saw her was Monday night when we got into the fight about you coming up this weekend. That was the last time I spoke to her."

I couldn't believe that it was Thursday, and the last time I actually saw my sister was Monday. My sister, who I was responsible for, my sister who lived with me. The room started to spin. I needed a drink. I got up and walked to the fridge where I opened a beer and chugged. Finally, the room stopped spinning and I gained some composure. Jacob was just staring at me from the hallway, a look of disbelief on his face.

"So let me get this straight; the last time you saw or spoke to her was Monday? Didn't you wonder where she was all week!?" he yelled at me.

I shuttered at his accusation. "Um, I don't really know. I was busy at work." It came out in a whisper and all I could do was stand there and stare at the boy in my living room who clearly cared more about my own sister than I did.

"Do you think she ran away?" I knew that I was grasping at straws, but I needed to make myself believe that maybe she did run away. "Maybe she was so upset after I told her that you couldn't visit, she decided to leave and go back to New Jersey?"

It was starting to make sense. My theory was possible. I had said some horrible things to her, things no sixteen-year-old should ever have to hear.

"No way." Jacob was shaking his head, not believing my story. "There is no way she would leave and not tell me. If she were going to run away she would come straight to me; I know it." As he looked at me, I could see all the color drain from his face, and he sat down on the couch slowly. He was staring at the ground and couldn't seem to find the strength to look up. "Just now in her room I saw you look in her closet, and I saw that all of her clothes are still in there and her laptop was still there, too. She would never have left without her laptop." He had a pained expression on his face, like he was gagging on the words.

He was right. When I looked in her closet I had seen all of her clothes hanging up and her laptop was still on her bed. I ran back into her room to double check what we had both already seen and knew was true, but the second time I walked over to her desk and picked up her phone charger.

I walked back out to the living room with the phone charger still in my hand and joined Jacob on the couch. When he saw the charger in my hand, I heard all the hope exhale out of his lungs. I couldn't breathe or think. I could only sit there with a sinking feeling in my stomach, unable to move. "I need another drink."

As I started to get up and move toward the kitchen, Jacob jumped up off the couch and yelled, "We need to call the police." He followed me to the kitchen and cut me off before I was able to open the fridge. With his hand blocking the fridge door from opening and a cold look in his eyes, he sternly said, "Stop." He reached into his pocket and got out his cell phone.

"Wait," I said. "Let's just think about this before calling the cops." I knew that if Jacob called the cops, and there ended up being nothing wrong, then it would get me in more trouble with Mitch than I was willing to think about. I'd known how upset Sam had been when I told her the truth about my childhood with our parents. It was rational to think she would run away.

"Are you kidding me? She has been missing for three days!" Jacob was getting belligerent. His face was bright red, and I could see the anger in his eyes. I needed to calm him down if we were going to figure out the next best move.

"Look," I said, trying to keep my tone firm but even, "we don't know where Sam is. We got into a big fight the other night. I knew that I upset her, probably to the point where she no longer wanted to be here with me." I explained.

"I know. She called me after your argument." Jacob was still fuming but wasn't yelling quite as loud. "You're such a douchebag. I can't believe that you think she would run away from you and not tell me. You know nothing about her. I know everything about her, and she wouldn't do that. Something is wrong, trust me."

Just at that moment, as if on cue, Mike walked through

the door. He was caught off guard by the scene in front of him and the stranger who stood in his kitchen. "What's going on here?" he asked with a hint of arrogance in his voice. "Are we adopting another misguided youth?"

"Something has happened to Samantha," Jacob said abruptly.

"Wait, what?" Mike paused with disbelief and then asked, "Who are you?"

"I'm Jacob, Sam's boyfriend. Who are you?" He looked back and forth between Mike and me, unable to disguise his surprised alarm that we both knew so little about the girl that had been living with us this last week.

"You're Sam's boyfriend?" Mike meant it as an insult rather than a question. He never addressed Jacob's question asking who he was. I needed to step in on this before it got ugly.

"Mike," I barked, grabbing his attention back to me. "Have you seen Samantha since Monday?"

He grinned. "Oh, you mean after your fight?" He hesitated as I sat there waiting for a response. "No, why? Who cares anyway?"

"She's missing, that's why!" Jacob yelled at Mike, who turned around quickly and shot daggers with his look.

"What is this kid talking about? She probably just ran off with some other guy." Mike started to walk down the hall toward his room and mumbled, "I always knew she was a whore."

That was all Jacob needed to chase after Mike. I ran after him, grabbing the back of his hoodie before he could get to Mike. The sudden jerk on his sweater sent Jacob to the floor, accidentally bouncing his head off of my foot.

"Jacob!" I yelled down, looking at the poor scared kid in front of me. "Just let him go."

I left Jacob lying on the floor, contemplating whether I wanted to chase after Mike, but decided it was best to just let him go, since he would be of no help to us. I heard Mike let out a little laugh before he closed his bedroom door.

I was freaked out that Sam hadn't been seen or heard from in a few days, but I admittedly didn't know that much about my sister. She could have run away and decided to hitchhike back to New Jersey. Or maybe she was at a new friend's house. She had been in her new school for a few days; she must have made new friends. Thinking of her school gave me a place to start. I took out my cell and searched for the main number to her high school. It was late, but I was hoping that someone might still be there. No answer.

"What are you doing? Who are you calling? The police?" Jacob was berating me with questions as he got up off the floor.

"No, I'm trying her school. I figure if she hasn't shown up all week, then they would've called me. And since they didn't then she must have been there."

"Are you sure they didn't call you?" Jacob asked.

"What do you mean? Of course they didn't call." I couldn't believe he was asking me this, and then I quickly remembered the missed calls on my phone, all from the same number. I hadn't checked my voice messages yet. I quickly felt the pit in the base of my stomach tightening and the queasy feeling start to return.

He must've seen the recognition hit me, since he quickly asked, "You have missed messages, don't you?" Before I could listen, he grabbed the phone out of my hand and put it up to his ear, walking across the room so that I couldn't stop him from listening. I could see the color drain from his face as he pulled the phone away and looked at the screen.

"You missed four calls from the school," he said, his voice turning faint. "They called each day and left messages."

I grabbed my phone out of Jacob's hand to look at what he was seeing. He was right. My mouth dropped open, and I didn't want to admit that I hadn't cared enough these last few days to see who my messages were from. As I listened to the first message, I realized why Jacob was so upset. It was Ms. Anderson, Samantha's principal. In the first message, left yesterday morning, she was calm, asking me why Sam wasn't at school that day, hoping she wasn't sick. She asked me to call her back, which of course I didn't. The second message, left this morning, she was more concerned. She said that she knew the flu was going around and hoped Samantha wasn't one of the students who had it.

The third message was left this afternoon. In it Ms. Anderson said that she was worried she hadn't yet heard from me and would be stopping by the apartment today to make sure everything was okay. The final message was left for me this afternoon. She must have called from outside the apartment. The message was more rushed and definitely more concerned. "Mr. Harris, this is Ms. Anderson again, the principal of Samantha's school. I am outside your apartment and can't get anyone to answer. I am extremely worried about you and Samantha. Please call me back at this number immediately or I will be forced to call the police."

I was suddenly so afraid that I couldn't breathe. I started to hyperventilate and I ran for Mike's room. I barged in on him at his laptop. "Mike!" I yelled, not sure what I was doing. "Are you sure you haven't seen Sam?"

He was startled and had a fading smile on his face. "No man, I haven't seen her." He started to get up, apparently noticing the worry that was painted on my face. "Is everything okay with that girl?"

I realized it was time. I picked up the phone and dialed the police.

Samantha

Darkness surrounded me. I couldn't tell if my eyes were open or closed. I thought that I had opened them but, wherever I was, the darkness was so overwhelming that I couldn't be sure. My head was pounding and my mouth was dry. I was lying on my stomach. I couldn't remember what had happened or how I ended up here. I reached out my right hand to feel around, but what I felt instead was the cold metal handcuffs tighten and cut into my wrist. My mind started to race as I tried to remember what had happened to me, but I couldn't. The last thing I recalled was walking home from the bus stop. I was distracted, not paying attention, caught up in my own thoughts about what had happened with Travis and what I was going to tell Jacob. The rest was...nothing.

I reached to feel what I was handcuffed to. It felt like a large pipe that ran up along the wall. With my left hand I reached out and found the edge of whatever I was lying on. It felt like a very thin mattress about two inches thick. I could feel the cold concrete floor beneath it.

I started to realize the severity of the situation and lost any bit of composure I had. My chest started to compress, and I couldn't breathe. I started to panic. Just then I heard a noise from the far corner of the darkness. It sounded like the clicking of a lock and I saw what looked like the door open to let in a bright light. My eyes hurt, not used to the light, and I shut them immediately. I took my left hand and covered my eyes, making a visor to try and see who it was at the far end of the room. It wasn't much help. I could only see a blurry figure getting closer. I couldn't really move much but scooted my butt as close to the wall as possible, huddling my body into a ball.

I couldn't scream, I couldn't beg, I couldn't cry. I could only get out one word. "No." It was so muted, I doubted that the large figure even heard me. I felt a sting in my arm. Whoever had come into the room was not here to help me but had injected me with something. A few seconds later I felt the darkness start to take over.

That was day one.

Travis

The police arrived about twenty minutes after I called. They sat Jacob and me down on the couch and explained that usually after forty-eight hours it was difficult to find a missing person. But I was numb to what they were saying. I could only think about how this was all my fault. I couldn't believe this was happening. I hadn't really cared about anyone or anything in so long, and now I'd gone and lost my sister after only a few days. I was the reason Sam was missing, I was the reason she left.

About halfway through the police talking to me about next steps and their plan of action, I needed to excuse myself. I ran to the bathroom and threw up. I couldn't believe what I was going through right now. It was all too surreal. I splashed cold water on my face but couldn't decipher between the water and the tears. What had I done? I would never forgive myself. My entire life was changing at this very moment.

During the time the police were at the apartment, Mike had only come out of his room twice. First when the cops showed up and again when they were searching his room. They needed to search the entire apartment in order to find anything that could help them know where to start looking for Sam. They had already taken her computer. They said that they could find out where she checked in last on Facebook and accessed her email, even if it was from her phone. They wouldn't tell me what they found and it was getting frustrating.

About four hours after they arrived, the cops left, saying they were on it and that we should trust them. They tried to stress that they had Sam's best interests in mind, but I didn't quite believe them. I mean, we were in Florida, and we all knew from the national news stories that Florida's missing children cases didn't usually end well. I also knew that no matter what they found out, they wouldn't tell me. I was their number one suspect right now.

It was 1:20 a.m. when Jacob and I found ourselves sitting on the couch alone and in a daze. I knew that he was just a kid, but I walked over to the cabinet and pulled out a bottle of tequila and two shot glasses.

"Care to join me?" I asked, knowing that we both needed something to take the edge off of what just went down.

He looked up at me first with disgust, and then I saw his eyes soften as he got up and joined me at the kitchen counter. Without saying another word, I poured the shots, and we both took one.

We stood in silence for what seemed like an eternity. Finally Jacob looked up at me, and for the first time tonight, he looked like a kid. "We are going to find her, aren't we?" I could tell by the pleading in his eyes that he wanted some reassurance and I felt the need to give it to him.

"I will never let this go until I find her." I put my hand on his shoulder and tried to look as convincing as possible. "We'll look for her ourselves. I know people that I can call. We will find her, Jacob, and she will be okay." He nodded, and I felt the knot in my stomach clench deeper. I was lying to him. "Now go call your parents. I bet they're worried about you."

I had no idea if we were going to be able to find Samantha. The only thing I knew for sure was that I wasn't going to stop looking for her.

Samantha

I had lost all track of time. My body was tired and aching from lying on this cold floor. My right bicep hurt from the needles, and my head was hazy from the drugs and lack of food. I had grown used to the darkness so much that whenever the door to my cell was opened I didn't even attempt to open my eyes, knowing that they wouldn't be able to adjust to the light in time to catch any good details of my surroundings. I called my little space a cell, since I was trapped in a prison. I had found a bucket and some toilet paper left next to me on day two. I was becoming an animal. The truth was I had no idea where I was and I wasn't thinking clearly enough to do anything about it.

The first few days here I tried the best I could to plan an escape. I would scream whenever my captor would enter the room. I would kick and fight the best I could to not have the drugs injected into my arm. I would cry uncontrollably and beg to be let go. I made promises that I knew I could never keep, like paying all the money I had and never telling anyone what was going on. I threatened that my brother would be coming for me, even though I had little hope anyone would find me, since they would have by now. After what seemed like a week, I gave up fighting and crying, realizing I was only using up the little energy I had left.

21 SEARCHING

Travis

I woke up to the sound of clanging glass coming from the kitchen. Since there was already a dull pounding in my head, the sound of breaking glass was excruciatingly painful. I slowly opened my eyes and rubbed the sleep away. My eyes were puffy and stinging, and in an instant the events of yesterday flooded back into my brain. I must have passed out on the couch, because when I sat up I was looking directly into the kitchen to see Jacob going through the bar and throwing away all of my alcohol. I immediately shot up off the couch, slightly losing my bearings, and ran in a somewhat straight line over to stop him.

"What are you doing?!" I tried to scream at him, but it came out more like a screech.

I was watching him empty each beer bottle into the sink and then throw it in the recycle basket. My eyes drifted over to the basket and I saw that he had already gotten rid of all my hard liquors and most of my beer. For a split second I thought about tackling him to the ground. The need for alcohol had never been as strong as it was this morning after remembering the events of last night. Then I realized that Jacob was probably right. I needed a clear head if we were going to find Sam. I couldn't risk any impaired judgment.

When I didn't respond to his comment, Jacob looked up at me from the sink. I simply nodded in agreement and walked out of the kitchen back to my room to wash up. As I walked past Sam's room I saw that her bed had been slept in. My mind raced for a second, thinking that maybe she was here. I quickly realized, after I saw his shoes on the floor, that Jacob must have slept in her bed last night.

After a quick shower, I headed out to the living room to see Jacob finishing up a call.

"Yes sir, thank you for the call. I will let you know if we hear anything from anyone." He looked at me as he was hanging up. "That was Detective Morales letting us know that they didn't find anything on Sam's computer that could help them find her. He did say her cell phone is turned off but they contacted the carrier to get the location of the last tower that sent a signal to her phone. I tried to get him to tell me the location of the cell tower, but he said that he couldn't give me any information about an ongoing investigation. Maybe you can call in a bit and he'll tell you more, since you're her brother and all."

"Sure, good idea." There was no way any detective on Sam's case was going to tell me anything. They probably suspected that I had something to do with this. I was a lawyer, I knew that the cops always looked at the family first. But, I didn't have the heart to tell Jacob. I walked into the kitchen and opened up the fridge. My normal morning beverage of choice would've been a beer, but seeing as we were out, I opted for orange juice and started up the coffee pot.

"So, is Detective Morales the lead investigator searching for Sam?"

"You don't remember meeting him last night?" Jacob asked from the living room.

I thought about it for a moment, but I couldn't remember anyone specific. "Honestly, there were a lot of people here yesterday. Was he the guy in the suit with the mustache?"

"Yeah." Jacob walked in and poured himself a cup of coffee from the piping hot pot. He turned to look at me after he took a sip. "So, what do we do now?"

I poured myself a cup, noticing that Jacob and I both took our coffee black. I looked up at him, not knowing what to say. I could tell that he was just as lost as I was. Taking in his appearance fully, I could tell why Sam liked him. He was tall and lanky, but he had a strong presence and wouldn't take any shit from anyone. His eyes were rimmed with red, like mine, from crying and lack of sleep. I walked past him, not answering his question, but patted him on the shoulder. I knew who I needed to call.

"Where are you going?" He looked confused as he followed me out of the kitchen.

I grabbed my cell phone from the charging station and selected Mitch's name from my favorites. "I'm calling my boss to let him know what's going on. He knows people, and I'm sure he will do whatever he can to help us."

I could see the understanding on Jacob's face. The reality was, Mitch probably already knew what had happened yesterday from Mike. Jacob still didn't know that Mike was my boss's son, and he sure as hell didn't know that they both didn't like the idea of Sam being here with me in the first place. I wasn't sure what Mitch would say, or if he would be willing to help me, but I was hoping that I'd known him and his family long enough that he could show some compassion. Mitch had a lot of friends in high and low places. I would probably need the help of both kinds if I wanted to find Sam.

He answered on the second ring, and I was surprised at how open he was to helping. He had actually been through a similar experience in the past with one of his clients whose daughter had been kidnapped. Not that we thought

Sam had been kidnapped for ransom, like his client's daughter, but he at least knew where I should start. He suggested that I go down to the police station and speak with Detective Morales in person. I had a better chance of getting information and convincing him that I had nothing to do with this if I created a personal bond with him. Then he said that he knew a private investigator who was good at "finding people who no one else could find," and gave me his number. He wasn't comfortable with calling him directly, since the guy didn't exactly do things by the book, but Mitch told me to mention his name and the guy would be more than willing to help. He owed Mitch a favor. I didn't ask why. Finally, he said how sorry he was and knew I had been through a lot this last month. After I hung up the phone, I realized I never asked Mitch what happened to his client's daughter. I guess subconsciously I didn't want to know.

Jacob and I headed down to the police station to meet with Detective Morales. As I remembered, he was a dark haired man with a mustache. He had on what looked like the same suit he wore last night. He didn't have much information to offer other than what Jacob had already told me. He did say that he would call me if they found anything else, and we exchanged numbers. I told him how important this was to me, and he promised that they would find Sam. As I shook his hand good-bye, I could see a mixture of suspicion and worry in his eyes. He was sizing me up. I loosened my grip and hoped that I portrayed as much worry and heartache in my face as there was in my chest. I left still feeling lost, but hopeful that maybe Detective Morales would trust me more than he had initially, and share information with me as he got it.

My next call was to Emanuel Simmons, the private detective that Mitch hooked me up with. He answered on the third ring and agreed to meet me at a local coffee house.

As I walked out of the police station, I found Jacob

sitting on the bottom step. He didn't want to meet with Detective Morales, saying that he'd already spoke to him and wanted to wait for me outside. As I walked up to him, I could see the tears in his eyes. He was pale and looked a bit green.

I sat down next to him and put my hand on his shoulder. I had been doing that a lot these last two days. "Hey, man, I know how you feel."

"Do you?" Jacob hadn't yet let any tears fall down his face, but I could tell that he was choking them back. "You don't even love Sam. You didn't know she was missing for three days! And now all of a sudden you care about her?"

Even though I knew he was right, his words hurt, and I got defensive. "Seriously? Are you going to keep throwing that back in my face? Just because I was busy with my own life doesn't mean I don't love my sister." Even as I heard the words come out and saw his disgusted reaction to them, I knew I was in for a battle I could never win. The reality was, I hadn't really thought or cared much for Sam these last few weeks. These last few years even. Definitely not like Jacob had.

"You have got to be kidding me?" Jacob got up, and for a second I thought he was going to punch me in the face. "You are such an asshole." Instead of hitting me, he turned and started walking away. I didn't know what to do next so I got up and followed after him.

When we got to the crosswalk, we had to stop and wait for the light. We were both looking ahead in silence. I spoke first.

"You're right," I had finally admitted it out loud. I could hear him exhale the breath he had been holding. I looked over and realized that he must've let one single tear roll down his face when he exhaled.

I had said enough. I looked straight ahead and when the signal changed we both crossed, heading toward my car.

When we got in the car, I drove us to the coffee shop.

"Where are we going?" Jacob asked.

"We are going to meet with the man I'm hoping can help us find Sam."

* * *

Emanuel Simmons was a big Latin man who stood about six foot two inches tall with broad shoulders and a bald head. He looked like either a boxer or a bouncer. He had potholes in his face and a crooked nose. I had texted him a description of what Jacob and I were both wearing, so he didn't even ask who we were when he sat down across from us at the coffee shop.

"What do you need help with today gentlemen?" he asked.

I hadn't imagined our conversation would start quite like this. Although, other than knowing he was a criminal, from what Mitch had implied, I didn't know what to expect. I just decided to get straight to the point.

"My sister is missing, and I was hoping that you could help us find her. Mitch said that you're good at finding people that no one else can find."

His eyebrows shot up, and he let out a low laugh. "Mitch told you that?" I nodded yes. "Did Mitch tell you anything else?"

"No," I replied sternly. That seemed to satisfy him because he went straight into asking me questions about Sam.

"Tell me what you know. Is she on drugs? Could she have run away with a guy?"

Even though Emanuel wasn't trying to be rude or offensive, I could see that Jacob was seething behind his clenched jaw. I elbowed him to get his attention and then made a motion with my hands telling him to calm down.

"She is not on drugs, and her boyfriend is this joker," I said, pointing at Jacob. He glared at me in return. "She was abducted earlier in the week, we think, while she was walking home from school." I went on to tell him everything we knew. What she looked like and what she had been wearing that day, which we got from her classmates, since I hadn't seen her. The last time someone had seen her was on the school bus. Jacob filled him in on what she liked to do, where she might have gone after she left the bus stop if she hadn't gone directly home, like the library or the mall.

Emanuel, who asked us to call him Manny, asked if we had gone to any of those places and showed her picture around. Like idiots, we both shook our heads no. Why hadn't we thought of doing that first? Probably because neither of us were thinking logically.

He asked us for more information, like what her cell phone number was, if she had any social media accounts, if she had a bank card or credit cards, etc. He also asked if she had a computer, when we told him that the police already took it he looked annoyed.

"The police aren't going to be able to find her," he said bluntly, after we finished giving him all the information we had.

Jacob looked confused. "Why do you think that? They told us they know what cell tower her phone last picked up a signal from."

"That's good information, but it doesn't mean anything now. She could be long gone. That was four days ago." He was telling us what we already knew but didn't want to really think about. "Honestly, I'm not sure if I'm going to be able to find her, since she has been missing for so long already. And usually I wouldn't take a case that the cops were already involved in. But I owe Mitch, and I always love a challenge." He had an evil grin on his face. Then came the moment of truth.

"How much?" I asked. Jacob looked at me, startled by the bluntness of my question, but I knew guys like this, and he wasn't going to help us out the goodness of his heart, even if he did owe Mitch a favor.

"You have to cover all my expenses while I look for her. On top of that, I want $10K whether or not this ends well." He looked me right in the eye, and I didn't flinch. The truth was, I was willing to pay as much as he wanted.

"Done." And that was that.

We shook hands, and he got up from the table.

"Wait a minute. Now what happens?" Jacob got up and grabbed his arm, realizing a second too late he shouldn't have touched Manny.

Manny looked down at Jacob's grip on his arm, and Jacob let go immediately. "Now I find your girl." And with that he walked away.

The rest of the day Jacob and I took Manny's advice and went to every place we could think of, showing Sam's picture, asking if they saw her recently. We went to the library, the mall, and the local Publix. At Publix, we did get a potential lead. The checkout clerk remembered Sam was there the Sunday before, the same day I had gone to Mitch's barbeque. She hadn't noticed anything out of the ordinary, but the store manager had noticed a young man following Sam around. When he asked him if he needed any help, he ignored him and followed Sam out of the store. Lucky for us, the manager kept an eye on the strange man as he walked through the parking lot and got into a red Chevy Impala. It could be nothing, but Jacob and I were desperate for leads so we texted the information to Manny.

Then we decided to go to Sam's school and talk with the kids that were on the bus that day. I wasn't looking forward to the school visit, since I was still ashamed that I'd missed Principal Anderson's calls and would now have to ask her for a favor. The kids had already been questioned by the police and most of them were little help, but one boy we spoke with mentioned seeing an old red car by the bus stop. When I asked the make and model, he didn't know. It could've been linked to what the grocery manager told us, so I texted the news to Manny.

After what ended up being a very long day, we walked into the apartment and saw a pizza box on the counter with half the pizza left inside. We hadn't eaten all day and both grabbed at the box. Mike was sitting on the sofa in the living room watching baseball. "I figured you guys might be hungry."

I walked into the living room to thank him and saw his face drop when he looked at me. "Damn dude you look like shit, and you're not even hung over," I smiled slightly. I'd bet I did look like shit.

I didn't say anything. I just shrugged my shoulders and took my cold pizza slice back to my room. I heard Mike get up from the couch and follow me down the hall. Before I got to my door, I stopped to turn around and face him.

"Hey, man, I just wanted to say how sorry I am for being such a dick lately." Mike had sincere pity in his eyes.

"Thanks," I said, as I turned to head into my room.

Mike kept talking behind me. "I mean it. I'm a pretty shitty friend. I thought maybe I could help you two look for her. If you wanted."

I didn't look back, but I nodded my head accepting his offer.

Before closing the door, I stopped and asked, "Do you happen to know anyone who drives a red Chevy Impala?"

He thought about it for a minute. "No, man, sorry."

As I lay on my bed that night, a million things raced through my mind, and I knew it would be a restless night of sleep. What was happening to Samantha right now? Had she just run away? Was she taken? Who would take her? Did I know them? Was it related to one of my cases? I went to sleep thinking about that red Impala, hoping Manny could find its owner.

22 CLUES

Samantha

I realized that my captor was male. I figured it out from his sweaty masculine scent and his rough hands on my wrists when he would clean the wounds caused by the cuffs. He hadn't yet touched me, but it was only a matter of time, I knew. I also knew that I wasn't only getting fed drugs through the needles. I hadn't been fed real food, only water, and I was still left with a little energy each day. That made me wonder what my captor did in the real world. Did he work at a place that gave him access to these drugs?

My captor never said anything to me. He never made any sudden movements or gestures. He only entered my cell two times a day, what I was guessing to be morning and night, and was never around at any other times. He must've had a regular life somewhere and been on a schedule.

In the darkness of my cell, I would lose myself in thoughts of what my life used to be like just a short time ago. I would think of the days when I would be hanging out with Jacob and Lisa at Mom and Dad's house. I would pretend that nothing bad ever happened to me and that I was lying in my bed at home, safe. I would let myself get lost in those timeless hours that you are so willing to waste away on a regular day. Envisioning myself in a new place with Jacob, or an old place with Jacob. I couldn't let the memories fade. I had to remember and keep hoping.

Travis

The next few days went by in a blur. We hadn't heard from Manny, even though I had texted and called him every day. I had been wiring money into an account he sent me to cover his expenses. By Sunday I was starting to think that he was ripping me off.

We had heard from Detective Morales yesterday. He asked that Jacob and I come in for a debrief, which I knew meant they wanted to question us to see if we had left anything out of our original story. On the drive over, we decided to share all of the information we had with him. We told him about every place we visited searching for Sam, the Publix manager lead we had, and the red Chevy Impala. We hadn't heard from Manny and if the cops had this information maybe they could do something with it. Unfortunately, they seemed uninterested in what we had to say. They took notes, but didn't get excited about any of our new information. They did share that they had the cell tower location, but it hadn't been much help, as Manny had suspected. The location had ended up being right around her bus stop, which could only tell them that after she got off the bus someone had shut off her phone and taken her battery and SIM card out. This meant that whoever took her did so at the bus stop, or near it. The other possibility that the police had suggested was that she did run away and shut off her own phone herself so that no one could find her. Jacob refused to believe that. I didn't know my sister all that well, but I knew that if she was going to run anywhere it was back to Jacob. She could have intended to run back to him and something went terribly wrong, but I doubted it. She would have called him to tell him she was coming.

It was Sunday afternoon, and Jacob and I were sitting on the couch in silence. We had exhausted every lead and were frustrated with the police getting nowhere. Finally, I got a call from Manny. As soon as I saw his number on the caller ID I shot up off the couch.

"What did you find?" I immediately asked, not wasting time to exchange pleasantries.

"I may have a lead, but I don't think you are going to like it."

"Just tell me." I was bracing myself, not knowing what he had to report.

"Well, it looks like she was taken right after she got off the school bus."

I cut him off. "We already knew that."

"Let me finish," Manny said with anger in his voice. "I hacked into the security camera at the bank across the street from her bus stop. I saw Sam get off the bus and walk out of frame. The surveillance footage showed a red Impala parked on the corner with someone in the driver's seat. It followed slowly after her a few moments later. There were no other cameras pointed in the direction of Sam's bus stop but that one, so it was the only footage I had to go off of. I wasn't able to get a clear read on the plate, but I did get the first three digits. When I looked through the Florida vehicle registry for plates with those three digits registered to any Palm Beach, Broward or Miami-Dade County residents, only a few came up. One was a red Impala."

As he explained what he had done, I was getting excited and Jacob could tell from my expression. "Okay, tell me." I couldn't wait to hear who owned the red Impala so I could hunt them down and kill them.

"The car is registered to a man named Charles Shipley." He waited for me to understand what he was telling me.

"Charles Shipley?" I couldn't believe what he was saying. Was the partner of my law firm involved in Sam's disappearance? "But he drives a Rolls Royce."

"Yeah, I see he owns a Rolls, but he also owns a red Chevy Impala registered to his son, Charles Shipley Jr.," he said.

"What?" I needed to hear the rest of what Manny was telling me. I sat down on the couch and placed my head in my hand, trying to comprehend what was going on.

Jacob was sitting next me, eagerly asking, "Who is Charles Shipley?"

Then Mike walked in the room and I heard him say, "What?"

Manny was still talking to me, so I needed to shush everyone in the room and focus.

"Sorry, keep going. What else did you find?"

"Well, I hacked into Samantha's Facebook account and realized that she hadn't friended Shipley Jr., but she also hadn't made her profile private, which means that anyone could view it. When I did some more digging, I found that he had been looking through her pictures and getting alerts on her status updates. He would've known where she was from her check-ins." Manny paused, but I could tell there was more information.

"Keep going," I encouraged. Now wasn't the time to ask how he knew all of this.

"I went to the places she had checked into in the last few days before her disappearance. There weren't that many, since it seemed that all she did was go to school and stay home. But just like you said, last Sunday she did go to the Publix down the street from your house. I got them to give me their security footage and guess who I saw at that same Publix?"

I already knew what he was going to say. I never even knew that Charles had a son. Then I remembered Mallory Shipley mentioning her family at the barbeque. And how she began saying that she'd shared my family's story with them. But Charles had stopped her from talking about it. Now I wondered if she was going to tell me about her son. Maybe Mallory had told him about Sam and how I had taken her away from her life in New Jersey and brought her to a place where she didn't know anyone and was left alone most of the time. Had Mallory Shipley unknowingly made Sam a target for her crazy son?

"I'm assuming that you don't know Shipley Jr.?" Manny asked.

I shook my head no and then realized he wasn't sitting right in front of me. "No."

"Well, I wanted to earn my paycheck, so I did some digging on this kid. He's twenty-six years old and lives in Coconut Creek." That wasn't far from here. "To say he's unstable would be an understatement. He was diagnosed with borderline personality disorder at age ten, and his father sent him off to private school at age eleven. His first arrest was at the ripe old age of fifteen for stalking a girl at his school. Of course, Daddy paid his way out on probation. He's been arrested on and off for the last ten or so years for a multitude of fucked up things: drugs, indecent exposure, public lewdness, stalking, you name it and this kid's been booked for it."

"So, you think he took her?" I asked, knowing his answer.

"I am ninety percent sure. I've been doing surveillance on his place since yesterday, but I haven't seen him come or go. I can tell you that his Impala's not there. I hacked into his computer, and he hasn't done anything strange. No weird search history, no blog postings, no moving of money, nothing. It doesn't even look like he's done anything on his computer other than check email in over a week." Again, I didn't want to know how Manny did all of this.

"So, what do we do now?" I sure knew what I wanted to do. I wanted to call Charles right away and find out where his son was and why he would take my sister. But if this was true, I also didn't want to tip off Jr. that we were on to him.

"Now I need to find out where this douche is. I don't think he's home. I know that the Shipley's have other houses, but I doubt he's stupid enough to take your sister to any of those.

He was right. "Charles has two other houses that I know of: one in Cape Cod and another in Colorado. Do you think they are driving to either of those? They could be on the road as we speak."

"Well, I don't think he would take her to a house that his father owned, where he could be easily found. I'm pretty sure he went off the grid." Manny sounded confident.

"Okay, but I've got to do something soon." I couldn't help the pleading tone in my voice. "I've got to—"

"Don't do anything. I just wanted to give you an update, since you've been texting me twenty times a day." His voice was commanding. And I didn't want to listen to him. But knew I had to in order to get Sam back, hopefully safe.

The line was silent and I thought maybe he had hung up. "Are you still there?"

"Look, Harris, I know you want to find your sister, and you seem like the stupid type to try something yourself, but I'm close. If you do anything to tip him off, we might lose him and her forever. Once I have a location, I will call you. Until then, let me do my job." With that the line went dead, and I knew he was gone.

I put the phone down and could see both Jacob and Mike waiting for my update. I filled them in on everything Manny had told me, and they were both as stunned as I was.

For the first time all week, Mike looked physically sick. He leaned against the counter to steady himself. "I remember Charles's son but haven't seen him in years." He looked up at me with pain in his eyes, "Travis, I really thought that Sam was playing a cruel joke on you this whole time. I never actually believed that she was in any danger. I'm really sorry."

I nodded at him and turned to look at Jacob. I didn't know him well, but I could see the sadness in his face. He was about to cry when I grabbed both of his shoulders and looked him in the eyes. "Don't, Jacob. This is good news. Call your parents and let them know. I'm sure they're worried about you."

He nodded and went out to the balcony to call them. They had arrived here in Florida Friday night and tried to convince Jacob to stay with them at the hotel, but he wouldn't go with them. He told them that he wanted to be here in case I got any more information about Sam, but I knew he also wanted to sleep in her bed to be as close to her as possible.

I did the only thing I could think of doing. I called Maddy. Maddy had known what was going on with Sam and begged to fly to Florida to help, but I didn't want her to see me like this. And I was afraid that if she did come I would really fall apart. I couldn't risk that right now. I had to be strong.

She answered on the first ring, and my chest tightened. I realized I couldn't talk. I didn't know what to say to her.

Before I had a chance to hang up, I heard her say, "It's okay, Travis, just tell me what happened."

Samantha

The first time I saw the sunshine, I was afraid of it. I had spent so many hours in the dark that my body didn't know how to react. He had carried me out of my cell and into a small room. The room was empty, except for a single wooden chair, which I could barely see through my squinted eyes and blurry vision. When he placed me on the floor next to the door and turned to leave, I tried to get a look at my captor, but my eyes were fighting me. I still couldn't see anything clearly. After sitting there for several minutes, I realized that the chair was holding a fresh change of clothes. Next to the chair was a red bucket with a washcloth hanging from the side of it. I realized that he was allowing me to wash up.

After being trapped in that room for so long, my legs were not very helpful getting me to the chair. I dragged myself across the floor and realized that the bucket was filled with water. As soon as I saw the water my mouth started to salivate. I had the most powerful thirst I'd ever experienced. I grabbed the bucket and started to chug down the water. I didn't care that it was in a disgusting bucket. I needed it.

I finished almost the entire bucket, leaving just enough water to soak and rinse the washcloth. Using the chair to support my weight, I slowly undressed out of the clothes I had been wearing since that fateful day. They were dirty and smelly. In fact, my body smelled awful. I looked down at my arms as I ran the damp cloth across my bloody wrists. My veins were bruised from all the injections and my skin was a very pale gray. I suddenly felt ill and bent over to throw up the water I had just desperately drunk. With my head over the bucket, I started to sob. What was I going to do?

I knew that he wasn't going to let me hang out in this room long. What was he going to do with me? Maybe this was my only chance to get away before he killed me. I quickly pulled myself together and dressed in the clothes he left me. They were too big for me and looked like something my mother would wear.

An hour or so later, he returned with some ointment for my cuts, a fresh bucket, toilet paper, a blanket and a pillow. He left them by the door when he walked in. I noticed that he was young. I wasn't sure how young, but I could tell he was younger than Travis. He was taller than me, thin, with light, soulless eyes and pale freckled skin. His hair was messy and uncombed. I knew that if I were feeling one hundred percent I could probably take him out, which was no doubt why he had to wait days for me to become weak.

He paused at the door. We were evaluating each other. I could immediately see the crazy in his eyes, as I'm sure he could see the desperation in mine.

He didn't say anything but walked over to the old clothes and picked them up off the ground. He walked over to the bucket and saw that I had vomited inside it. He looked up at me with disgust in his eyes and walked out.

23 FINDING ANSWERS

Travis

I ended up telling Maddy everything from start to finish. Why I had brought Sam back with me to Florida. What I had spent my time doing since I had been back. How I had made so many mistakes. I poured out my soul like I never had with anyone before. She listened the entire time, never judging me. She just let me put it all out there.

I told her all about Sam and what Jacob and I had been through this week. I told her about the information that Manny had found and asked her what she thought I should do. She told me to listen to Manny. I was paying him a lot of money and he seemed to know what he was doing.

She cried with me when I told her the thoughts that ran through my head of what was happening to Sam if she was with that psycho. Again, she asked to come to Florida to support Jacob and me, but I told her not to. I knew how stressed we already were. She reluctantly agreed.

The truth was I wanted Maddy here with me. I wanted to hold her and feel her warmth, but I couldn't do that to her. This last time, I had been the one that walked away from her, and she deserved better than me.

I woke up Monday morning groggy from the previous night's phone call. I checked my phone, it was 6:30 a.m. and no calls from Manny. I knew it was too early to hear from him, but I was getting impatient. He told me not to get involved and to let him do his job, but I couldn't just sit around all day waiting. I needed to do some digging of my own and find out all I could about Shipley's son. I got up quickly and went straight to Sam's room to wake up Jacob. I let him know my plan and told him to get ready. I did the same with Mike, and then I got myself ready.

Samantha

When he left me in my new room I decided that my apparent good behavior had gotten me out of my cell. The first couple of days I had been fighting it, but lately I just didn't have the strength.

The next time I saw him he brought food in with him. Real food. I could smell the peanut butter right when he walked in. I wanted to jump up and attack him to get to the food, but I held back. He left the plate on the now empty chair and glanced at me before he left, closing the door behind him. I could hear the dead bolt lock and the sound of his footsteps get softer as he walked away. I got up and approached the chair. Before I attacked the peanut butter sandwich, I pulled it apart and smelled it. I knew that he must've drugged it, but I didn't care. I was so hungry. After I ate it, I curled up in a ball in the corner with the blanket wrapped around me, waiting for the drugs to take effect or my stomach to reject the food like it had the water earlier. Surprisingly, nothing happened.

The next morning when he entered my room he didn't have any food with him. He just stood at the door and looked me over. Suddenly, I was overwhelmed with fear about what he was thinking and wondered if this was the moment he was going to try and touch me. All day yesterday I thought about how strange his behavior had been. Letting me out of my cell, encouraging me to wash myself, giving me clean clothes and food. I knew that he was preparing me for something and the only thing that made sense was that he was getting ready to rape me. And probably kill me afterward. However, as my panic set in, he didn't move. I was sure he could tell by the look in my eyes that I was scared. I was leaning up against the far wall clutching my legs close to my body. Tears started to gather in my eyes and suddenly he also looked sad. It was only for a brief moment and then gone, but I did see it…the sadness.

He turned around to walk back out, but this time he didn't close the door behind him. He left it open as if to tempt me to leave. I was so scared and in shock that even though the door was open, I didn't move. I felt like this was a test and, if I did run or move, that something bad was going to happen. I sat there just staring at the open door. After a few minutes passed he returned with a peanut butter sandwich, which I ate after he left and locked the door behind him. As soon as I heard the deadbolts turn and lock, relief rushed over me. I was safely locked away, alone.

Travis

I was heading into the office, and it wasn't even 8:00 a.m. I was never in this early but knew Shipley was. It was the best time to try and catch him off guard. He wouldn't be expecting me, and we would be the only ones in the office this early.

Jacob and Mike followed me through the long, empty halls of the firm. Jacob had never been here, so he lagged behind, but of course Mike and I knew them well.

When we got to Shipley's office, he was just where we thought he'd be, sitting at his desk with his coffee mug in hand, reading through briefs.

He was startled when I knocked on the door. At first he looked up at Mike and me with a smile, which quickly faded when he saw the determined faces before him.

"Good morning, gentlemen. I am surprised to see you both here so early on a Monday?" He slowly took his glasses off, no longer interested in the brief.

I spoke first. "We are here to talk to you about your son Charles."

Shipley was thrown by the statement. The last thing he probably imagined talking about this morning was Charles Jr. His brow furrowed as he looked at me with contempt in his eyes. "What about my son?" The word son came out stressed.

I approached his desk, with Mike and Jacob following in step. "He has my sister," I growled.

Charles shook his head in confusion. "I don't know what you're talking about. I heard your sister was missing, and I am truly sorry for that, but what does CJ have to do with it?"

Hearing Charles shorten this monster's name like he was a normal person made me shudder with anger.

"Your CJ took my sister last Tuesday. Almost a week ago." I wasn't yelling, but my voice was getting loud. I could feel my blood pressure rising as spit was flying out with every word. "Now tell me where I can find him."

Charles looked down at his desk and his initial response of confusion turned into desperation and anger. Looking back up at us he said, "I know that your sister is missing and you're probably going out of your mind with worry, but who told you CJ was involved?"

"Stop calling him CJ!" I yelled, "Just tell us where he is."

"I don't know where CJ, Charles Jr., is. I disowned him years ago after he stopped taking his meds and started getting into trouble with the law." Shipley slowly rose from behind his desk and walked over to the family pictures that were on his side bureau. I had never noticed them before.

"He's sick, Travis. He has borderline personality disorder. I can't help him if he doesn't want to help himself."

Shipley picked up a picture of what must have been Charles Jr. and handed it to me. I wearily took it and angled it back so that Jacob and Mike could see the monster that had Sam. In this picture, he was just a kid, probably no older than fifteen. He was tall and thin like his father, but had his mother's light eyes and pale skin. He had a baby face covered in freckles. I could hardly believe this was the kid who'd abducted had my sister.

"You're lying!" I yelled at him. "We know about the place in Coconut Creek. We know about the red Chevy Impala. He has her!" I was starting to lose control.

"Why would he take her? He doesn't even know who she is?" Charles asked.

Before I could stop myself, I cocked my arm back and swung at my boss. Mike jumped in and grabbed my arm before it connected. He grabbed the picture out of my hand and set it down on the table.

"Charles, he has Samantha." Mike spoke slowly stressing the word has so that he understood this was still going on. "You have to help us."

Shipley's face was now as white as his hair. "How do you know this?" This question was directed back at me.

"I hired a private investigator that—" I was about to tell him that Mitch had recommended, but I didn't want to get Mitch in any trouble. I quickly glanced at Mike and covered up my blunder, "...was recommended by an old client. He found video footage of Sam being taken at her bus stop, and the car in the video was a red Impala that is owned by you and registered to your son." This was clearly a fabrication of the truth.

Charles didn't say anything.

Mike jumped back in. "We know that Charles Jr. lives out in Coconut Creek. Do you know if he's there now? Do you know of anywhere else he could have taken Sam?"

"I don't," he said almost in a whisper, looking at Mike

instead of me.

Mike approached him slowly, reaching out his hand and placing it on Shipley's shoulder. Mike had known Charles for years, since he was a little kid. "I remember CJ. I can't imagine that you could just cut off your child one hundred percent." He was talking in a low voice, trying to gain Shipley's trust.

"I did Michael. One hundred percent." Mike's strategy backfired, and now Shipley seemed angry and eager to get us out of his office. He turned back to me. "Listen, Travis, I really wish I could help you, but I haven't spoken to or heard from my son in years. I didn't even know about a house in Coconut Creek." He was still lying, I could tell.

"What about Mallory?" Mike said more sternly, probably realizing the kid gloves had to come off if we wanted to get answers.

Shipley quickly turned back to Mike. "You leave her out of this, Michael. You know that she's sick and can't be told about any of this. It would kill her." He turned back to me. "You don't even know if CJ has your sister. I'm a bit insulted that you think you can come into my office and make outrageous accusations like this." He herded us all closer to the door. "Please leave."

We stared at each other for a few seconds before I turned to leave. I grabbed Mike and Jacob and we walked out of Shipley's office. Jacob had been quiet the whole time, but as we walked down the hallway back to the elevators he was pleading with me to go back. We didn't have any more information than we came with. But what Jacob didn't realize was that I had done what I wanted to do in Charles's office. As I heard Charles yell my name from down the hall, I knew my plan had worked.

When I looked back, I could see him standing in the hallway just outside his office. "I hope you find your sister soon and that she's safe." I could hear the genuine sadness in his voice. I nodded at him but didn't say anything else.

When we got to the elevators, I pulled out my cell

phone and called Manny.

Manny picked up the phone on the third ring but didn't say anything. I was learning this was typical for him.

"I didn't listen to you. I went to talk to Shipley Sr. I have a feeling he knows where his son is, and if he doesn't then his wife does. Tap their phones. I'll text you their numbers and address. Get it done quickly because he's probably calling her as we speak."

"No need. It's already been done. Do you think I didn't anticipate you going rouge on me?"

I didn't answer him. I just hit END.

Samantha

It was getting dark out, and my stomach was grumbling. Even though I had my sandwich earlier I was still starving. Without the drugs, my body was returning to normal and it needed replenishment.

Then I heard his footsteps approaching the door. I went back to the far wall and wrapped my arms around my legs tightly. This could be it, I thought to myself.

He opened the door and once again had no food with him. For the first time, he spoke to me. "If you're hungry, then your food is on the kitchen table." And then walked away, leaving the door open behind him. I had to go through the same dilemma from this morning. Should I follow him or should I just stay here? Almost as if responding to the question in my head, my stomach growled. I decided I needed to take the risk.

I slowly stood up, taking time to gather my legs underneath me. I hadn't walked much in days, and my legs were wobbly. I made my way to the door and grabbed the doorway to steady myself. I looked out into the hallway. It was a narrow hall that led straight to the kitchen. I could see the kitchen table at the end. It had two plates with sandwiches. I slowly walked down the hallway, keeping one hand on the wall to steady myself the entire way. I passed two other rooms, but both doors were closed and locked. Were there others here?

When I got to the kitchen, my captor was leaning up against the counter, waiting for me. I looked over at the table and saw my sandwich. I took a seat and started to eat. He sat down next to me and started to eat his sandwich, not once looking up at me. I took these moments to quickly survey the house. It was small, and there was a living room off the kitchen that led to the front door. It wasn't far from where I was sitting, but I knew I could never make it there without him catching me. I also noticed that there were three dead bolts on the door, all locked. Next to the kitchen table was a sliding glass door that lead out to the backyard. I realized that wasn't locked.

When he got up to throw away his now empty paper plate, a sudden rush came over me. Before I could think about what I was doing, I grabbed the vase that was on the center of the table and hit him in the head with it. I didn't wait for him to hit the ground before I turned to the sliding glass door and ran for my life.

Once out of the house I realized I was in a fenced backyard. I tried to run to the side and find a gate, but with my wobbly legs I didn't get far. I felt him grab my ankle, and I fell to the ground. He must have lunged at me because he was also down on the ground. I could see a trickle of blood running down his forehead. He crawled on the ground toward me as I screamed as loud as I could for help. I was frantically kicking at him, but as hard as I tried I couldn't get out of his grasp. He got up and towered over me. With one powerful punch, I saw darkness.

Travis

Twenty minutes after my call to Manny, my phone rang. "He called his wife just after you left his office, asking where their son was. She said she didn't know, but from the pressure that Shipley was putting on her, I don't think he believes her. She didn't make any calls after she hung up with him. I tapped her phone too."

"Damn it," I cursed under my breath. "We're at their house now and she isn't here. She left about ten minutes ago."

Right after we left the firm this morning, I headed straight for the Shipley's house. Luckily, they lived in the same community as Mitch, so Mike knew the guard and they let us right in. Unfortunately, the first thing we noticed when we pulled up was that Mallory Shipley's car wasn't in her usual spot in the driveway. Just to make sure, Mike buzzed the gate and spoke to their housekeeper, saying he was there to visit with Mallory, knowing she hadn't been doing so well. Their housekeeper let Mike know that Mrs. Shipley had just left for her doctor about ten minutes earlier. When she said this, Mike and I looked at each other. We both knew she probably wasn't headed to the doctor.

"Manny, you still have a tap on her phone?"

"Yes."

"Can you get one on her cell phone too?"

I could hear Manny chuckle. "Man, who do you think I am?" He paused. "I already cloned her phone, so when she gets or makes a call, so do I." I knew he was grinning through the phone. "I told you I liked a challenge."

"Okay, great. The Shipley's housekeeper told us that Mallory headed to the doctor ten minutes ago, but we doubt she was telling the truth. Just to be safe, we're headed there now. Let me know if you find anything else out." I went to hang up before Manny caught me.

"You're wasting your time, man."

"What do you mean?"

"Her cell is on in her purse, which means I can track her exact location." I couldn't believe this guy was that good. "I'm following her silver Lexus on the Sawgrass Expressway right now. I will call you when she arrives at her destination." Then he hung up.

I sat there staring at my phone.

Jacob was in the back seat yelling at me. "Travis! What did he say?!"

"He cloned her cell phone and tracked her exact location. He's following her down the Sawgrass right now. So, unless her doctor is in Plantation, she's headed some place out west."

Mike hit my arm from his passenger seat. "Well, then let's get going. We might not be following her exactly like Manny, but we can at least get a head start."

My mind started to race, thinking about what we were going to do once we got to her. "Don't you think we should bring a gun?" Mike was big into shooting, a sport I'd never really gotten into. He'd taken me to the shooting range a few times, so I knew he had several guns, some of which he kept at his parents' house.

A look of recognition came over Mike's face, and he nodded at me. "Head to my parents' house, I have just what this psycho deserves."

Thirty minutes later, we were on the Sawgrass Expressway heading west toward the Everglades. Mike only had two guns at his parents' house, which was good since I didn't want Jacob having a gun. I knew that if there were more than two he would want one. He had been very quiet today, and I needed to make sure he was ready for whatever was about to go down.

"Hey Jake," I said, getting his attention. "Are you all right back there?" I could see he had a snarky look on his face, probably doubting the sincerity of my question. "I just want to make sure that you know what might happen today."

"I know. We might find Sam," he said, and returned his gaze out the window.

"I just want you to be prepared for how we might find her and what we might have to do to get her." My voice cracked halfway through my statement, and it didn't come out as strong or confident as I had intended. Mike shot me a side glance, and I caught his eye for a second. Even though I was saying the words to Jacob, I was really trying to prepare everyone in the car for what might happen, even me.

Samantha

After my attempted escape, I was put back into my cell. I woke up with my head throbbing and once again engulfed in total darkness. I reached up to feel the bump on my head, and my hands felt wet. I must've been bleeding.

I cursed to myself, knowing that running was a stupid move. I saw freedom and went for it, not thinking. At least he hadn't cuffed me to anything this time. I slowly got up and felt around. I took a few steps forward, barely lifting my feet off the floor. After about six shuffle steps, I realized that there was a wall in front of me. I felt around the wall and could tell that it was made of cinderblocks. I figured this must be a hurricane room, knowing that in Florida there were no basements because of the sandy foundation and being so close to the ocean. I followed the wall around the room until I came to a corner and kept going to see how big this room actually was. I bumped into my old mattress and felt the piping that I was previously handcuffed to. I continued on through the room and came to a switch on the wall. I quickly clicked the switch, foolishly thinking the light might work. It didn't. I should have known he would disconnect the power or unscrew the light bulb. I felt past the switch and found the door. I grabbed the handle, but of course it was locked. I put my ear up to it, hoping to make out any sounds on the other side, but I couldn't.

I realized that there was no light coming from underneath the door and sunk to the ground to find out why. Feeling the bottom of the doorway with my fingertips, I found that there were towels on the other side to block out the light. I'd always had small fingers, so reaching out with both my pinky fingers I was able to move the towels slightly, letting a little bit of light through. I still couldn't see much, but at least I would be able to hear better. The dull thumping in my head had taken over and the coolness of the floor was a welcome feeling, but I knew I didn't dare close my eyes.

Travis

As we were driving down the Sawgrass Expressway, my phone rang, it was Manny again. He told me where Mallory Shipley had gone. I knew the place. We weren't far. There was an exit off the highway that led into an old community built in the '50s where the houses were on acres of land. It was right between civilization and the Everglades.

I increased my speed, and when I turned off the exit, I ran every red light to get there. I didn't care if a cop started following me. It would probably be better. I could see Mike in the passenger seat, not saying a word, just holding onto the side bar to steady himself. Jacob was in the back seat talking to Detective Morales. I told him to call once we had left Mike's parents' house to fill him in on everything we had learned. I yelled out the address that Manny had given me, and he relayed it to the detective.

We pulled up to the house minutes later to see Manny's black SUV blocking in a silver Lexus sedan. Next to the Lexus was an old red Impala. This was it.

I looked down at my sweaty palms wrapped around the handle of one of Mike's guns. Even though I had fired a gun before, I'd never thought I would have to use one on another human being, but I was ready if I had to. I ordered Jacob to stay in the car, but he wouldn't listen to me. He followed right behind us with a stubborn, but scared, look on his face. Stupid kid. I couldn't stay to argue with him; I needed to find Sam.

As we got closer to the house, Mike drew his gun, ready to shoot. Manny was at the front door, listening to what was going on inside. He saw us approaching and motioned for Mike to go around the back of the house. They had never met before, at least I didn't think they had, but the way Mike handled a gun showed he knew what he was doing. I assumed Manny could see that. Mike turned to look at me, "I'm going around the back, just in case." He headed to the right side gate.

Jacob and I walked slowly up to the front door where Manny was still listening closely. When we got closer to him, he put his finger to his lips to tell us to be quiet. We could hear Mrs. Shipley screaming inside the house.

Manny, who was also armed, mouthed to me, "You ready?"

I nodded. He looked at Jacob and sternly mouthed, "Stay here." I could tell through Jacob's tough exterior he was scared and nervous, he conceded and shook his head yes.

Manny was about to turn the door knob, when we suddenly heard Mrs. Shipley stop screaming and say something in a lower scared tone. I couldn't make out what she had said, but a second later we heard a single gunshot.

Samantha

I lay on the floor in front of the door to my cell for what felt like hours. I was desperately clinging to the hope that someone had heard me yell when I ran outside earlier. He had to have neighbors. All of the houses that I had seen so far in Florida had little to no privacy. This house couldn't have been much different.

Suddenly, I heard the slightest sound like a door closing. Then I heard talking. I wasn't sure how many voices I could hear at first, since they seemed to be whispering. I concentrated harder and heard a woman's voice. She wasn't whispering anymore, and I could hear their argument more clearly. My blood started to pulse through my veins, as my heart sped up with the realization that there was someone else here. A woman. I hadn't remembered seeing a woman, even though I hadn't been let free to roam the house.

I listened more intently to try and hear what they were arguing about.

"Do you have a girl here CJ?" she shouted at him. His name was CJ.

I could hear my captor let out a laugh. "What are you talking about, Mom? The chemo must be seeping into your brain. Oh, wait, it is. Maybe it's making you crazy." I could hear him laughing again.

"CJ, do you understand what you've done? Do you understand who you took? I can't save you this time. No more hiding! This ends today!" She was frantic.

"What are you talking about? I didn't take anyone." He was still trying to deny it.

"Where is she?" I could see from the small crack under the door that the woman was starting to move around the house. "You took Samantha Harris, CJ! I told you about her story and her loss to show you how important family is, and how we have to treasure it while everyone is still living. Not for you to push us farther away." I could hear her choking on her own tears.

The realization of what was happening started to piece together in my mind, but I was stunned speechless. My captor, whose name I finally knew, was arguing with his mother, who apparently found out he had taken me. And she knew who I was!

Then something stopped her from yelling. He must have grabbed her because their feet were close together now. "I know what you were trying to do, Mother. But when I looked her up and saw her beautiful blue eyes looking back at me, I knew right then that she was the one I've been waiting for my whole life. She's different from all the other girls. I was weaker back then. I know you tried to protect them and warn them about me, and because of that none of them ever had the chance to love me back. Well, she will."

The woman was sobbing now. "Oh, my sweet boy. What happened to you?"

Finally, I snapped out of my daze and I did the only thing I could think of, I started yelling. Screaming for someone to help me, knowing that if I could hear them, then they could hear me, too. She was here to help me. I desperately screamed with all of the energy I had left in me. I was yelling so loud that my throat hurt, when finally, I heard something that made me freeze. One single gunshot.

Travis

Jacob's face drained of all color and his look of dread made bile start to creep up my throat. I couldn't breathe, trying to figure out what had just happened inside the house.

Manny didn't hesitate, even though I did. He turned the doorknob and ran into the house, gun drawn.

"Stay here," I said sternly to Jacob, pushing him back a few feet.

As I entered behind Manny, more apprehensively, I could see Mallory Shipley lying on the linoleum kitchen floor. Blood had started to pool around her chest and I could tell she was either dead or dying.

Manny started screaming at Charles Jr. to drop his weapon, but the kid didn't move. When I finally saw his face, I realized that even though he was twenty-six, he looked more like he was sixteen. He had a baby face, but his baby face was covered with blood splatters, and his eyes were filled with a raw rage I had never seen before.

Then I suddenly heard Sam screaming. I lost my bearings in the room and looked around, trying to find her.

The screaming was coming from right behind Charles Jr., and when I looked in his direction we finally made eye contact.

He knew who I was; I could tell from the recognition on his face. "You have her eyes," he said faintly.

All of the sudden the raw rage I had seen in his eyes, only moments earlier, was suddenly coursing through my body. Without thinking I rushed him.

Samantha

The next few moments seemed to happen so quickly. I heard more yelling, men this time, and more gunshots. I lost count at five. Then silence. I started to hyperventilate. Was someone here to save me? Was it the cops? Has someone shot my captor? All of these thoughts were going through my mind as I desperately looked through the crack of the door. Then I saw footsteps approaching, and I frantically slid away back into the far corner of the room.

When the door flew open, my heart stopped. It was him. My captor.

He reached down and grabbed my arm. I couldn't tell if he was covered in his own blood or someone else's. When we exited my cell, the scene in front of me became clear, and my body crumbled to the ground. My captor released his grasp from my arm, and I lunged toward my brother who was lying lifeless on the floor in front of my cell door. My captor wrapped his arm around my waist and hoisted me up, I was kicking and screaming Travis's name.

As he dragged me through the rest of the house, the passing scene was horrific. Everyone in the house was lying there bleeding…dead. After we passed Travis, I saw a woman's lifeless body lying at the end of the hallway, surrounded in a pool of blood, my captor's mother. I gasped trying to fight off the shock.

Then we turned slightly to the front door, and I saw Mike lying in the kitchen, a few feet in front of the open sliding glass door. I wasn't sure, but I thought I saw him move slightly as I started to scream his name. I was still struggling to break free from my captor's grasp, adrenaline taking over, when we passed the body of another large man I didn't recognize.

Then I saw Jacob, lying next to the front door with blood trickling from his forehead. Bile came up my throat. I hadn't eaten much in days, but I still leaned over and vomited all over myself, and my body went limp. I could only whisper his name, "Jake".

My captor got me out of the house and into a black SUV easily. After seeing Jacob, my body went into shock and I couldn't move. "You have nothing left now so stop trying to run."

He was right. I sat there shaking, realizing that my world had just ended. I had absolutely no one left.

3 months later…

It was a warm summer day as I walked hand in hand with Maddy through the farmer's market in Myrtle Beach, South Carolina. I had been broken these last few months, literally, and Maddy had been the one to put me back together.

A couple of weeks ago, when I was finally starting to feel normal again, Maddy suggested we take a vacation. I had been obsessed with finding Sam. It was all I did anymore. We came to the only place I could think of, Myrtle Beach. I knew it was crazy, and probably not healthy, to come to the place that reminded me most of Sam, but I thought maybe it would help me relax and remember better times.

We were deciding what to make for dinner that night, when I caught a glimpse of her out of the corner of my eye. I had seen Samantha so many times in my nightmares. In my nightmares, the image of her was always the same, the last time I saw her being dragged out of the house kicking and screaming.

I replayed the events of that day over and over again in my mind. In reality, everything happened so fast, but in my dreams, it played out in slow motion. As I rushed Shipley Jr., he freaked out and shot twice, just missing me and hitting Manny behind me, who took a bullet to the chest and shoulder. Manny had returned fire while going down, but Shipley Jr. ran toward the kitchen. Away from me and the bullets. As I chased after him, I heard Samantha screaming. Without thinking, I turned down the hallway and ran in the direction of her voice. In retrospect, I should have focused my attention and my gun on Shipley Jr., but in the moment, I wasn't thinking clearly. Her voice sounded so helpless and scared. I can still hear it echoing in my head.

I made it half way down the hall when the first bullet pierced my back. It felt like I had been leveled by a brick. I landed hard on the floor, unable to move. I heard what I thought was the back slider open and then two more gunshots. As footsteps approached my body, I tried desperately to crawl toward Sam's voice, which was coming from behind a door at the end of the hall, several feet from where I landed. But I couldn't move. That's when the second bullet hit me. I felt the cold start to take over and closed my eyes. I faltered in and out of reality for several moments. Just long enough to hear two more gunshots. After that, I lost consciousness. I regained it long enough to see Shipley Jr. carrying Sam, kicking and screaming out of the house.

Later, while I was recovering in the hospital, I found out happened after I had been shot in the back. Mike had entered through the back slider, but Shipley, being in the kitchen, was right there and shot Mike twice in the stomach before he even had a chance to take a shot. Then, Shipley walked over to me, shooting me a second time in the back. He did the same to Manny, to make sure that none of us were left alive. But, he wasn't expecting Jacob.

Jacob had entered the house once the shooting stopped. Shipley Jr. tried to shoot him, too, but had no more bullets left in his gun. He rushed Jacob, they struggled, but ultimately Shipley Jr. kneed him in the crotch, and then used the butt of the gun to knock Jacob out. Jacob was the only one not shot, but did have a severe concussion.

When Shipley Jr. took Sam that day, he thought we were all dead. All of us except Jacob. What he didn't know was that we all survived. Manny had been wearing a bullet proof vest, so the only wounds he really had were in his shoulder and on the back of his head. When he got knocked down by the impact of the first two shots, he slammed his head against the tile floor and was left unconscious. Mike, had a tougher time. He had been shot twice in the stomach and lost a lot of blood. He was with me at the hospital for a couple of weeks after the incident.

I had the toughest recovery though. The first bullet that hit me had gone straight into my spine, temporarily paralyzing me. The second ripped through muscle, stopping only inches from my heart. The pain during recovery was unbearable, but over the last few weeks it has become more manageable. My physical pain is nothing compared to my mental anguish. It was my fault that Sam was still missing.

Since that day, I haven't stopped looking for her, and neither has Jacob. I moved back to New Jersey to be closer to Maddy and Jacob. I knew that Shipley wouldn't stay in Florida anyway. I left the firm, even though Shipley Sr. had resigned; I was useless to them. My main purpose in life had become finding Sam. I spent all of my time and money focused on finding her. And I will never stop until I do.

As we continued walking through the market, Maddy squeezed my hand a little, knowing that I was lost in thought like I usually was these days.

"Come back to me, baby," she whispered in my ear.

I smiled and looked in her direction. Then I saw her again, Samantha, the silhouette of her face, through the flowers that were displayed to my left. I turned my head quickly and followed in the direction I saw her. Could she be here in Myrtle Beach? Or was my mind playing tricks on me? Why would Shipley bring her here?

I let go of Maddy's hand and quickened my pace so that I didn't lose her again. The market was crowded, since it was Sunday and a lot people stopped here after church. I found myself pushing through families, excusing myself for my rudeness. I could hear Maddy calling my name behind me, but I didn't have time to stop and explain. I couldn't lose her again.

As I searched desperately through the crowds of people for her wavy brown hair, I spotted her near the produce. I could still see only the side of her face. Her hair was very short, and she was thinner than I remembered. I knew that it had to be Sam, so I called out her name. She turned her head. We locked eyes, yes, we both had the same blue eyes, the recognition not registering on her face as it had on mine. I yelled her name again and saw someone grab her arm and pull her in the opposite direction.

I set off running after her, weaving in and out of people, trying to catch up with them. I saw her cross the street. I could now see that the man she was with was in fact Charles Shipley Jr. He'd changed his hair and had a beard now, but it was him. He had her arm and was dragging her into a black SUV, similar to Manny's but not exactly the same. She turned her head to look back in my direction, but I didn't get there in time. The car jolted out of the spot and started to speed away.

I could see her watching me through the side mirror, still looking lost and confused. I thought I could see tears in her eyes. It was Sam; I knew it now.

With my hand on my knee trying to catch my breath, I grabbed for my phone and hit the speed dial. Maddy finally caught up to me, we were both breathing heavily. Maddy looked desperately into my eyes, questioning my sanity.

Jacob answered the phone on the first ring. "She's alive; I just saw her."

Travis and Samantha's story continues in *Spirit Away*. Available today in both digital and print!

ACKNOWLEDGMENTS

I couldn't have done any of this without the love and support of my family and friends, always pushing me to follow my dreams and take a chance.
A special thank you to the best focus group a girl could ask for: Mom, Loren, Michelle and Brittney. I am so lucky to have you all in my life. You took time to read my book and give me your honest opinions. You will never know how much that means to me. I couldn't have gotten this far without you

Made in the USA
Columbia, SC
12 June 2021